Unwitting Accomplice

A Kim Barbieri Thriller

Sid Meltzer

Published by Rogue Phoenix Press, LLP
Copyright © 2021

ISBN: 978-1-62420-580-4

Credits
Cover Artist: Designs by Ms G
Editor: Deborah C. Day

Dedication

In memory of Sandy Rosenberg. *Unwitting Accomplice* wasn't a book until she said it was.

Sandy, we did it!

Chapter One

Friday, March 24
11:15 AM

One envelope stood out from all the others competing for Kim Barbieri's attention. All it had was her name and address. The rest was blank. Clearly, it was meant for her eyes only, the note inside demanding to be read.

Wondering who would write her a personal letter, she put down her cup of coffee, opened the envelope and took out the single sheet of paper inside. Savvy as she was, she was completely unprepared for its stark, ominous message.

I intend to commit a murder.

There was no *Dear Kim* above the line, no *Sincerely yours* below it. Like the envelope itself, there was nothing to tell her the identity of the writer, or why it was sent specifically to her.

"Hell's this?" she whispered to herself.

After a long, brutal winter, the sun had chosen that morning to come out and give New Yorkers a hint of the warmer weather to come. It was one of those early spring days, a little too chilly in the shade, yet absolutely glorious in the sun. Barbieri welcomed the retreat of winter, lying out on her patio for the first time since before Thanksgiving, enjoying her ritual first cup of morning coffee while listening to Verdi's *Il Trovatore* on her ancient record player.

It was an opera she knew by heart, and as it came to an end, she forced herself to get up off the lounge chair, take the LP off the turntable and pour a second cup of coffee. Her too-brief escape was over, and it was time to attack the backlog of mail that piled up whenever she was too worn out from chasing cops and robbers all over the city to wade through it. *It's not going to go away by itself.*

She first tossed the ninety percent that was junk, then put aside the bills she had to pay. She saved for last the once-in-a-blue moon personal correspondence, like the mystery letter.

What am I supposed to do with this? What does it mean? Why did I win this particular lottery?

She put the disturbing note back in the envelope to examine it again with a critical eye, as if opening it for the first time. While she had not been called into work that morning—a slow news day evidently—she never stopped looking at things from a journalist's point of view. *Sweat the details. Always. They tell a story all by themselves.*

It was a standard, plain vanilla business envelope, white or close to it, with no embossing, watermark, or logo that could have given her the thinnest of threads to pull. *Probably from Staples or Walmart. No help at all.*

Printed on the front were her name, street address, apartment number, and zip code—all correct. The writer knew of her by seeing her byline, she assumed, which meant he also knew what she did for a living. Her stories appeared just about every day in the *Daily News*, the tabloid whose circulation pretty much ended at the city line. She gave her fellow New Yorker a small nod for accuracy.

Whoever sent it had chosen a standard business typeface, and the envelope looked like it came out of a cheap home office printer you could get anywhere. Canon perhaps, or HP. *They're all pretty much the same anyway.*

In the upper right corner was a common Forever stamp—Elvis before he became a lounge act—precisely aligned with the envelope's top and side edges. Its postmark revealed it was mailed two days before, on Wednesday, and meant it was placed in her mailbox by a mail carrier rather than the sender. Had the postmark been completely legible, it could have helped her track down the post office where it originated. Unfortunately, only the last two numbers—0 and 9—were clear. The rest was an unreadable blur. *I can't even tell which city it came from. All in all, the envelope itself is giving me next to nothing to go on.*

She took the letter out again as if she had not done so only a minute before, putting the now empty envelope aside. It was standard letter size and appeared to be the same stock as the envelope. It was folded in thirds, business style, by someone who took care to line up the edges perfectly.

One neat and orderly fellow. Or should I say lady? Lord knows men have no monopoly on weirdness. The opportunity to judge people was both an occupational hazard and a perk of the job. After so many years of interviewing cops, witnesses, victims, and assorted dirtbags, she could not help herself.

The sinister warning, *I intend to commit a murder,* was printed on the top inside third of the letter, flush left, in the same typeface as on the envelope. She noted again how the middle and bottom thirds of the paper were left blank.

As unsettling as the message was, there was something else creeping her out. *This is an unwelcome invasion of my privacy. Somebody out there knows my name, what I do, and where I live. What else does he know about me? My account numbers? My passwords? My family?*

She put the letter back in the envelope, careful not to leave any more of her own fingerprints or ruin any the writer had left. Tempted as she was to toss it out as a waste of time, she chose instead to hold on to it for now. As a reporter, she knew better than to dismiss a promising lead. Besides, she did enjoy a good mystery, and the killer-in-waiting might decide to give her clues actually meaning something later on.

The mail all taken care of, Barbieri poured herself a fresh cup of coffee, grabbed her copy of the *Times* and reclaimed her prime sunbathing location on the lounge chair. She had finished reading the paper earlier in the morning, but was never really done with it until she filled in every last square of the crossword. A few more minutes of warmth provided by Mother Nature herself, rather than the down coat she had worn all winter, sure beat rushing to yet another savage crime scene.

Chapter Two

Barbieri grabbed her cell off the kitchen counter. She had put the mystery letter aside the day before, but could not put it out of her mind. For twenty-four hours, she had thought about little else except her new anonymous pen pal. Her best course of action was to hash the message out with the one person she could trust to keep his mouth shut.

"What?" Pete Delaney was not known for idle banter or witty repartee. Social skills were not one of his strengths. Speaking in monosyllables was. With these two, small talk was kept to a minimum by mutual agreement, if not dispensed with altogether.

"Come over."

"Now?"

"Now."

"Twenty."

Kim Barbieri was as good as any male with man-talk. She spoke it fluently and was comfortable distilling conversation into its purest form with her partner. When she and Delaney communicated with each other, they competed in waxing ineloquent, and the duels always induced a small smile she found hard to suppress. *Reminds me of the stupid secret codes I used to dream up with my girlfriends after school.*

Delaney was a photographer for the same newspaper, a stringer like Barbieri. Stringers were usually assigned to work together at random, based on who was up at the time. Except for homicides. To the metro desk editor, these two were the go-to team where dead bodies were involved. Working stories together sometimes ended with them hanging out together afterwards, which over time morphed into a sort of friendship.

Not romance, certainly. There was no chemistry between them, only a high level of mutual comfort, respect and trust, which was why Barbieri decided to loop him in on the anonymous letter.

Delaney was strictly a news photographer, and he looked the part. On the short side with long brown hair, a scruffy beard that defied grooming and what seemed like a permanent cameraman's squint, he went about his work with a brusque, no-nonsense demeanor he had cultivated on the job. Rain or shine, night or day, his camera vest, bulging with lenses and filters, was his security blanket. No shot was impossible as long as he wore it.

Growing up in the suburbs he had imagined himself leading camera safaris in darkest Kenya, where he could apply his photographic skills and critical eye to capture the brutal symbiosis of big cats and their prey. Life had other plans. Until he made it to the Serengeti, the dark urban streets of New York City would have to do.

While she waited for Delaney, Barbieri checked her mailbox. No second mystery note. Her mind went back to the troubling message. *How did the sender, whoever he or she is, know how to pique my interest? Why would the writer send it to me and not some other journalist? New York has plenty to choose from. Hundreds, I bet.* She wanted no part of a planned murder. That much she knew. Yet she was not a fan of loose ends. She liked closure. The sinister message left a lingering bad taste she could not get rid of.

In her decade or so of covering crimes, she had seen only a handful of homicides go unsolved. The open cases still kept her up some nights, long after the white shirts in the NYPD decided to stop working on them. Cold cases seemed like a waste of manpower when there was never a shortage of new homicides needing to be solved. No matter how much she tried to block them out of her memory, Barbieri could never stop thinking about what the investigators might have missed. *Was it the follow-up call they didn't make? Maybe the witness who decided he didn't recognize the perp after all? The DNA sample disappearing off the face of the Earth?*

Blue lives mattered a great deal to her. When cops and reporters meet day after day, night after night, over stiffs from the seemingly endless supply the city offers up, a bond forms. Maybe a morbid bond, yet a bond nonetheless. When she was with them, she spoke their language, the slang they used only among themselves, not her own. *Where else would I get to slip "badge bunny" or "Duracell shampoo" into a conversation?* Her empathy for the stiffs and the cops came with the territory.

"Got something," Barbieri greeted Delaney at the door. So much for pleasantries. They went right into their shorthand.

"What?"

"Patience, young man."

Delaney followed his partner to her desk in the study, a literate woman's version of a tormented writer's man cave. Books were piled on every shelf not covered by yellow writing pads, each virgin territory after the first few pages, and atop the center of the desk was an old bargain-basement Dell laptop good for word processing and email, and not much else. She and the Dell went way back. Even after she finally succumbed to peer pressure and treated herself to a Macbook, she could not bring herself to toss it. *One day I'll get around to discarding the old apps and files. Then it'll run faster, won't it?*

She took out the envelope from the drawer, opened it, gingerly removed and unfolded the one-page letter and placed both next to each other on top of the desk. Delaney's eyes went from one to the other until he focused on the message. "*I intend to commit a murder.*" He waited a nanosecond before asking her, "What the fuck does it mean?"

"What it says."

"When?"

"When did I get it?"

"When will he kill?"

"Could be a she. Not anytime soon, my guess."

"Nothing to ID the sender."

"Could be anybody."

"From anywhere. Professional, maybe."

"Educated."

"Grammar counts for something."

"One perp, acting alone."

"One victim, not more. Singular."

"Mental case?"

"Worker going postal?"

"Computer literate."

"Uses Word. Sends file to the printer."

"Home office. Not safe for work."

"Definitely. Probably online. Maybe leaving a trail."

"Leading back to him. Her."

"What now? Police?"

"Not yet."

"Nothing they can do."

Barbieri folded the letter, put it back in the envelope, and left it on her desk. As she followed Delaney out to his car, she fought the urge to remind him to keep the anonymous threat just between them. There was no need to; she knew he would not say a word to anyone.

The reporter was not impressed with the brilliant deductions they had made based on some generic stationery and a single sentence. It was simple logic at work and it did not really bring her any closer to identifying the sender. Regardless, by bringing in her loyal sidekick, she now had a better picture of the person threatening to commit a capital crime. The would-be perpetrator morphed from an abstraction, a cipher, into a human being with a name, a family, an address, and perhaps an online history, waiting to be exposed. She felt they had inched the cryptic note closer to becoming a critical piece of evidence in an out-and-out criminal case.

On the other hand, their brilliant deductions could all be bullshit, and she knew it. The whole thing could be a hoax some sicko was playing on her. They had been wrong one or two times before, on matters a lot more trivial than murder. They could have been just reinforcing each other's sloppy thinking. If not, it could turn out to be Barbieri's first opportunity to cover the premeditated part of premeditated murder. *How many reporters get the chance to put a story like this in their scrapbook?*

She was not sure how exactly, but she felt herself being drawn into a game with an element of danger to someone else, not herself or Delaney. This game might or might not have a lethal ending, and she wanted to know how it would turn out if it was just the three of them playing.

Bringing my playmate into this arena is complicating my own involvement. Her mystery guest was now communicating with two outsiders, not just one, and Barbieri was not sure if he would appreciate Delaney becoming her full partner just yet. While she trusted Delaney more than anyone to keep quiet, the writer himself would have no reason to trust him. Her photographer could go to the cops if he ever got spooked.

Telling them about her new pen pal was something her inner control freak would not allow just yet.

Chapter Three

When did I start thinking it would be a good idea to murder a complete stranger in cold blood?

Can't say for certain, but I do know things really started to get ugly for me when I put in my papers, posed for pictures with my new Rolex, and realized I'd made myself useless. If my plan to stick a knife in someone's chest had a start date, this was it.

That's why you drove all the way up here to almost Canada, isn't it? To hear my side of the story? Trust me, I've wanted to tell it as much as you want to hear it.

I used to be a real big shot, you know? It took a few years to escape the grunt work, but eventually I turned into a pretty important guy in the office. I was a big swinging dick, and I rather enjoyed it.

Me, I was old-school. I started at the bottom, sharing a tiny cube with another peon. I watched how my bosses made money, and eventually *their* bosses let me into their world. I worked alongside them, shadowing them. Then one day, I found myself making money like them. King of the world, I felt like. I became my own little profit center for the firm and took off from there.

See, as far as the higher-ups were concerned, my job description was very simple—*make money*. Make sure the company had more in the bank when I clocked out at night than it did when I'd clocked in in the morning. Simple.

I was what the corporate world called a *rainmaker*. It's a horseshit word for someone who knows how to drum up business and rake in the bucks. I don't want to brag, but I made a ton of money for the company—

a *ton*. They let me keep a big chunk of it to make sure I didn't jump ship; between salary and bonuses, pretty soon I was taking home more than I knew what to do with, quite frankly.

As long as I made it rain buckets, the gods were never angry. In my world, money definitely equaled love. You bring in money for the company, and the company shows you how much they love you by giving some of it back to you. They got rich, and I got raises that meant a lot and fancy new titles that meant nothing.

Let you in on a secret. All the client wanted from me was to dig him out of the hole he had somehow dug for himself. Help him get home before his kids went to bed once in a while and help him sleep a little more soundly. This was what he was paying me for. You do this for him, you're golden.

Guys in the office looked to me to make the big decisions. They had the business degrees and connections, while I had the kind of wisdom you only get from hard times. I had the scars and bruises, they didn't. I could spot opportunities. I came up with ideas, set goals, planned. I budgeted, motivated, negotiated, and I sold. I assembled teams, assigned tasks and managed resources. I cut costs, anticipated roadblocks, put out fires and made gut calls. I made plans, then executed them. To the HR guys who have a box to fill in the org chart, this job description would've been all I needed to get me in the door for an interview.

The upstart MBA types I was forced to work with spoke a language the Navajo Code Talkers couldn't break. Say one of them needed you to pitch in on a project. He didn't ask if you had the time. He asked if you had *extra bandwidth*. Seriously, *bandwidth*? Whoever made this a word, they should bring back the death penalty just for him. My colleagues used ten-dollar words like *resource allocation* and *immunization strategy* to describe our job, bullshit terms created to make their work seem harder than it was, and impress outsiders who didn't speak the language. Gave even our junior guys instant authority, as if they knew what they were talking about.

Personally, I never knew what they were fuckin' talking about half the time and I was their boss.

Consulting in retail was never hard as cutthroat businesses go. It was always challenging, sure, and I could always come up with gimmicks to help stores keep customers coming back and keep their doors open. Everybody thought I'd eventually make partner, even me. *Especially* me.

Then Amazon came along, followed close behind by Josh Kelleher. There wasn't much I could do to make my clients competitive with Amazon. You want to see what that monster's done, just walk up Broadway. About the only thing missing is the tumbleweed. There wasn't much I could do to keep my company from making this douchebag a partner, either. Kelleher was the CEO's son-in-law, and all my earnings suddenly meant squat in comparison.

I worked; Kelleher coasted. He got my partnership; I got a watch. Life's unfair. I was more than a little pissed, so I walked.

Of course, I had to remind myself my company didn't put me out to pasture when I reached mandatory retirement age. I'd stopped working on my own—my decision, not theirs. They didn't fire me; I fired them. Maybe I was too angry at being passed over to think clearly. Maybe I should've eaten crow and stayed. But this didn't make my new carefree existence any easier. To my mind, it wasn't just that things weren't working out the way I'd planned. Like everything else, my retirement was a work in progress. You tried one way of doing things, one new set of routines. If it didn't work out, you went to plan B. No big deal.

All I could do was hope it would all be okay in time. I'm sorry, *bandwidth*. Being home all the time, I spent many hours thinking about where I'd found myself and imagining taking a whole new direction no one could've predicted—least of all me.

Chapter Four

See, the problem wasn't my self-imposed exile, exactly. It wasn't twenty-four/seven domestic bliss, either. Sure, I ran out of things to fill up my day sometimes, but there was always some part of the house I could convince myself needed painting or patching. If they didn't, I'd just take another nap.

No, there was something far more negative weighing on my mind. It was a little harder to pin down than my empty day planner, the absence of order defining my days and me, in some way. Eventually, though, I did manage to figure it out. Or rather, them. Plural. See, there were two problems creating a perfect shit storm brewing inside my skull.

First was, I'd reached the ripe old age of fifty-two without having done anything worth remembering. I mean zippo. Never invented anything, written any book, or made any kind of contribution to society. No discoveries. Sure, Helen and I had a great marriage, which is something. She was a high school science tutor, always pretty busy. In our neighborhood, there was an inexhaustible supply of parents who'd pay anything to get their idiot kids into the right school.

While I made a lot of people a lot of money, most anyone could've succeeded there. Consultants are a dime a dozen. They don't put up monuments in Central Park for people in my line of work and nobody ever won a Pulitzer for a PowerPoint deck. I could die tomorrow and nobody would miss me. It would be as if I was never here on the planet.

I knew my limitations, and it was pretty likely the goals taking up valuable real estate in the back of my mind wouldn't be crossed off my bucket list. I didn't have the talent, to be honest with myself. There was no award ceremony in my future.

So this was one bulb lighting up, my unchecked-off to-do list. Still, there was something else gnawing at me, bubbling up to the surface. After more than five full decades on the mother ship, I'd stopped earning my keep. I was no longer a productive member of society, at least not the way I defined it. I wasn't producing, just *consuming*. I had become a taker, not a maker, as some right-wing nuts put it.

This was a flagrant violation of my Protestant ethic, and it sucked.

By opting out of the workforce, I had made myself irrelevant. Useless, even. Nobody above me was dumping problems on my desk, waiting for me to pull their butt out of the fire. No nobodies below me were competing to show me how brilliant they were. It's like I had the know-how and no way to put it to good use. Life went on without me, and the world kept spinning on its axis. I was expendable. Worse, I was disposable and the one who did the disposing was me.

That was the real eye-opener, the unpardonable sin. Ask anyone who was sent to the sidelines before their time. I needed to be doing something, anything, to make myself feel like I was contributing again. Something I could accomplish using the same business skills I'd used when I was reporting for duty every morning. I wanted desperately to be *back in the game*.

Creeping from the back of my mind to somewhere in the front was an idea telling me there was one thing I hadn't done. A project, a challenge of some kind I could run, and should run. Had to be. I didn't know what it was, not then anyway. I knew it would come to me and I'd know it when I saw it.

That the project would involve committing a capital crime wasn't on my radar. Not consciously, anyway. Kill someone? Me? Not in a million fuckin' years. While I'm not sure if anyone can tell exactly when a subconscious force becomes a conscious force, mine remained well hidden at the moment.

Chapter Five

Kim Barbieri always gave as good as she got.

The cops, lawyers and criminals she dealt with on her job were all pretty hardcore, yet she had no problem going toe-to-toe with the most alpha of males and females. She met attempts at mansplaining, indeed any form of male-pattern boorishness, with a shrinkage-inducing glare. Offenders backed down and learned to mind their manners soon enough.

Barbieri never played the gender card, ever, to men or women. She played the competency card, the needs-no-adult-supervision card, and she played it well. *No story of mine ever has to be retracted, no correction ever has to be printed. Accuracy is never in doubt when my byline goes on top.*

She did not dwell on being female and hoped nobody else did. There was nothing she could do about it. *I want my colleagues to think of me as a good reporter, not a female reporter, and I never give them opportunity to think otherwise.* Yet she also knew it could not hurt, sometimes, if she came across as a woman not to be messed with. She had earned a well-deserved reputation for directness and knew exactly when to make it work to her advantage. She set it loose only when needed, never otherwise. Nobody in their right mind messed with her.

One-hundred-percent Italian on both sides, Barbieri was tall and slender, with olive skin, brown eyes and a mop of curly brown hair she had stopped straightening out years ago. She was closing in on forty, and a few gray hairs were popping up here and there, yet she did not mind. Maturity was definitely an asset in her line of work, as it seemed to be in short supply among her colleagues and competitors. *I'm the designated adult in the room. Work it.*

She was no delicate flower who shied away from the darker side of crime reporting, especially when the crime was homicide. Victims were sometimes thoughtlessly left outside in the middle of the night, in the middle of the street, in the middle of a driving rain. The story must still be filed. Murderers did not keep office hours. Homicides did not always take place in weather cold enough to freeze bodies, and victims were not always found right after death. The potent stench of decomposition mixed with fermenting body waste she was sometimes exposed to stayed on her clothing long after she sent in her story and went home. Nevertheless, she persisted.

This particular Monday, three days after the mystery letter landed in her mailbox, she was sitting in an all-night coffee shop near the Seventy-Ninth Street boat basin on the West Side, nursing a cup of hot mint tea as she struggled to write a story about two bodies found taped together in the Hudson River. It was 3:40 a.m., with the temperature hovering just above freezing. She did most of her work outside, talking to cops and witnesses, and lousy weather never made her job, or her mood, any better. She had forty-five minutes before deadline, and her mobile-office-slash-diner was empty except for her and her journalist tool kit—Macbook, iPhone, batteries, chargers, earphones, notepads, and a dozen or so pens and markers—arrayed on the table. The officers at the scene and the EMT team who hauled the stiffs off to the morgue had already been dispatched to parts unknown to handle the next 911 call.

All she saw staring back from her screen was *"Today the bodies of two unknown females, bound face-to-face with tape at their waists and ankles, were found on the Manhattan side of the Hudson River."* Good start, although a little skimpy on the details. It was not nearly enough to satisfy her own standards, let alone her editor's demands. She knew exactly what she had to do to whip it into shape, but her mind was otherwise engaged.

Nothing in the mail today. Again. Why? Has he aborted his mission? Did he actually go out and kill someone? Nothing in the paper or on the local news. Is he going to communicate with me again? Or with someone else?

Try as she might to keep them separate, her personal life sometimes threatened to barge its way into her professional life. As the mystery letter was now doing. She thought of such distractions as a contest of wills, and hers was pretty powerful. She was always able to summon the inner strength to block them out and get the job done. *"I intend to commit a murder."* So what do you want from me? Commit it. *I've got a story to write.*

After being briefly hijacked by thoughts of the letter, Barbieri went back to the task at hand. She knew the drill. With a few quick calls to all the first responders who caught the 911 call about the floaters, she coaxed the details she needed from each one while they were busy first-responding to the next emergency. She managed to cobble together a professional-grade story, proofread it to make sure she had told the whole truth and nothing but, and submit it with five minutes to spare. Cool as a cucumber. No feathers ruffled. She closed the computer, filled her messenger bag with all her stuff, finished her cup of tea, and headed home. Factory shift over.

Nobody at the paper cared how she did it, as long as it got done.

Chapter Six

"How was work?" asked Captain Timothy Brennan, commanding officer of Brooklyn South Homicide.

"Five borough grand tour," Barbieri replied. "Construction worker on West Twenty-Third was killed. Presumed killed, anyway. Wall they were putting up collapsed, and he was buried under tons of mud and concrete. Fire department's been digging and they still haven't found the body."

"Poor bastard. I don't remember getting a report."

"You wouldn't have. The accident was in Manhattan. Chelsea, not Coney Island."

"Illegal, I bet. From Mexico or Guatemala."

"Close. He was from Honduras. Been here only about seven months."

"Probably not in any union. I bet the company didn't have a construction permit, either. These builders, they don't give a shit about safety. If one of their illegals is killed on the job they find another one to take his place. Nobody cares."

"Only his family back home he was sending money to. That was at nine. By eleven I was up on Fordham Road. Obese old woman died weeks ago. Landlord discovered her only this morning, body glued to the sofa. Not glued, exactly. More like woven into the fabric."

"Aroma lured him, no doubt."

"She must've been stuck there a long time. Never moved. Technicians from the ME's office had to cut away her flesh so they could get her into the ambulance."

"I think I need a shower."

"Not more than I do, Cap'n. I actually went into her apartment."

Barbieri's assertiveness toward alpha males did not apply to one in particular. Timothy Brennan had the body of a linebacker—six-four, two-forty, ramrod-straight posture—with piercing blue-gray eyes able to see right through a suspect's bullshit alibi. *If he ever suspected I was holding out on him, he'd have my confession in a nanosecond.*

"That all? Construction accident and the obese couch potato?"

"In the morning, yes. By two I was in Queens Civil Court for the Kramer thing."

"Tenants suing their landlord, right? Holes in the ceiling. Broken everything. Rats."

"Slumlord. Bitch should be shot the way she neglects her buildings."

"My luck she's shot in Brooklyn. I did have one new arrest today, for a lethal overdose. I can't decide if it's murder or manslaughter. Woman's in excruciating pain from cancer. Pancreatic, I think. Her oxy prescription runs out and they won't let her refill it for some reason. Her junkie son gives her some of his heroin, thinking it'll put an end to her suffering. He means well, but the heroin turns out to be mixed with fentanyl."

"Drug's a hundred times stronger than heroin, isn't it?"

"At least. Now the mom's dead from an overdose, and the son's charged with felony murder. I would've charged him with man one, tops. I'm just a cop, so what do I know?"

"Kid's an orphan and a defendant at the same time. Nice. I thought the DA usually lets accidental overdose deaths go."

"New policy. No death goes uncharged."

"Any unsolved homicides today? Killers on the loose?" Barbieri still had not heard anything from her writer pal and curiosity got the better of her. There was nothing on any news sites about a newsworthy homicide in Brooklyn, and the NYPD sometimes withheld information from the public. Maybe no one asked.

"Nope. All perpetrators are accounted for. My job is too easy sometimes."

Barbieri and Brennan were friends with lots of benefits. They had met over and over again for months, usually over murder cases important enough, or bizarre enough, to require the higher-ups to make an appearance. Gang murders, usually, or bias crimes. Occasional naughtiness by Page Six types. Though she covered the entire metropolitan area for the paper, she came to prefer assignments in Brooklyn in the hope she would run into him. They talked as cop and reporter, at first. Then as man and woman. Now as lovers.

It was not his power alone that turned her on. Or his composure. Or his obvious intelligence. It was the way he used all three to make sure what he wanted done got done. Brennan never had to throw his weight around or raise his voice. With her, quiet authority was an aphrodisiac, and it never failed. Maybe it was jealousy, as it was the one quality she wished she had more of.

There was yet another benefit Brennan brought to the relationship she came to appreciate, if only grudgingly. It was politically incorrect, a complete betrayal of her oath to the sisterhood. *He never resorts to "I'm the man, that's why" macho bullshit with me. He doesn't need to. He's okay with letting me be me. Still, he does make me feel safe. Nobody's going to bother me, or worse, with him around. If women have a problem there, screw 'em.*

~ * ~

They had agreed to spend the night at his place after work, a studio on Staten Island she had no desire to mark as her territory. She had realized early on, after only a few evenings there, her feminine touch would be lost on him. He was perfectly at home with the Ikea touch. Blond wood platform bed and sofa, surrounded on three sides by matching blond wood wall-to-wall and floor-to-ceiling bookshelves jammed with books on history, science, philosophy, religion, politics and a heavy dose of criminology. He was taking this captain business seriously. It was seriously eclectic stuff, not just for show. Barbieri had sensed his scholarly side early on—it was one of the things she was attracted to—so she was not at all surprised by his personal library.

"I also caught the hit in Mill Basin. Body was found on his cabin cruiser with a bullet in his head."

"Mafia, right?"

"Organized crime. The new policy is we're not allowed to use the Italian word when an Italian member of an Italian gang kills an Italian member of another Italian gang."

"Makes sense."

"Does to me."

Past girlfriends had no doubt tried to turn Brennan's man cave into a she shed and had clearly failed. For him, home was simply a place to escape from work, learn about the world, and catch up on his sleep before his next all-nighter. Getting promoted to captain was taking its toll.

It was the end of a long, exhausting day for both of them, and they wanted nothing more than to crawl into bed and stay there awhile. As Barbieri claimed her share of the covers, she caught sight of the book on his nightstand and started leafing through it.

"Fascinating," Brennan whispered to her as she scanned the first few pages. "Two brothers. One's a writer, author of the book. One's a guest of the state."

"For?"

"Murder. The brothers took slightly different career paths."

"Drugs? Gang?"

"I'll let you know when I get to that part."

For her, his studio was a place to indulge her urge to merge with a hunk who had no problem with her no-strings approach to modern romance. She did not need commitment. She was not about to let herself fall in love with him. She was not interested in talking about her feelings, or hearing him talk about his. She did not need a soul mate who understood her. There was time for that later. Still, she was a human being. A person who from time to time needed a hug or to fall sleep in another's arms. In Brennan, she found someone who was glad to oblige. Animal attraction, plain and simple.

Have dinner. Talk about their murder cases and news stories as foreplay. Do the Posturepedic polka. Repeat as necessary.

Whenever they wound up there, in his place, she was not worried about running into someone she knew. She did not know anybody who lived in Staten Island. When they ended the night in her neighborhood, Fort Greene, which happened maybe half the time, she could tell nosy parkers they were both on duty. Maybe they believed it, maybe not. Plausible deniability, if only to her.

They were determined to keep their relationship a secret and live by the rules they had both agreed on. Sack time was not worth ruining their careers over. She did not use him as a source for her stories, and he did not give her exclusives or use her to send a message to the community. Their thing was nobody's business but their own, and they would do nothing to make it public. She even managed to keep it a secret from Delaney, and she spent more time with him than just about anybody.

Barbieri thought it was safer on her part not to tell Brennan about the anonymous threat, at least for now. If it turned out to be some kind of bullshit hoax, he would probably take it out on her. *It's my problem, not his. I will deal with it. Rules are rules. There's nothing he can do anyway, and he'll just think I'm an idiot for wasting his time.*

Chapter Seven

In her career covering all things judicial for the *Daily News*, Barbieri made a decent living reporting on all manner of mayhem only *after* it occurred. She was never invited to the scene of the crime before it became one.

She wrote her pieces the old-fashioned way, following the standard get-to-the-point-and-get-out format. It was a rule drilled into every student in tabloid reporting school. Make sure to answer the questions: Who? What? Where? When? Why? and How? Then ship the story right over to her editor.

Editors edit. Given half a chance, she had learned the hard way, they would edit the life out of a story. Barbieri had trained her editor at the *News* well, sending in well-crafted stories that gave him no chance to scratch this particular itch. About all he had to justify his existence was writing an oh-so-clever headline that would grab a reader for a whole nanosecond.

She covered almost every type of criminal and civil case the public feasted on, from libel suits and celebrity divorces to today's councilman-on-the-take and deportations of illegals. While all manner of dumb-as-a-bucket-of-hair miscreants managed to find their way into police custody, and into the crime section of the *Daily News*, murderers in particular kept her busy. The good citizens of Gotham kicked one or two dead bodies to the curb almost daily.

All too often, their stories became the fodder for fill-in-the-blanks journalism. *"On blank day, at blank time, blank name was found blanked to death at blank address in blank borough."* All my bachelor's degree in *journalism qualifies me to write are Mad Libs news stories. Does anyone still play this word game?* Barbieri was not quite okay with that. Believing she had earned the chance to graduate from beat reporter to investigative reporter, she wanted to dig deeper into every story and give her readers more than the bare bones. Her editor, Cavanaugh, wanted her to stay right where she was. He did not want to have to replace a proven reporter, a known quantity who delivered every time, with an unproven one who would deliver once in a while.

"Your career growth is your business," he told her. "Getting the news out is mine. Stick with what you do best and we'll both be happy."

She knew investigating the victim's background, or the perpetrator's, or even the neighborhood where the incident took place was not quite the same as investigating the incidents themselves. She was not about to step on any detective's toes. *No suspect is going to point a gun at me to avoid arrest. Nobody is going to prison or getting acquitted due to anything I write.* It did not much matter to the higher-ups at the paper if her stories were unread by attorneys, officers, or judges, or anyone else in the criminal justice system, as long as the circulation grew.

~ * ~

The anonymous letter Barbieri had received was an invitation to a form of law and order simply not included in her job description. She always applied the strictest form of if-mom-says-she-loves-you-confirm-with-dad journalism on every story she wrote. Now she found herself in a fact-free zone.

I've just been informed, in writing, a murder is being planned. All my friends know what I do for a living, and one or two of them are not above a practical joke. Then again, it could be a prank pulled by certain demented colleagues of mine, in which case payback will be swift and merciless.

The threatening letter could also have been written by some psychopath simply begging to be put away for his own good. Dealing with them was an occupational hazard at crime scenes, where officers had to sort out the dangerous ones who needed to be in an institution from the harmless ones who merely wanted a little attention.

Still, there's a chance the threat to commit murder is genuine, in which case someone's life might actually be in danger. Barbieri had no idea who the soon-to-be-killer might be. She had no way of knowing who the victim might be, or the reason why the murder was being contemplated. She did not know where or when the murder would take place, or what weapon the killer intended to use.

All I have are those six words.

Chapter Eight

"Hypothetical." Barbieri continued to resist the urge to confess all to Brennan, even though she knew it could one day become a police matter. She had boundaries, and he respected them.Yet she could not let it go. She felt it was safer all around to try the side door.

"Okay. Hypothetical. I hypothesize all the time when facts are scarce."

"Person A tells Person B he is planning a murder."

"Do these somebodies have names?"

After five days, there had still been no more communication from whoever had written her. *The letter has spooked me, though, and he is a top cop who would come to my rescue if I called for help.*

"The person planning the murder does not. Not yet, anyway. The person hearing about it does. What does Person B do?"

"There. Between my shoulder blades. Perfect."

Barbieri and the captain were in her bathtub, scrubbing off each other's residue from their respective days at the office. It was an old-fashioned, freestanding tub with claw feet she had rescued from a nineteenth-century mansion about to be gutted, and was plenty big enough for both the five-foot-eight woman and the six-foot-four man.

"What can Person B do? Not much I can see." Brennan replied. "I guess he can go to the police, but they—we—couldn't do anything. There's nothing to go on."

"Nothing."

"It's not a crime to think out loud, Kim. The First Amendment still applies. Now if Person A actually *does* something…."

"Like point a gun or pull a knife."

"Or stalk his victim, or threaten him with physical harm, then it becomes my problem. *Our* problem. The department's. That's all this hypothetical individual said, he's planning to kill? Not who he's going to kill? Or when? Or where?"

"Nope. Nothing except his intention." Barbieri did not like lying, even by omission, to an interrogator who was quite good at making liars regret lying. "Not where he's going to commit the crime, either. Guy looks like he's thinking this through."

"If we knew where and when he'd murder someone, we could send men there. If we knew who was planning the crime, we could tail him—unless he lawyered up. Without all that...."

"Point taken, Cap'n."

"My experience, he's going to make a mistake. They always do. He'll brag to the wrong person. Trust someone he shouldn't. Half the crimes we solve, three-quarters, are the result of the perp's stupidity, not great police work. Or luck. Which is okay, if it makes our job any easier."

"It's all hypothetical anyway, as I said."

"This hypothetical Person B? Is it anyone I know, hypothetically?"

"I'll get the fire going."

Their bath time abruptly over, Barbieri pulled herself out of the tub, dried off and put on her bathrobe. She went over to her record shelf in the living room and took her recording of Puccini's *Madama Butterfly* out of its sleeve, wiped it gently with a record cleaning cloth and carefully placed it on the turntable.

She had inherited her father's record player and large collection of opera recordings when he passed. His old vinyl LPs were a little scratchy, and sometimes hissed and popped, yet that was okay. Those little imperfections gave them character. She liked character. Keeping her dad's turntable in good working order, and handling his well-worn records with tender loving care, were a way of honoring him she was certain he would appreciate. They were still his and they were in her care.

Brennan was not the huge fan of opera she was—few people

were—yet he was more than willing to indulge her passion for it. It earned him a gold star in her boyfriend rating book. As *Madama Butterfly* began, she walked over to the fireplace and got a fire started. The apartment was not really cold, in truth, but she never needed an excuse to snuggle with him while staring at a roaring fire. The fireplaces in her building had been bricked up and plastered over for years, until the latest renovation uncovered them and got them working again. Major selling point.

Barbieri had felt it was safer all around to feel him out, and she was right. He has real homicides to solve, not hypothetical ones. *The police won't get involved if a crime is just in someone's head. Which means it's up to me to stop this demented bastard. If I don't, an innocent person will be killed. I've fallen into a trap this guy, whoever he is, set for me. An absolutely goddamn diabolic trap.*

Chapter Nine

Barbieri was merely a visitor to the dark side of life, albeit a frequent one, whenever a crime was deemed important enough to warrant a story in the paper. She was a full-time resident in a much more decent world, one measured not by how much pain was inflicted but by how much normalcy was shared.

A devout compartmentalist, Barbieri made it a point not to let one world intrude on the other. She left the awful misdeeds of others outside when she returned to her home on Vanderbilt Avenue in Fort Greene and shut the front door behind her. The lone exception to this rule was with Brennan, out of necessity. Outside of physical attraction, about the only interest she and the captain shared was the latest gruesome death. *He's gorgeous. I'm shallow. He'll do.*

Fort Greene, a newly gentrified neighborhood in brownstone Brooklyn, was now home to a new generation of immigrants. Not the wretched refuse of a century ago, but young, aggressive masters of the new gig economy with perfect children to grow and artisanal, sustainably farmed Kenyan coffee to savor.

Her home, like all the others in the area, was within shouting distance of the old Brooklyn Navy Yard. Once, the Yard churned out mighty battleships like the *Missouri* and the *Maine*, and the neighborhood teemed with sailors and welders, seedy hotels and even seedier bars. After the Navy decided they had no use for it, the Yard was turned into a super-sized industrial park where Gen-Xers with the next big idea went to make their fortune.

Barbieri was the proud owner of a fully-paid-for two-bedroom condo on the parlor floor of a restored four-story townhouse. It had been born a single family home for a family of means, spent its middle age divided into tiny studios with zero light and less charm, and finally bounced back into lovingly restored—and obscenely overpriced—luxury units. Her bedroom and dining alcove were furnished with old, yet sturdy hand-me-downs rescued from friends whose tastes had changed. The rest of her apartment was filled with vintage items picked up in neighborhood antique stores she could not walk past without stopping in. Brand-new did not speak to her.

She loved where she lived. More than anything, Barbieri enjoyed living life on her terms. Being a freelancer was pretty close to being her own boss. Part of her had simply wanted to be a sole reporter on a one-person newspaper, one goal she sort of met. *I really am a mild-mannered reporter for a once-great metropolitan newspaper. I work when I feel like it. New assignments never pile up in my inbox. I have no inbox.*

While Barbieri was not yet the great journalist she wanted to be, she had no doubt she would be some day. Neither was she about to make the leap, as many of her role models had, from print journalism to cable news punditry. Reporters from the *Daily News* were not usually invited to that particular party. On the other hand, she was not working for a lame trade journal, either, writing breathless prose on the latest robotics upgrade in metal fabrication.

Kim Barbieri was in a good place. Still, the sinister message continued to eat at her. *I didn't sign up for this. Why would I even want to be pulled down this murderous rat hole? Why upend my life because someone I don't even know dares me to? How would I go about solving a crime that hasn't happened yet?*

Where would I start?

Chapter Ten

For the sake of keeping sane, I was going back to doing what I knew best. Setting up shop, running a business of some kind, managing a project from start to finish, where I could plan and strategize all I wanted to get some satisfaction for a job well done.

Set a goal. Execute the plan. Watch money go from someone else's pockets to my own. Buy a Maserati and drive off into the sunset. Simple. Still, I prefer doing one item on the to-do list at a time, checking it off when it's done and moving on to the next one. Pretty soon the job's done and I can kick back a little.

The other stuff, the bucket-list stuff, I was pretty sure I'd never get to anyway. I wasn't checking out anytime soon, and running an operation of some kind, being the boss, was something I could do right away.

I lived for that. Yet it's where I parted ways with my usual way of doing things. At work, I was always a team player, which I happened to think was one business buzzword that actually stood for something. When you're taking on a new client, you're always part of a team of maybe five or six guys, and each person has only one job to do. When you fall down on your job, say market research, the rest of us can't do ours. When you're all pulling together, there's no dead weight.

Back then, in the office, I was in charge, first among equals. Experience counts for something. Here, on my own, I'd be leading a team of one: myself. Now I had to ask myself, what business should this one-man team go into? The one I know, the one taking up every waking moment for these many years?

The one thing I knew backward and forward, unfortunately, was the one thing I had no interest in doing—helping merchants out-cutthroat their competitors. My old boss, I knew, would take me back in a heartbeat, except I wasn't ready to go back there. Not as long as I'd have to breathe the same air as Kelleher.

I had no choice but to look elsewhere. I knew of no reason why I couldn't take my skill set, which always worked wonders for me, and put it to use in a whole new enterprise. It really didn't matter which. The things I'm good at—planning, analysis—I'd now use to meet a goal I never had before. What, exactly, I couldn't say. Managing is managing, in my opinion; what you're managing doesn't matter.

I decided to ask the experts, guys I have coffee with from time to time over at the Greek diner. I'd ask them what they'd do in my shoes, pick their brains a little. I'm still not sure why I even bothered, given the employment opportunity I was actually pursuing involved a capital offense. Maybe I was looking to bury those dark impulses I was having more often. Put a stake into them so they never come back to haunt me.

Didn't work.

Chapter Eleven

To anyone exposed to the fruits of man's dark side, as Barbieri was every day, dealing with death at the hands of one's fellow man was simply another day at the office. Practically her job description. She had seen way too many dead bodies, emptied of life in ways both pedestrian and spine-chilling. As she followed the cases through trial and sentencing, she took some satisfaction whenever bad guys learned they were about to spend the rest of their days doing some serious penitence in a maximum-security prison.

While seeing shitheads taken out of circulation warmed her cockles, the city the cops were protecting had a richly deserved reputation for mass-producing new shitheads for the cops to search for after they committed their heinous crimes. Not like the good old days when the lives of hundreds of New Yorkers came to a grisly and untimely end every year, certainly, yet still respectable. Knowing there would always be a demand for her services was one of the compelling selling points of her job.

There was one insight into the human condition Barbieri was never allowed to forget: *under the right set of circumstances, if pushed hard enough, anyone is capable of taking a life*. The truism guided her thinking as she tried to conjure a mental picture of the wannabe who was planning to commit murder. *Could be a man or a woman, rich or poor, Ivy League graduate or a high school dropout, devout or agnostic. We're all sane, and we all know taking a life is wrong. Yet an odd look, a few nasty words, an aggressive move could cause the unthinkable. The deranged animal hibernating inside could be roused and let loose. Someone's life must come to a sudden end. Stranger or loved one, it wouldn't matter.*

She had also made the acquaintance of killers who were simply out on assignment. Some poor bastard had a contract put out on him for wearing a wire, and a gun-for-hire was sent out to let him know his transgression had not gone unnoticed.

Barbieri's killer-in-waiting fit neither of those profiles. The inferences she and Delaney made told her he was definitely in control and his own boss. *He's firmly in charge, pushing himself. He isn't carrying out anyone's instructions except his own. None of the usual suspects—greed, jealousy, rage, hatred—seems to be motivating him. If anything, the murder won't be an act of passion, but an act of impassion. A thrill kill.*

It never surprised her how the detectives who caught the cases she covered spent more time proving the bad boy's guilt than on finding him and putting him in jail. In this sense, the crimes she wrote about were no mystery. Though the perp may have been unknown when the cops got to the scene, their initial investigation—interviewing witnesses, watching crime scene tapes—pointed them right to the bad actor.

Once he was picked up, they would work to nail down means, motive, and opportunity to make the ADAs happy and the defense lawyers miserable. "The policeman's lot," Brennan once confided to her over breakfast at his place, "is escorting perps from a life of crime to a life of sodomy. Take him off the streets and put him behind bars. Everything else is someone else's job, not mine."

All of which made Barbieri realize she should not give a whole lot of weight to the image she and Delaney had conjured up based on a single letter containing a single sentence. *Anyone could've written the threatening message, because anybody's capable of murder.*

Chapter Twelve

"Kim! *Mia cara.*" Aunt Estelle greeted Barbieri with a great big hug after she let herself in. There was no need to knock; Estelle had an open-door policy every Thursday morning as far as Barbieri was concerned.

Estelle Apuzzo was her mom's older sister, with the same smile, the same mannerisms, the same mom-ness. Talking with her aunt, in a home very much like the one she herself had grown up in, was as close as Barbieri could be to talking with her own mom, except without any mother-daughter complications creeping in.

"Hey, Aunt Estelle. Good morning." Barbieri still called her "Aunt Estelle" because it defined her own place in the Barbieri family. Codified it for all time. Likewise, her aunt was one of the few people who called her by her first name. Aunt guidelines allowed for it.

She joined her aunt in the kitchen, a cramped space filled with appliances and cookware that had changed little since she and her late husband, Seb, had bought them a half century before. They sat with their cups of espresso at one corner of the kitchen table, a plate of homemade anisette cookies between them.

"Those bodies in the river. What'd the autopsy say, Kim? Double homicide, right?" Aunt Estelle loved getting lurid details from her niece the paper left out. She was immensely proud of her niece, the successful *Daily News* reporter, and scoured the crime blotter every morning for her byline. Until the name Kim Barbieri appeared in the wedding announcements section, it would have to do.

"Sorry, no. It looks like suicide. Sisters from Saudi Arabia. They decided to end it all and jumped off the bridge together. They didn't want

34

to be sent back home, apparently." Barbieri hated to disappoint Aunt Estelle.

"Muslim sisters? Jesus…." Aunt Estelle hated to be disappointed.

The discovery that the girls were Saudi was exactly why Barbieri wanted to be an investigative reporter. *I need to write about these girls' lives, not only their deaths. Why did they come here? Who was sending them home? Why would they rather kill themselves than go back there?* Barbieri kept the thoughts to herself, because she was not quite ready for her aunt's career counseling.

"I did pick up something about the math teacher who got busted."

"The lesbian at Madison High School? Bring it."

Her aunt's home was a standard-issue two-story postwar house, red brick outside with a small porch in front for people-watching, an alley not quite big enough for a car on the side, and a postage-stamp backyard hemmed in by her neighbors' yards on all three sides. If all you wanted was to mind your own business, you could not do it there. Inside, Barbieri found everything as it had been forever: the well-worn sofa, the aroma of Italian cooking wafting from the kitchen, the same black-and-white photos of her mom and dad and grandparents, aunts and uncles and cousins, on every surface. It all made Barbieri feel ten years old again, held tight in a warm embrace as close to the home she grew up in as she would ever get.

Barbieri had emigrated years before from the part of Brooklyn her aunt still called home, a neighborhood a world away from the upscale uniformity in which she was now immersed. Her homeland was maybe a half-hour train ride away, a few miles down on the elevated Brighton line, in a neighborhood of unruly extended families crowded into single-family homes, tiny mom-and-pop stores and comfortable old diners, and a crazy quilt of ethnic enclaves seemingly changing from one block to the next.

Here, the melting pot of old gave way to a hodgepodge of languages and cultures and religions. Immigrant Chinese, Pakistanis, Poles, Orthodox Jews, Bajans, Haitians, and other refugees from shithole countries shared a few square miles of geography and nothing else, and plain old American English did not stand a chance.

It was the world Estelle Apuzzo had been born in years earlier, and where she continued to live for as long as Barbieri could remember. Her first neighborhood was the only one she knew.

Barbieri had gotten off the local at the Avenue M station at nine in the morning and started walking over to her aunt's house. Halfway there, though, the skies opened and the wind picked up, causing a driving rain that soaked her from head to toe. She ran into Starlight, the Greek diner on Coney Island Avenue her mom and dad used to take her to as a kid, to try to dry off and wait out the sudden storm.

Barbieri knew she would be having espresso and cookies later in the morning, but nursing a mug of mint tea at the far end of the counter usually offered a much-needed moment of aloneness before the enhanced interrogation techniques to come. This time, however, she did not feel alone. *Who's staring at me? Why?* Someone or something had gotten her attention. She was not alarmed, exactly. Or scared. She assumed it was just someone who thought she looked familiar yet could not quite place her. This was where she grew up, after all, and a few of her neighbors from way back when had never left.

Still holding her mug, Barbieri glanced to her left. There was no one else at the counter. Looking around, she noticed four older women at one table and an older couple at another. Nobody she recognized. Over at the table by the window, she saw four men deep in conversation. Again, nobody was paying her any attention at all.

Get a grip, girl. You're imagining things.

When the rain finally stopped, Barbieri finished her tea and signaled the waitress for the bill. After leaving a generous tip, she resumed walking to her aunt's home.

"So, are you seeing anyone?" Grilling her niece about crime was merely a prelude to the main event. Barbieri's marriage prospects were item number one on the agenda this Thursday, as they were every Thursday.

"Couple. One looks like a keeper." Barbieri was not being especially truthful. Timothy Brennan was only a placeholder. Their relationship would never keep and she knew it. That was perfectly fine with her, even if it would never be for Aunt Estelle. Barbieri cared entirely about what people did, and nothing about whether they were part of a boxed set. Besides, he was not even Italian, so why make trouble?

Before she grew into the person she would become, she had had a few relationships, usually with men a little too much like herself. They were the opposite sex, true, but she and they were almost too alike in everything except junk. *The near clones always come with strings attached. I don't want strings. The only baggage I can tolerate is my own.* Brennan brought none to their relationship.

Her aunt would have none of it. She came from an earlier generation and had never stopped embracing traditional ideas about marriage and family. Barbieri was fully prepared for her Thursday morning earful. She told friends she hated every minute of it, while reluctantly admitting to herself she loved it.

"This keeper, Kim? What does he do?" Barbieri knew Aunt Estelle did not believe her for a second. Her aunt knew better than to pry, yet she went ahead and pried anyway.

"I'm not going there. How are Uncle Phil and Aunt Lo? And the twins?" Barbieri had learned how to deftly change the subject by shifting the discussion to her aunt's second most interesting topic of conversation.

Their game of hide-and-seek over espresso and cookies continued for a few hours, until it was time for her to head back home. Barbieri gave her aunt a great big goodbye hug, which they both badly needed, then retraced her steps back to the Avenue M station and Fort Greene.

Chapter Thirteen

Guys I get together with every few weeks or so could easily be mistaken for a Viagra focus group. All late fifties or early sixties, white, of sound mind and body. Some are already retired, like me. Others are counting the days till they can join us. Far as I can recall, we all first met through our wives and learned to play nice without the womenfolk.

Usually we sit over coffee and doughnuts and shoot the exact same breeze we shot last time we met. Talk therapy where nobody gets better and no problem goes away. They say guys don't really like confiding in one another, but in situations like this, where one of us has something on his mind, we turn into a kind of support group.

Trust me, my compadres are never shy about weighing in on issues they know next to nothing about, of which there are plenty. They all mean well, I know, and once in a blue moon, you hear something actually constructive from one of them. Happens.

It's raining this particular Thursday morning, a real soaker. Biblical. Everybody's plans for the day, especially anything outdoors, are put on hold, so nobody has anything better to do than kill a few hours dispensing wisdom at the Starlight diner. It's on Coney Island and M, been there since forever. I don't know if there's actually an American cuisine in this country. If there is, it was brought here by Greek immigrants.

Starlight is one of those places straight out of the diner manual: mirrors everywhere, long red counter and red vinyl stools opposite the door, a few tables for four in the middle, and a long row of booths with worn-out and taped-up red vinyl seats by the windows. You walk in and right away there's the aroma of hot coffee being poured into every other mug, and when they seat you, you're handed a menu with a thousand variations of the same dish: comfort food. Starlight's not a restaurant you go to for atmosphere, what with the noise level and everything, yet regular customers like the guys and me don't seem to mind at all. The place is always packed.

At the appointed hour, 'round nine in the morning, we all drive over, pull into the lot, run in out of the rain, dry off best we can, and commandeer our usual table between the counter and the side window. All the other regulars seem to be in their assigned seats. Four old ladies at their table yakking away, old couple who've never said a word to each other at theirs. Must've taken a vow of silence when they got married. Also a tall brunette at the end of the counter nursing her mug of tea. Nice-looking. For some reason I can't take my eyes off her.

Then it hits me. I could swear it's the reporter I wrote to, from her picture on the *Daily News* website. Faces are one thing I don't forget. I make a mental note to go back online when I get home, see if I'm hallucinating.

After the waitress brings over our orders—iced coffee and key lime pie for me—I bring up the topic of the day, my next career, and open the floor to discussion. They know I recently walked away from my job, so I'm sure they have a thought or two on the subject.

One of them suggests IT. I tell him, "I know my strengths, and being twenty-five isn't one of them." Another suggested making some kind of military gear, which is actually a good idea considering the skill set I bring to the table. Nothing came of it, though, as I've decided to pursue this other opportunity involving assault with a deadly weapon.

We ride this occupational therapy merry-go-round a while longer, until the rain lets up and we can all go back to our loved ones. The guys all meant well, and their ideas could've pointed someone in the right direction. Not me, though. Still, the round-table symposium of village elders isn't a complete waste of a miserable morning; by offering up their conventional ideas, they actually helped me turn in the right direction.

It hit me during our breakfast that one way to make it big in business, any business, is to think outside the box, yet another corporate horseshit word of the day. Experiment. Innovate. Be creative.

If you really want to break out, you have to be willing to take a risk. You need to walk miles away from your comfort zone, the area where you've proven yourself time and time again, and explore a whole new field.

As I'm doing now. Escaping my comfort zone is fine with me, perfect even. For the first time I can remember, at least since I was in knee-pants, I'm ready to entertain an idea way, *way* out of the box, an impulse of mine that's always lain beneath my goody-two-shoes surface. Some kind of dark urge I can't quite put my finger on, even though I'm certain it's there.

I'm not going back into the same business, but into a whole new line of work. Illegal. Criminal. Fuckin' violent. No venture capital is needed, of course. It would be a low budget operation if ever there was one. No networking involved. In fact, working alone is pretty much mandatory. I'm also pretty sure I'll have the market to myself. There are no competitors out there who'll try to steal business from me.

Chapter Fourteen

Friday, March 31
3:34 PM

Barbieri recognized the sender's second message the instant it caught her eye. The envelope came on a Friday, exactly one week after the first. Same paper stock, same typeface. It was definitely sent by the soon-to-be killer, if that was what he really was.

Careful not to leave any prints this time, she put on gloves, slit open the envelope with a knife, removed the new letter and compared it with the first, which had never left its premium location on top of her desk. They also appeared to be indistinguishable, save for one critical difference—the sentence on the top third panel.

The initial assignment is to identify the gender and age of the victim.

She grabbed her cell and called her partner.

"Another one?"

"Another one."

"Right over."

Twenty minutes later, Barbieri buzzed him into the building. Upstairs, Delaney let himself in, took off his overcoat and cameraman's vest, and hung them up on hooks in the hallway. The sun had gone back into hiding after its brief appearance the week before, and the cold, damp weather had decided to make everyone miserable a while longer. He walked right over to Barbieri's desk in the study. She had already placed the envelopes and letters side by side for him. Without prompting,

Delaney scanned both envelopes first and confirmed everything was identical except the date on the postmark. Like the first letter, it had been mailed two days before.

"Identical."

"Identical."

He then turned his attention to the letters, scanning back and forth between them. They also appeared to be identical, save for the message.

Delaney read the sentence aloud. *"The initial assignment is to identify the gender and age of the victim."* Then he read it again. He waited a nanosecond longer before stating what was now obvious to both of them. "He's back."

"Getting serious."

"Initial assignment?"

"His, not ours."

"Doesn't know the victim."

"No relationship."

"Not the wife. Or anyone he works with."

"Not any neighbor."

"Rules out act of passion. No revenge."

"Cold-blooded murder."

"A hit. Holy shit."

"Holy shit indeed."

"Probably of sound mind and definitely methodical."

"Don't know about the sound mind, but I'll give you methodical."

"Going step by step to carry out—"

"An assassination."

"Termination with extreme prejudice."

"No Mafia hit."

"Terms he uses. Intend, commit, initial, assignment, gender, identify. Precise, formal…."

"Teacher, maybe. Engineer, businessman."

"Never killed before."

"Agreed."

"What now? Call the police?"

"Not yet. Maybe after letter number three."

"You sure there'll be one."

"Hundred percent."

"Could be too late. For us, I mean."

"Explain."

"Not telling the cops about a murder in the works?"

"Point taken."

"Crap."

"What?"

"Postmark."

"What about it?"

"This one's clear."

"11209."

"Fuck me."

"Not gonna happen, Barbieri."

"He's a Brooklyn boy."

This last bit of information took things up a notch for Barbieri and Delaney—especially Barbieri. On top of the profile they had already conjured up about the killer-in-training, they now had a location for him—a neighborhood off the Verrazzano Bridge called Bay Ridge. White ethnic enclave since forever. *Our guy either lives there, or works there, or visits there at least once a week. Is he passing through on the way to somewhere else? His part of the borough isn't far from mine. Maybe fifteen minutes away by car, give or take, on the Gowanus and BQE, longer on the subway.*

Their great-minds moment took the sender's involvement in her life from fairly abstract and remote to concrete, immediate, and ominous. It moved her from feeling in control of things to feeling vulnerable.

I do not like feeling vulnerable.

Chapter Fifteen

Kids are always doing stuff they'd never do later on. I know I did. Use a magnifying glass on a sunny day to start a fire or roast a caterpillar, maybe. Sneak into the movies. I was always doing stuff I had no business doing.

It's stupid, dangerous, and that only makes you want to do it more. Think you'll never get caught, one, and two, if you do get caught, you'd maybe get sent to your room or not get your allowance for a week or two. No big deal. It's a rite of passage almost all of us outgrow eventually—at least the ones who don't grow up psycho—but maybe I haven't.

This dark side I had as a kid seems to be inching its way back, or maybe never went away. Look, to be clear, I'm not comparing taking a human life with the stupid pranks I pulled as a kid. I can't even say for sure where this evil side of me is coming from. I'm merely speculating here, but the thrill of actually getting away with doing something wrong is pretty much the same.

I know the stakes are much higher now, both in the magnitude of the crime I'm thinking about and in the punishment I'd receive for it. I know I might live to regret it, sense it deep inside. I've decided to go with it anyway, see where it takes me.

I have no models to follow, no textbooks to pore over. People in this line of work don't write them. If I go ahead with this, I know I'll be acting alone, a one-man start-up in a business liable to get pretty nasty, where the risk-reward ratio is almost all risk and almost no reward. I dare not tell Helen what I'm thinking. I dare not tell anyone, for that matter. The law frowns upon such things.

And the tall brunette at the diner, sitting by herself at the counter? It was her, definitely. The reporter. I didn't know what to make of it, though, her being in my neighborhood. Pure coincidence, I swear.

Chapter Sixteen

So now I've found myself open to committing a criminal act, an evil deed the average guy, if he was having a bad day, would entertain for a few minutes before coming to his senses. Or if not open to it, at least putting it up for a vote.

Maybe I'm being dishonest. In truth, I opened myself up to it. I'm not avoiding responsibility here; I'm the driver, not a passenger. Cold-blooded murder. Nuts, right? If this is what shrinks call a desperate cry for help, they'd need a lot stronger word than *desperate* to describe it. Sick, maybe. Or pathological.

Murder is evil. Even thinking about taking someone's life is evil. I know this. My mental gymnastics is leading me to believe maybe I'm not nuts. I'm too much of a control freak. Evil... perhaps.

This impulse of mine has barely flickered to life and it's already screwing with my head. Do I care enough about my emerging dark side to stop? Not really. As long as I'm not caught, I'm fine with it. I think. Again, this acceptance of my darker self is taking place when it's barely formed. Like one little germ cell deep inside your body which, if you don't take anything for it, might grow into a full-blown fatal infection. We're talking dark-where-sunlight-goes-to-die dark.

Though what I'm thinking about hasn't really gone beyond idle thoughts, I'm not trying to suppress them at all. If I'm not careful, they could take on a life of their own, easily. It's like trying to start a fire by rubbing two sticks together and you gently blow on the spark, trying to create just enough wind to breathe life into the fire, just not enough to blow it out. Before you know it, whoosh. House is engulfed in flames and there's no escape. Guess this is evil, too.

I'm okay, as far as my own opinion of myself goes. At this point I'm telling myself I don't care one whit what *I* think of me, only what my family thinks of me. Helen, my sisters. Far as they're concerned, I'm starting to live one huge lie. Not happy about that, but I figure as long as they have no idea what I'm up to, it's all systems go. That's the truly scary part.

I know taking a life is somewhat un-Christian, yet it won't stop me either. Though I was raised Episcopalian, I'm not a big fan of organized religion these days. Take it or leave it, makes no difference to me. Yet I know without a doubt my church has a problem with murder, in no uncertain terms. Thou shalt not kill. Couldn't be plainer.

Every culture in the world knows killing is wrong. The priests didn't pull this stuff out of their asses. They insisted it was the word of God, and if thou break the rule of the big fella, thou shalt be punished big-time.

Even if I stopped going to church years ago, which I did, the church's teachings, its morality, are deeply imbedded in me. Murder is the most sinful thing you can do, isn't it? It's one of the mind games going on in my thick skull. Crazy as it sounds, murder's made the journey from being a major crime, the absolute worst thing you can do, to a sin against my religion. Simply another sin, like stepping out on your wife.

Morality is how you act when no one's watching you. Isn't that how the saying goes? Well, if no one's watching me except me, it's all good in my humble opinion. Immoral, certainly, but good. If you can live with yourself after, go right ahead. You only have to answer to yourself, no one else.

I'm not much for introspection, never been one to look too closely at my emotional side, peel away the layers to get at my deep psychological issues. If you can live a normal life despite your inner demons, let them be, I say.

This idea I'm becoming open to homicide is no one-off impulse, I'm certain. It's not suppressed rage that can't wait to get out. Well, I'm not completely certain, to be honest. The thing with being passed over for partner, I'm pretty much over it. Joshua Kelleher may be a moronic boor who married his way to the top, but it's not a capital offense. There's no death penalty for being a son of a bitch. I still think about it, though. I still go over the conversation I should've had with the board in my head, and I still get angry.

I don't know if a shrink would see a cause and effect going on here, but I don't think my lethal ambition has anything to do with Kelleher. The fuck.

This urge to kill I'm nurturing—not an urge exactly, more like a ride to destinations unknown I'm willing to take—is a whole other animal, dangerous territory I no longer wish to control.

I'm not motivated by greed, to be sure. I wouldn't kill anybody for a million bucks. If I do act on this notion and take some guy's life, it would be a crime without any passion whatsoever. For me, the thrill would be in the planning of the hit and not getting arrested for it, not the hit itself. The idea I could commit the perfect crime is rewarding in itself.

This drive to take a life started out as not much more than an idle thought, yet now I've let it totally preoccupy me twenty-four/seven. Whenever it feels like it, it takes control of my thinking, like I'm at its mercy. I can be with my wife, my buddies, the neighbors, yet my mind is elsewhere, and no one's allowed to join me there.

"Hey, we're waiting here. You in or out?" a poker buddy named Bert asks me during one of our weekly card games. Practically has to poke me in the ribs, I'm so far out there. I love the game, maybe my only vice—correction, my only other vice—because it allows me to let my risk management skills out for exercise.

"Sorry," I reply, trying to focus again on my hand. "I see you... and raise you," I add, tossing in two bucks' worth of chips. I'm not sure if it's the smartest move on my part, and frankly I don't care. My mind is otherwise engaged.

"Let him stay in the twilight zone," one of the other guys weighs in. "Better for us. I might even win a hand."

This is the way it works, evil. When you let the dark side out, it tends to engage in mind control. It becomes all you think about, from the moment you wake up. The guys notice it, for sure, like my wife does. I certainly notice it. I know what's happening. I'm actually fine with it, perfectly okay with letting myself be pushed around by my own dark creation.

Someone is going to die on account of me. It doesn't really matter what the other party in the transaction did to deserve it. I have no motivation, no real reason at all, other than to take on a challenge and see it through.

Not personal, just business.

Chapter Seventeen

"Captain."

"Miss Barbieri. Nice to see you again."

The reporter and the commanding officer had run into each other at the Starbucks a couple of blocks from Manhattan Criminal Court, where they were working on unrelated cases. To keep up appearances, they shook hands when they met, like they always did. As if they were colleagues, nothing more. The last thing they needed was to be the subject of courthouse gossip.

After a brief stab at seasonably warm, the temperature had continued its return to damn cold, and Barbieri was back to wearing her winter uniform—black-lined trench coat, muted tweed jacket, simple white blouse and black wool pants. She also had her trusty messenger bag, filled with the computer and accessories print reporters cannot survive without.

Brennan was wearing the uniform he wore every day, rain or shine, on duty or off—blue sports jacket, white shirt, red tie, and black pants. *Somebody needs to take him to Nordstrom.* His shield was visible, clipped onto his belt, and his gun was out of sight, hidden by his jacket. Of course he was also carrying a book, the one by his bed she had leafed through last time she stayed over. There was a lot of waiting-around-with-nothing-to-do in the courthouse.

Running into each other all the time became close to inevitable, given their respective beats, and they had both learned to be pretty blasé about the whole thing. Hot and bothered at home; cool, calm, and collected by day. Just part of the job. If the pair ever broke up, they could not stop seeing each other if they tried.

After picking up their coffees from the barista, they took adjoining stools at the counter and sat facing the window. Neither of them was worried about their conversation being overheard; they would only be talking shop.

"What are you here for, Captain?"

"Homicide in Chinatown last night. Looks like it's tied to one in Sunset Park last Thursday. We like the same guy for both. You?"

"Hate crime. Puerto Rican kid threw an Indian man onto the subway tracks early this morning. Grand Street station on the D line. Bunch of good Samaritans helped him climb back on the platform before the train came, and held the kid until the police came. Told the arresting officer he hates Muslims, apparently."

"Victim isn't a Muslim. Indians are Hindu. They have less use for Muslims than he does. Idiot."

"If I get to interview the idiot, I'll let him know his effort was wasted." She heard the ding of an incoming text message, her cue to take her cell out of her coat pocket and glance at the display. "Arraignment. Gotta run."

Barbieri put the lid back on her coffee, grabbed her messenger bag, and hurried off, leaving Brennan sitting at the Starbucks counter. Ordinarily Barbieri enjoyed these chance encounters with Brennan, yet she was actually relieved this one was cut short by the just-in-the-nick-of-time text. It meant she did not have an opportunity to tell him about the two letters. She was leery about doing so, yet did not know precisely why.

Is it because dragging him into this might force him to reveal this thing he has with me to the department? Or do I want him to know I'm a big girl who can take care of things all by myself? Or is it for an entirely selfish reason, a possible story in it for me? Scoop of the century.

If I get another letter, I'll tell him. I swear. No, I will. Definitely.

God, the murder hasn't even happened yet, and it's making my life way too difficult.

Chapter Eighteen

So I'm trying to figure out where my urge to end someone's life is coming from, and I've convinced myself anger isn't to blame. I keep telling myself I'm over Kelleher because this is what I believe. Then something happens to make me think maybe there's something there.

Helen and I are in the city. Nothing's on our schedules, so we decide to spend the afternoon in SoHo in lower Manhattan. The designer boutiques there, they should be paying her to model their clothes. On the tall side, like me, with a great figure, blue eyes and long black hair going gray. Helen never let herself go. A real knockout, let me tell you.

SoHo's a zoo, jammed with tourists who think they're saving money by spending every last dime they have at outlet stores. About three fifteen, three thirty, we're leaving a place I never heard of before called Celine, on Wooster Street, I think. We're loaded down with shopping bags and are both a little tired and cranky, so we decide to take a break and stop somewhere for coffee. After a while, shopping becomes a drag, even for her.

Helen and I are at the corner of Spring and Greene, waiting for the light to change. We're right at the edge of the curb, trying not to be pushed into the street by the shoppers jammed right behind us. All of a sudden, a motorbike zooms past us, inches away. Driver's turning the corner way too fast and practically jumps the curb. We both flinch and sorta lean way back, like you do when you're reacting to a brushback pitch. I recover and bounce back up. I'm okay, except Helen keeps falling backward, like she's losing her balance. Luckily, a couple of people catch her before she hits the ground and lift her back onto her feet. I swear to God I thought she got hit.

"You okay?" I ask, inspecting her from head to toe to see if she's injured anywhere.

"I'm fine," she says, looking herself over to see if she's in one piece. "He didn't hit me. I got startled. Motorbike seemed to come out of nowhere." She's not hurt, only stunned, thank God. I eyeball her again to make sure she's all right, then turn away from her and look down the street. I spot the guy on the motorbike, stopped at the light one block away. From the back, it looks like some kind of cheap mystery machine messengers ride these days, an ordinary mountain bike with an electric motor stuck on with duct tape and spit and more duct tape. The drivers are all unlicensed and don't seem to have much regard for traffic laws. Or sidewalks.

I leave my bags with Helen and race over to him to keep him from riding off. I stand right in front of the bike, my body language telling him I want to have a word with him, and I start screaming at him at the top of my lungs. "Off the fuckin' bike! What the fuck is wrong with you?" I can see he's a middle-aged Chinese man who clearly doesn't understand a word of English and has no idea he almost ran over somebody, but I keep yelling at him anyway. He's obviously scared to death, not seeming to understand why this lunatic American is about to beat the crap out of him.

"Dave! Stop!" Helen's now standing between me and him, trying to keep me from making the situation worse than it already is. The confrontation hasn't escalated beyond yelling, and she doesn't need me to start hitting the poor guy. I stop screaming although I don't stop fuming. I'm overreacting, I know, but I can't help myself.

"Calm down. Look at me, Dave. Nothing happened. I'm okay." She escorts me back onto the sidewalk, trying to maintain eye contact with me, and I'm looking down, trying my best to avoid it like a kid being punished. After a few more moments of this fragile ceasefire, she's confident I'm not going to attack the driver and signals to him to go. He nods in response to her sign language, says something in Chinese, sounding like it could mean "thank you," and drives off looking relieved. International incident's over. She looks me up and down, clearly alarmed at the way I lost it, and reaches out to hold my hand as we resume our walk to get some coffee.

"Sorry, Helen," I attempt a preemptive peace offering.

"You scared the crap out of the poor man... and me."

We buy two cups of espresso to go from a tiny French bakery on West Broadway and sit outside on a small bench surrounded by our shopping bags. This conversation isn't going to be easy for me.

"I said, 'I'm sorry,' hon." My apology works every bit as badly the second time.

"Not enough, David. The way you acted was way out of line. Where is all this coming from?"

"Don't know. I thought he hurt you."

"Bullshit. C'mon, David. I told you I wasn't hurt, and he didn't hit me. I think you already had anger inside you, and this poor man gave you an excuse to express it. It's not healthy, and you know it." She's talking to me as she does with her students, which makes sense considering I'm acting like a kid having a temper tantrum.

I keep staring into my cup of coffee, not saying anything. Other than the thing at work, I am the un-angriest guy in the world. At least I think I am. Besides, she doesn't know the real reason I retired when I did. I always used to talk with her about my work, but only the good parts. I never brought my office problems home with me.

"I'm not going to make you open up, Dave. I wouldn't even try." She reaches out and grabs my hand as a peace offering. She isn't mad at me, her gesture is saying, but at how badly I behaved. Hate the sin, love the sinner. You want to know why I love her? That's it right there. "Please don't do this again."

We drink the rest of our coffee in silence, thank heaven. I'm not sure if it's because I don't know what to say to her, or because I want to keep hiding my anger issues from her.

~ * ~

This anger thing Helen was seeing for the first time was nothing new to me. Like I told you before, I was mad as hell at my company for not making me a partner, and I wanted to strangle Kelleher for cutting to the head of the line. I had told myself to man up and get over it, which I honestly believed I did. Yet clearly this anger wasn't suppressed. It's there all right, inside, seething.

To be honest, I had a lot of hostility churning inside me at work long before Kelleher got there. There were plenty of times I wanted colleagues to suffer, feelings I wrote off at the time as nothing to worry about.

A tad too hotheaded for my own good, I had a bullshit detector that landed me in one too many arguments. I'd been known to rub colleagues the wrong way, guilty beyond a reasonable doubt of expressing my opinion—contempt, usually—a little louder than the situation called for. That's just not done, and I had a hard time letting go of this particular little habit. It was one of the reasons the bosses gave me for not making partner. They had to justify their decision without mentioning the heir apparent, and it was justification enough. Least it's what they said.

Maybe I should've taken it as a warning sign, my tantrums. Some fights I got into, I wanted to grab the guy by the throat and strangle him. I wasn't going to, of course, and maybe everyone has this touch of evil once in a while, if they're provoked.

One time some numbskull trying to make a name for himself was giving a presentation to me and the other managers. I never much liked the guy. His presentation, though, was really impressive, one slide after another showing the huge opportunity our competitors had overlooked and the incredible profits we'd make by seizing it. He made it all seem as easy as picking the low-hanging fruit, except I could see the whole thing was full of holes, beginning to end. Complete waste of everyone's time.

Rather than tear him a new one in public, I held my tongue—bit it, actually—although the doodling I was doing on my notepad was another matter. While he was waxing stupid, I was drawing him getting absolutely flattened by a steamroller. Not in a comic book way but in a completely gory way. Blood everywhere. Vital organs squashed. Brain matter splattered.

I guess no matter what I showed on the outside, call it professional indifference, inside I really wanted him to suffer. Again, only a fantasy, like the urge I sometimes had to throttle Kelleher for no reason. Still, looking back, my evil intent toward others was definitely a warning sign able to be interpreted two possible ways. One, I had a lot of anger in me I could control if I really wanted to, or two, I was one demented psycho who needed to be locked away before I killed someone.

Unfortunately, it was a sign I used to always ignore. Not now, though. If all goes according to plan, I'll soon be crossing a line from model citizen to stone-cold killer. I'll be turning into a criminal, as if merely thinking about murder doesn't make me one already. Guilty way, *way* beyond a shadow of a doubt.

Look, I can tell you in all honesty I'm not driven by rage, yet it's there. Definitely.

Chapter Nineteen

With only the two letters as their guide, Barbieri and Delaney had a pretty solid hunch her fellow Brooklynite had never killed before. He must be some kind of academic or executive, based on his command of language, if nothing else. Had to be.

The second letter told them the killer had reached his first decision point, choosing whom to kill. *Whose life is going to be snuffed out only minutes after he runs into the killer? Or she. This maniac's going to have to choose between male and female, too.*

Barbieri decided to try answering the question without her partner. It seemed to be a question of logic, her strong suit, and she was always up for challenges forcing her to think things through to the logical conclusion. Being methodical, she reasoned, the mystery man had probably already put together a list of decisions he would have to make: ideal victim, location of the crime, weapon, et cetera. He would then have to make a sort of decision tree where he went one direction if he chose option A and another if he chose option B. *How I'd do it. Knowing who the victim would be will help him decide how he'd be killed, which tells him where he'd be killed, which in turn tells him when he'd be killed. Just go with the flow.*

He was new at this, of course, so he could not know for sure if he was making the right choices. He might resort to trial and error, making things up as he went along. Once he made this first decision, though, Barbieri believed he would stick with it unless it turned out to be a real problem he had not expected. Like anyone taking on a new challenge, he would find a way to deal with drawbacks he had failed to plan for.

The second letter said the killer is going to select the victim's gender, which tells me he doesn't know the victim. If he does, the gender would already be decided.

Barbieri guessed that as a rookie, and as a male, he would not kill a woman unless he had some deep psychological hang-up about the fairer sex. Hatred, maybe, or some kind of male insecurity. *I may be projecting a little too much, using my girl mind to think like a boy, but you make do with the tools you have.*

There was one fact, though, bolstering her hunch the victim would be male, something she had picked up in her on-the-job training—probability. *With most men who kill a stranger, the victim is another man. By a wide margin. Men killing women makes the news more, except they're few and far between. God, men are so fucked up.*

She also surmised the victim would not be old or disabled, or a child. *Maybe I'm projecting here too, in terms of my own beliefs, but I can't see my guy killing someone who doesn't have a fighting chance.* As for race, Barbieri did not have any insights on the subject. *Does he have a bias? If not, does he want the cops to think he has a bias?* So far, at least, this act appeared not to be based on any kind of prejudice toward one minority or another. There were plenty in New York to choose from, hundreds maybe, so this lack of bigotry did not help her any.

Based on what Barbieri's inner Kreskin told her, the victim her killer was driven to murder would be an able-bodied adult male, race TBD. Call it woman's intuition, maybe. She was so sure she did not see any need to confirm it with Delaney. *I know I could be wrong, but it's where I'm putting my money. Do I cave and tell Brennan, though? If I do, he's going to insist on seeing the mail I'm getting. Or worse, take the whole damn thing off my hands.*

~ * ~

So how, exactly, do I go about deciding who'll stop breathing right after making my acquaintance?

Tell the truth, I'm not really sure. What I am sure of is by making the right choice in this process of elimination, pardon my pun, I could help make my plan a success. Making the wrong choice, on the other hand, could cause it to fail big-time. In which case I'm going to jail for a long, long time.

The soon-to-be deceased could be someone I know, or a complete stranger. Male or female. Young or old or in between. Black or white or yellow or another color entirely. American or otherwise. High class, middle, or low. Straight, gay, or bi. He could be gainfully employed or down on his luck. Filthy rich or dirt poor. Didn't matter at all, at least to me. I could put my homicidal urge to good use and reduce the city's homeless population by one, but if I do, it'll be purely by chance. I don't care one way or another.

Another critical variable: size and strength of the victim. Myself, I'm a pretty strong guy and in pretty good shape. Five-eleven, one ninety-five. If I have to use brute force, like if I decide to strangle the guy, he'd have to be weaker and smaller. If the victim decides to lodge a protest against his imminent demise, we don't want him to be able to overpower me, right?

Lots of factors to consider, so I'm tackling this problem the way I always have—weigh the pros and cons of each type of victim, rule them in or out. Knowing *who* the victim is will drive the rest of my decisions. All of this will culminate in his death by my hands.

First, familiarity. Could I kill someone I know? Someone I play ball with or do business with or run into from time to time at the mall? I don't hate anyone badly enough. Frankly, I don't personally know anyone who deserves to die, although I have to admit one or two come close. The act of murder would also be way too personal, I think. With a friend or acquaintance, I'd also know way too much about the person's family. About his personality. His quirks.

I also have no desire to make a widow of his wife, who I might know, or take away his kid's father. They haven't done anything wrong. I also know it couldn't be someone I know because of who I am. I couldn't and wouldn't ever intentionally hurt a friend. Don't have it in me. Would I want the last person he sees to be me?

Also, I don't want anyone else blamed for the murder, or even suspected of it. Person of interest, in police speak. If I know the victim happens to have made a few enemies from time to time, I wouldn't want the cops looking too closely at them, or worse, arresting them. No need for collateral damage. Likewise, I wouldn't want my name picked up by any detectives asking about the victim's friends and neighbors. I want to keep myself out of it. Completely under their radar.

No, it would have to be a complete stranger. Much easier, right? This stranger could be male or female. Another decision to make. Could I kill a woman as readily as I could a man? Size and strength, or rather the lack of them, work in women's favor as far as I'm concerned. If it gets physical and she fights back, I'm pretty sure I could overpower her.

On the downside, I couldn't kill a woman. I've always been an old unapologetic sexist. In a good way, I mean. I hold doors for them, give them my seat on the bus. Honest. More and more, all I get for my gentlemanly manners is a dirty look from the lady I'm being a gentleman for, which I can never understand. Never stops me, though. Can't help myself; it's how I was raised.

I also admit I have a big problem with violence against women. I have no problem at all with women police officers or soldiers, except something inside me thinks they shouldn't be anywhere near the front lines. Women aren't supposed to kill or be killed. They shouldn't be maimed or incinerated or dismembered in the line of duty. That's what men are for.

No way could I bring myself to kill a female. It would have to be a male. Pretty much sums up my relationships with the fairer sex. Chalk me up as an unrepentant sexist, but I couldn't do it. Sue me.

His sexual orientation is also his business, not mine. What do I care who someone sleeps with? Couldn't tell one way or the other by looking at him anyway, to be honest, although there are a lot of gays out there, and a lot of haters. So if I did happen to kill one, the police might think it's a hate crime—which it definitely won't be—and find some homophobe to pin it on.

What about age? How old would this male stranger be? I couldn't kill an old man, simply out of respect. Not disrespecting your elders was always drummed into me by my mom and dad, and what could be more disrespectful to a senior citizen than moving up his expiration date? I also couldn't kill a boy. Children are put on this Earth to be protected. Until they're able to fend for themselves, they're very much a work in progress. Let them learn, play, explore, have a crush. There's plenty of time to be a victim of violent crime later.

Nope, no women, no boys, no old men. Also no disability, like he's blind or uses a walker. He's already suffered plenty without being attacked simply because he's there.

The victim would have to be an apparently healthy adult male, probably middle-aged. Does his race matter any? Not that I can see. An ordinary, run-of-the-mill African American doesn't deserve to die any more than a plain vanilla Caucasian. Neither does a homegrown American versus a recent immigrant from Syria or Mexico. I've decided I could kill a black or Hispanic or white or Asian male without giving a thought to their gene pool. For my purposes, it doesn't matter which ethnicity box he checks on the census form.

All in all, if he's a healthy adult male I've never met before, he's fair game. I can't ask her, but I'm pretty sure the reporter lady would approve. Of course, it may not be a total coincidence that "healthy adult male" pretty much describes the individual who screwed me out of my promotion. I ain't stupid.

Chapter Twenty

One tool of the trade in Barbieri's line of work was reading people, at least to the extent said person would help her write a better piece. *A colorful person brings a lot more to the story than a tree stump does.* If she sensed a person she was interviewing was sane and credible and gave her a nice, juicy quote, she put him in the story. If not, she would give him a good citizenship medal, thank him for his time, and keep looking until she found someone who was.

Murder suspects were a lot harder to read. It was not so much because they were dangerous, but because they were often crazy to boot. Not criminally insane, just old-fashioned insane. Flat-out nuts. The topic happened to come up in the middle of a romantic conversation she and Brennan were having about capital cases. *My dear correspondent could turn out to be a total nutjob. Brennan's not going to be suspicious if I bring the subject up.*

Coming back to her living room carrying a bottle of white wine, with *Otello*—the earlier version by Rossini, not Verdi—playing just softly enough to let them talk, she brought up a story she had done on a kid in Bed Stuy who joined the killing fraternity while barely out of elementary school. "It's like he'd been born to kill, and no one could talk any sense into him. Not his mom, not his minister, not even his older brother doing life in Attica. Kid's a born psychopath in my book."

"Maybe he's simply well-adjusted, Kim. Ever think of that? Where he grew up, killing is little more than a gang initiation. He'd execute a kid he never saw before on orders from above to fit in with his peers."

"You pass, little man. Have a cookie."

"It's the life he lives. He only wants to belong. It doesn't make him a psychopath, necessarily. A sociopath more likely. A wannabee career criminal with no conscience. One thing most murderers have in common is they've seen someone they know get killed. Not poverty, or no father, or crack. They witnessed a murder. The guy who got killed has a long rap sheet himself, most times."

"Go along to get along. Is that it, Cap'n?"

"Kill or be killed, more like it. Think of the boy as a conformist. A better example of crazy enough to kill is road rage. Temporary insanity. Like the officer who got himself arrested on the Cross County Parkway last week."

"Was he in your squad? Homicide?"

"No, Computer Crimes. He's a regular cop, no hint of trouble. Never been written up for anything. Out of nowhere he gets cut off, catches up to the other car, opens his window, and shoots the driver in the head. He's not evil or anything, just an otherwise sane person who lost it and happened to have a Beretta in the glove compartment."

"Happen to anybody."

"Half of the people we arrest are mental. They live for years on the boundary between merely eccentric and dangerously psychotic. They cross it one day when a voice tells them to. The sicko listens, and some poor bastard minding his business is pushed in front of an oncoming bus. Who wrote the story I saw about the lady on Eighty-First Street found dead last week? Murdered?"

"The ad exec? Not me. Editor gave it to someone else. Nutjob did it?"

"Yep. Guy living two floors up. Arrested him last night. Crazy but harmless, everybody thought."

"Then he snaps. Your neighbor one day, your executioner the next."

"Maybe he got the wrong change at the bodega. Who the hell knows?"

"The choice is prison or a mental hospital. What are we supposed to do, Timothy? Flip a coin?"

"Perps like them don't need to be punished, Kim. Which is what society is good at. They need to be treated."

"Which is what we're bad at. We turn our backs on crazy."

"We incarcerate crazy, actually. Our prisons are filled with inmates who really belong in the hospital. I've put a lot of them there myself, unfortunately. You heard of Aaron Hernandez? Football player sent to prison for murder?"

"Sure. Patriots. He committed suicide, right?

"Hung himself. The autopsy revealed he had severe brain damage, the worst the ME ever saw. Probably from being hit in the head a thousand times. So how was he responsible for his actions?"

It was a rhetorical question, and Barbieri had no ready answer.

"Officers have to be taught how to handle people like him. Last year we had a really tragic case out in Queens. This man was insane. Completely. Officers in his precinct all knew him and knew how to handle him. Neighbors called 911 on him nine times, and each time he was taken to the hospital. Last time the neighbors called, officers from another precinct responded. They didn't know his history. He waved a knife around, and they shot him."

"What they were trained to do. Topic's always been a little too complex for me, Cap'n. If a guy shoots up a kindergarten and kills a bunch of five-year-olds, he's a psychopath. Period. Yet if an old man starts hallucinating, kills his wife who he no longer recognizes, he's a psychotic."

She had interviewed a few therapists for stories she had written who threw out diagnostic terms that were pretty close to a foreign language for her, like schizophrenic and delusional. She'd learned just enough to write about them without embarassing herself, or her editor.

"I'd brush up on psychiatry if I were you, Kim. Outsiders like us, we know next to nothing. I don't know as much as I should, and I have to get these people out of circulation all the time." *You know some lunatic's been writing me, don't you? Why don't you come right out and ask?* "I've got a book, sort of psychiatry with training wheels, which I'll give you next time we're at my place. It'll help you at least tell one disorder from another. It's always a good idea to understand who you're dealing with."

"So you're part of the problem, Cap'n?"

"Only following orders. Like I told you before, my job is to get the guy off the street. Where he goes from there is someone else's responsibility. Call the loon a psychotic or a psychopath or whatever, and let the shrinks sort it out."

"Coward. I broke off a relationship one time with a guy who had serious issues and was clearly getting worse. I did everything I could to prevent *his* craziness from becoming *our* craziness. It reached a point where I gave him an ultimatum."

"Get help or you're gone?"

"Exactly. I moved on."

Chapter Twenty-one

"Think he's nuts?"

"Who?"

"Professor Moriarty."

"Literary allusion. Clever."

"Respect me now?"

Barbieri and Delaney were outside a Bronx courtroom, covering the arraignment of a building inspector who interpreted the title "inspector" to mean "I can be persuaded to look the other way." She was patiently waiting for his attorney, who seemed to be arguing with someone on his cell, to make the mistake of making eye contact with her. Getting a statement from him would allow her to add some much-needed balance to the story she was about to file. *With any luck, he'll spout something besides the standard-issue "My client is completely innocent and we expect to be fully vindicated at trial."* Until she got the attorney's attention, she had no problem batting about the mystery man's mental state with her partner.

"Insane. Occurred to me."

"It's possible. Definitely."

"If he's nuts?"

"Then maybe he's not as rational as we thought."

"Separate but equal. Insane *and* rational?"

"Don't they rule each other out?"

"Depends on what disorder he has, my guess."

"How do we diagnose a man we haven't met?"

"Where do we even begin?"

"Online. I'll look into it." *I'm a reporter, not a shrink. Brennan's made me realize I have a lot to learn about psychiatric conditions. He's right. I've never even been to a psychiatrist, unlike more than one of my friends.*

About all she knew for sure about mental illness, outside the lunatics she reported on, was that Riker's—the jail so close to the airport that inmates could feel the jets rumbling right above them—was jam-packed with crazies. *Might as well change the name of the place to Bedlam. At least it'll be accurate.*

She had not yet gotten the book Brennan had mentioned, so she turned to the internet. Covering the courts, with all their delays and downtime and two-hour lunch breaks, gave reporters a lot of time to kill. No use wasting it. Like every other subject on Earth, everything ever written on mental illness was stored in the cloud, and very little of it looked to her to be original.

She herself suffered from a common psychological condition many writers were susceptible to: the inability to read somebody else's writing without finding fault. Online, she found fault everywhere she looked. *This isn't writing. This is cloning.* If the authors were not copying and pasting each other, they were disagreeing. There were a million illnesses which seemed to morph from one to the next. No two experts seemed to agree on where one ended and another began, and no two descriptions of an illness seemed to match. *Maddening!*

Barbieri was no dummy. She had always aced science exams and never let complex subjects push her around, yet she found psychiatry to be a discipline with no discipline whatsoever. Black and white were alien concepts.

About all the hall of psychiatric mirrors did was make her realize she needed a source able to dumb the subject down, way down, to her level. As Brennan promised his beginner's psychiatry book would do for her. She decided she could not wait until the next time they wound up at his place, so they arranged to meet later in the day in the Manhattan Supreme Court building.

~ * ~

Brennan was right. Clearly written for lightweights, the baby-steps guide to psychiatry spoke to her as if she knew nothing, which was pretty close to the truth, and gave her a pretty solid grasp on a subject sane people had a hard time relating to.

Insanity did not simply pop up, full-blown, out of nowhere, the author explained. Nobody was normal when they woke up in the morning and a candidate for the straight jacket by afternoon tea. Not how it happened. *It's a long, slow descent into madness, with no starting point you can see. This much I understand.*

Insanity began slowly, barely noticeable by the patient or anyone else at first. He or she might say something a little off-kilter a few times, maybe blurt out something inappropriate. No alarms would go off. After a while, though, it would build up little by little, one weird behavior or crazy outburst after another for a few months, until boom. Here was your certificate of psycho. Welcome to our gated community.

Another tidbit she picked up was insanity was not a zero-sum game: all or nothing. People could be a little nuts, a whole bushelful of nuts, or somewhere in between. It was a continuum of crazy, and whether he needed psychiatric treatment or a week in the Bahamas could all be in the eye of the beholder.

If his family or friends were tolerant types who dismissed his occasional no-nos as harmless quirks, he was home free. Everyone would say he was eccentric, maybe make like they are too busy to come over for dinner, and leave it at that. No heavy-duty sedatives, no psychiatric care, nothing. If family and friends were not so tolerant and were creeped out by the man's antics, then he was crazy as a loon and should be committed yesterday. Totally subjective. When it came to mental illness, everyone's reactions counted as much as the symptoms they were reacting to. Just the way it was.

This wasn't hard at all. It's a start, but a good start. I've graduated from a know-nothing to a know-at-least-something, in a subject doctors have a hard time mastering. Insane.

~ * ~

There's crazy, and there's crazy. Which one am I dealing with?

Is the guy writing me crazy to actually think he could pull this off and get away with murder? The answer, as far as she was able to tell, was, yes. Absolutely. *"Let's do this and go out for pizza after."* The kind of crazy she could wrap her head around.

But what if Brennan and Delaney are on to something? What if the man's certifiably insane, non compos mentis, looney-tunes crazy? Maybe he's schizo—not that I would've seen any sign of the disease in his letters. Could he have a Jekyll and Hyde thing going? Mister Rogers one day, Hannibal Lecter the next? She had heard the term used a thousand times in movies and books; schizo,[1] and she herself had used it a thousand times since she was a kid, usually as a generic form of crazy.

It turned out schizophrenia was not at all what she thought it was. The way Brennan's primer explained it, this particular illness had nothing to do with two personalities sharing the same body. Dr. Jekyll and Mr. Hyde were not roommates on the top floor.

Being schizophrenic simply meant the patient had lost contact with reality. With all this imaginary stuff popping up inside his head, he would become withdrawn or afraid. He would see things that were not there, or speak gibberish, or feel paranoid. Someone was out to harm him, or someone was always watching him. Nobody was, yet it was how he feels.

That's not him. My man of mystery is definitely not schizo. Not at all. He isn't delusional or paranoid. Not yet, anyway. She knew schizophrenia was only one form of insanity, and there were a million other forms of it people could have. If he was in fact something other than schizo, maybe a demented psychopath of one kind or another, Barbieri had no idea what it would be. *Maybe there's a home psychiatric diagnosis kit on Amazon. They sell everything else.*

One thing she was pretty sure about—whichever version of lunacy he had, the killer would not go to a professional to help him work through this attempted murder business. Treatment would blow up the mental contraption he was holding together with Krazy Glue. A therapist would be bound to go to the police, as the confidentiality rule did not apply when the patient was about to put someone's life in danger. Besides, if the therapist tried to find something interesting about him, the killer would not give him much to go on. Therapists ask questions. They probe. They pry. They peel away layer after layer to get at the underlying problem. *The one thing the therapist would need to know about the killer, the most important thing, is the one thing he could never reveal. "Oh, Doctor, don't tell anyone, but I'm planning to kill a perfect stranger. Problem?"*

If the killer did not reveal his plan, the therapist would only see the usual garden-variety neurotic tormented by the usual garden-variety neuroses.

Chapter Twenty-two

I'm beginning to think of myself as a perfectionist determined to commit the perfect crime.

When you leave a business, no matter if you're canned or you quit, your most important assets aren't handed in to HR along with your ID card and your low opinion of your bosses. Your experience, your skills, your savvy, your intuition—they all go walking out the door with you. It's absolutely true in my case. I'm still an experienced exec with solid credentials, and as far as I'm concerned, those assets are all upstairs ready to be tapped. Sort of like a sleeper cell of some foreign enemy, biding their sweet time until the day they get the signal to activate.

With me, at this particular moment in time, the signal's not to show yet another shoe store how to keep from going under, but to end an as-yet-unidentified schmuck's life.

I know in my gut I have all the skills I need to handle this quote-unquote project without going to jail. All this due diligence, it's all in a day's work far as I'm concerned. I used to get a pretty nice paycheck just for doing homework like this.

And strangely enough, now that all this has sunk in, I know in my gut this little adventure is just another project to take on and manage. I'm fine with being evil, without question. I have a dark side. Fine. You can rationalize anything, I guess, even homicide. I'm becoming a bad senior dude, at least to my mind, but can I seriously go ahead and apply my skill set to a completely bizarre purpose? To actually take someone's life? This is the sixty-four-thousand-dollar question.

I'm not a criminal mastermind. I'm no evil genius. I'm an old pro who knows how to get things done. A plodder who thinks through every detail to minimize errors and maximize success. You have a goal: You plan, prepare, then you execute. It's the only way I know how to do things. You don't want surprises. You anticipate every possible thing that can go wrong, then make sure it doesn't.

For a graduate of the old school, like me, it's the elixir of life. I'm confident once I pull the trigger—in a manner of speaking—put the plan into motion, I'll be able to perform as if I never stopped. Prioritize, strategize, anticipate, focus, all that. All to meet the goal at hand— murder, instead of a nice fat bonus at Christmas.

It'll take more courage than I've ever had, certainly. It'll take guile. I'll have to avoid every possible error that could foil my fiendish scheme. I'll have to evaluate every possible weapon and anticipate every possible snafu. I'll be doing it all for myself, by myself. There'd be no executives to whom I would pitch ideas, no peons to dump the drudge work on.

It has to be totally anonymous, beginning to end. No paper trail leading back to me and no DNA evidence able to put the final nail in my state-sponsored coffin. The deed has to be done quietly and quickly. I have to be able to get away as if I was never there to begin with. No one can hear the crime I'm perpetrating, or see it, or record it on a security camera. No one can recognize me at the scene of the crime, or give the cops a good description of me after the victim doesn't wake up. To the NYPD, I have to be a person of absolutely no interest. None. Zero. Forever.

This business I'm about to undertake won't be committed by me and whatever emotional baggage I carry. Only me, sans baggage. I'll approach it totally rationally, as if it were a project, an assignment—one completely novel to me, admittedly—executed by a skilled company man.

While I could make it seem like an accident, what's the point? Everyone's always wanted a little recognition for what they've done, haven't they? Gold star, pat on the back? I'm no different. I want the gratification of everyone knowing precisely what I've done, knowing there was a master at work. Even if nobody knows who this master was.

It's all on me, and I am all in.

Chapter Twenty-three

By now, see, before I've done absolutely anything illegal, my mental state is really starting to do a number on me. Or to be more precise, I'm being driven to distraction by the idea I'm crazy in some way. The question dogging me is, am I making the transition from perfectly normal to criminally insane? Am I leading two lives?

No warning signs have gone off in me, other than the hissy fit in Soho, and none of my friends have ever said anything. Which is probably the clearest sign of all I'm fine upstairs. If I'm not psycho, then what about all the other entries in the catalog of crazy? At least the ones I've read up on in the library.

From the little information I have, I think of myself as a completely normal person about to do something totally abnormal. So I'm pretty sure I could rule out psychosis without further ado. Reality and I have always had a pretty tight relationship. I don't have delusions, and I know I'm not manic-depressive. I suffer no ill effects from any childhood physical, sexual, or psychological abuse, which I don't believe I ever had. No mood swings: steady as she goes. If I ever show signs of any of those things, Helen will be on my case big-time. Guaranteed. When I flipped out on the messenger in Soho, she didn't think I was crazy. She was afraid I was carrying around this anger. My wife's always been a pretty good judge of these things.

From the outside I look normal, I know. I act normal, nothing like the filthy, smelly nutcases you see sometimes in the subway talking to themselves or screaming about persecution at nobody in particular. Folks don't start crossing the street when they see me coming down the block.

There's the definition of insanity that goes, "It's doing the same thing over and over and expecting a different result." Einstein, maybe. I totally buy it. Still, in my line of work, you had to break the mold, shake things up in order to make a dent in a problem. On this level, at least, the oddball's the one person in the room who's normal, usually.

Sometimes the stuff I used to come up with at work even gave me the heebie-jeebies. Yet it's okay. Way I see it, if I'm not seizing every opportunity to push the envelope, I'm not earning my keep. Clients ain't paying me for off-the-shelf ideas they can get from any generic consultant.

But this dark urge is way beyond eccentric. This is a Pandora's box I have no business opening. I mean, I'm taking a rational approach to a completely irrational notion. Cold-blooded murder. Irrational, bordering on insane. The sane part of me enabling the part of me that's bonkers, to the point where I can't stop myself. It sometimes feels like there's a battle raging inside my head, a tug-of-war between what I know and what I fear.

I happen to be the referee in this contest, and I've come down firmly on the side of being of sound mind. If I do have some kind of mental illness, I'm still safely inside the sane side of the scale. I'm troubled, maybe, but I'm still playing with a full deck. My opinion.

Chapter Twenty-four

"Spot."

"Where?"

"Lady pulling out. Right side."

"Got it."

It was the Wednesday after the second letter, and Barbieri had persuaded Delaney to drive with her over to Bay Ridge, the neighborhood known postally as 11209. The two notes had both been mailed on a Wednesday from that post office and delivered two days later. They apparently needed a couple of days to ship a letter maybe three miles to her neighborhood. Two days for a fifteen-minute journey.

If the killer stuck to his schedule, she expected letter number three to come in two days. She had a choice—do nothing until then, or do something, *anything,* which might take them a step closer to preventing a murder. *I never have been the waiting-for-something-to-happen type. Standing still gets me nowhere. Maybe we'll get lucky and catch the guy in the act of mailing the third letter. Worth a shot.*

The gentrification juggernaut was not going to reach Bay Ridge anytime soon. Insulated by New York Harbor on one side and the Gowanus on the other, it was a quiet neighborhood of mom-and-pop stores and modest one-family row houses in the same family for generations.

They got out of Delaney's three-year-old Forester near the post office on Eighty-Eighth and Third, a dreary, unwelcoming dead-letter box of a building. Close to the waterfront, the area was chillier than they had planned for; the coat and hat each of them wore were no match for the icy wind coming off the water.

They went inside, figuring the guy might leave his letter right at the post office itself. They had no idea who they were looking for, or what he even looked like. All they could hope to see was some odd behavior or expression, which might give him away. If he had none, they would be out of luck.

"Anything?"

"Nope."

"Nothing to see here."

The post office interior, a weary space adorned with tired posters on walls badly in need of a paint job, was a beehive of inactivity. Ordinary men and women standing patiently and silently in line to buy stamps or send packages. Indifferent postal workers standing behind the counter to sell them stamps or toss their packages into a bin, where they became someone else's problem. There was an automated kiosk sitting forlornly on the side customers could use, avoiding human interaction entirely, yet did not. The marketing term "early adapters" never quite fit residents of the outer edges of the outer boroughs.

That was about it. No obvious madmen or homicidal maniacs. No tells. Nobody looking the least bit suspicious. It took about a half hour of this mind-numbing surveillance to make Barbieri rethink their strategy.

"Walk?"

"Sure. Where?"

"Around the neighborhood."

"Might see something."

"Unlike here."

Just as they began to head for the door, the feeling took over again, the sense she was being watched. Only this time it was different. Visceral. *He's here! I'm being stalked. By him*!

A primitive part of her brain called the amygdala had pulled the alarm, which alerted her nervous system, which in turn caused a surge in adrenaline, sending her body into panic mode. Her heart started racing. Her hands started trembling. The hairs on the back of her neck stood up. She looked around, yet saw nobody who looked even remotely like a homicidal maniac. There did not seem to be anybody she had ever seen before, either, at the Starlight diner or anywhere else. *So where is he? Who is he? Is he even a he?*

She was checking out the line of customers waiting their turn when one man caught her eye. He turned his head toward the clock on the wall so he faced away from her, left the line, and walked over to the mail slot by the front door. He dropped a single business envelope into the slot and exited the post office seemingly without a care in the world.

With him gone, her body returned to normal. The alarm went silent and the panic faded away.

"Why'd we stop?"

"Thought I saw something. Someone."

"Guy just left?"

"Yeah. Why did he leave the line?"

"Remembered he had to be somewhere?"

"Gave me the willies. I thought it was him."

"Looked okay to me."

From where she and Delaney were standing, off to the side, she had had a glimpse of just a sliver of his face, little more than an inch or so from his hairline to his chin, for maybe a nanosecond. He had been walking away from them, and whether intentionally or not, he never turned his head toward them. He seemed to be a generic middle-aged male, probably white, of average height and weight. Ordinary jacket and jeans. No peculiar posture or gait she recognized. Did she know him? Was it *him*?

It was too late to find out. He was gone. She let it go, hoping it would come to her later. Maybe in the shower.

Barbieri and Delaney spent the next hour or so braving the cold, hiking up and down the main streets of Bay Ridge. They made a big loop around the neighborhood, up Shore Road by the harbor, across Fourteenth Avenue, and down Eighty-sixth Street, hoping they would get lucky and see some fiendishly evil body-snatcher looking over his shoulder as he put a single piece of mail in one of the corner mailboxes, then scurry away like a rat. No luck. They caught only a couple of people in the snail-mail act, and there was nothing fiendishly evil about them.

"Missed him."

"Apparently so."

"Or he spotted us first."

"Two idiots out in the cold doing nothing. Possible."

"Undercover work sucks."

"It does. Give it another hour?"

"Getting late."

"Okay. We'll head back."

"Wait to see what the mailman brings on Friday."

"We tried."

The expedition was a bust. The mystery man remained completely unknown, just as he was before their day of playing junior G-men. They found their way back to Delaney's Forester, parked near the post office, and he drove her back home. It was a quick ride, and a quiet one. They chose not to discuss their next move and instead respected each other's unspoken wish to be alone with their thoughts.

Barbieri imagined what would happen if she actually went ahead and called the police, and the conversation she made up sounded like a bizarro-world version of an old Abbott and Costello routine.

"911. What's the emergency?"

"Someone's going to kill someone."

"Who is, ma'am?

"I don't know."

"The location, ma'am?"

"I can't say."

Delaney dropped her off at her building. The only thing left to do was wait the two days it took for the mail to get from the killer's neighborhood to hers.

~ * ~

As much as I try to avoid going anywhere near my post office, I happen to mail the third letter to the reporter right from there. Helen reminded me we were running out of stamps on my way out the door, so I'd be there anyway. I don't know if they have guards behind one-way mirrors there, on the lookout for suspicious packages or maybe suspicious customers, but why would they suspect anyone just coming in to buy stamps?

I'm waiting in line, maybe three or four people ahead of me, holding the letter in my hand. I'm wearing gloves, which I'd never bothered taking off, so there's no danger of leaving prints on it. Then I spot her—the reporter, Barbieri, with some other guy I don't recognize. I guess I wasn't really surprised she showed up there, based on the postmarks on my letters. It was a lead no decent reporter could ignore. The two of them are both clearly on the lookout for yours truly, and while they're eyeballing everyone else, I'm sneaking glances at her. Totally oblivious. I'm right in front of her, and she can't see me.

Just as it looks like they decide going there was a big waste of time and get ready to leave, she stops like she senses something. Me. I'm too far away to hear her, though I can tell from her body language she's got some serious heebie-jeebies. Now, it's not my intention to scare her, certainly not to scare her off from the murder I'm planning, so I stop looking her way and make my exit. Slowly, so as not to draw attention. I drop the envelope in the mail slot right before I go out, making sure I'm facing away from her as I leave. Last thing I want is for her and her friend to get a good look at my face.

Either way, if I frighten her off or let her ID me, it could ruin everything. Yet the fact that she senses when I'm around gives me something to think about. I'm just not sure if I want to use it against her or just have a little fun with her. From now on, I'm putting the mail I send her right in the mailbox. No more post office. Or I'll switch from snail mail to email. I remind myself to check if the *News* allows readers to email their reporters.

The post office itself has cameras everywhere, for one thing. The other thing is by using the mail, as in the United States Postal Service, the murder I'm planning could become a federal offense. These guys don't like it when you use their mailboxes to commit mayhem. I don't know how the hell I missed it.

Means if I screw up somehow, I'll have postal inspectors coming after me, along with the NYPD. If they ever put my letters under a microscope, they could find evidence pointing right to me. Hair, saliva, prints—who knows what their lab could turn up? I mean, I've been very careful so far, so why push my luck?

Chapter Twenty-five

Okay, my self-diagnosed sanity out of the way, what I'm still unsure of, what doubt I have, concerns the little matter of guts. As in, do I have the stomach to physically take a life?

Murder... killing... homicide. I've known all my life it could be done by bad guys and enemy agents, even good guys if they're backed into a corner. I watch violence on TV and in the movies, and I have to turn away. Blood and gore gives me nightmares. A little ironic, I know, given what I'm about to do, yet life is full of such contradictions.

I'm trying to imagine what it would take to actually end someone's life. Could I hold a guy's head underwater until he stopped struggling? Could I wrap my hands around a man's neck and squeeze the life out of him? That would take some hefty cojones, wouldn't it? Am I cold-blooded enough to watch my victim thrash and twist and struggle as his life comes to a slow, violent end?

I'm not sure, at all, if I could stick a gun in someone's back and pull the trigger. Or watch some poor bastard suffer a long, slow death if I slip cyanide into his coffee. I have no idea if I could lie in wait in a parking lot and run a guy over, then run over him again to make sure.

Truth is, I may not have it in me to do any of those things. Or maybe I simply don't want to admit it to myself if I do. Bravado only carries you so far.

I don't think murder's in my blood, so to speak. Far as I know, no uncles or aunts or cousins ever spent a day behind bars, for any crime at all. I would've definitely known, as it would've been the number one topic of discussion over the dinner table back home with Mom and Dad.

Gruesome as killing is, ordinary folks do it all the time. Pick up the paper. You got abused wives who were abused one time too many and stabbed their husbands while they slept. Fired employee coming back to work to shoot the boss who did him wrong. Some woman who kills the other woman trying to steal her man.

What I have in mind isn't a crime of passion like theirs were, though. Unlike them, I'll make damn sure I won't be caught. What we do have in common, though, is they were all amateurs, first-timers like me. I could plan and prepare all day long, yet I'm still an amateur in this particular area of expertise. I've convinced myself if they could do it, I can do it. First time for anything, even this.

There's one other thing I cling to, one other rationalization I use to convince myself I'm not a completely soulless son of a bitch. Ordinary people kill someone by accident all the time and learn to live with themselves. Mostly, anyway. They turn their back for a second and their little nephew drowns in the pool. Pedestrian crossing the street looks left instead of right and he's a stain on the crosswalk. They weren't killed on purpose. Nobody's going to jail for taking their life, yet they were killed nonetheless.

Accident or not, poor shmucks kill innocent human beings and still manage to go about their lives. Conscience won't leave them alone, maybe. They might lose sleep for a few months, yet their life eventually returns to something approaching normal. I've decided if they could carry on a normal life after their tragedy, so could I. Again, maybe I'm fooling myself, since the death I'm going to bring about will definitely be intentional on my part, but it's what I believe.

And this is why I've come to believe, or rather willed myself to believe, psychologically I could do it. I have the cojones. I won't know for sure until the deed is done, will I?

Chapter Twenty-six

Kim Barbieri was lying in bed, alone, when she was jolted awake by her cell phone. It was seven in the morning and sunlight was flooding her bedroom, making it far warmer indoors than it was outside. It was a welcome sign spring was completing its annual migration back to New York City.

She checked the caller ID to see if it was her editor, Cavanaugh, calling to see if she was available to cover whatever crime du jour was worth an article in the paper. It was the only call she expected at this ungodly hour. Her friends knew she worked nights sometimes and never bothered her before noon.

It was not her editor this time. It was Brennan. Which made her a little reluctant to answer the phone. She knew why he was calling.

"Cap'n," she said after the third ring. He would not take kindly to making him leave a message. It would only make things worse for her.

"Wake you?" Brennan asked. Without waiting for her to answer the question, he asked the next. "Anything you need to tell me, Kim?"

He was just being protective, giving her an opportunity to dump whatever she had on him, and on the NYPD. Barbieri knew two things. She was not ready to let him take over something she was fully capable of handling, and she did not want to send him on a wild-goose chase. All she could possibly tell him was a murderer she knew nothing about, might someday, somewhere, kill some adult male she also knew nothing about. And even that was just a guess.

"No. I'll take care of it."

"Okay. Understood. Now, if those hypotheticals you mentioned turn un-hypothetical—"

"They won't. If they do, I'll bring you in. You have my word." *Why do I keep telling him these small lies? They'll only make things worse for me.*

"I'm not waiting for your invitation, Kim. This is serious stuff. Don't be surprised if you see some men following you over the next couple of days. I sent them."

"Unsend them! I mean it, Brennan!"

"I don't want you to get hurt, or get in over your head. Are we clear on this?" He didn't wait for her answer. "Go back to bed, Kim."

With the call over, he hung up. She went back under the covers, yet was unable to go back to sleep. Her hypothetical discussion with him had tipped him off, as she sort of expected it would. She did not know how, but it did.

Am I pissed he's prying his way into my business? Or am I pleased? Doesn't matter. He knows I'm up to something. No crime has occurred yet, but he knows.

Men.

Chapter Twenty-seven

In the realm Barbieri covered, attorneys had to choose their words carefully. Even more than journalists like her. If she got something wrong, the worst thing was her editor might exile her to the end of the stringer line. Consequences were a little more severe with prosecutors and defense lawyers.

When attorneys parsed the differences between the words used for taking a life, the impact was measured in years inside a cell. Ten or twenty versus life. This was why she wanted to make sure of what her new pen pal was getting into, and maybe getting her into as well. *Which crime am I letting myself be sucked into? Murder one, murder two? Which could I soon find myself complicit in if I don't watch my step?*

She had seen plenty of arrests for homicide, maybe hundreds. Drive-by shooting, tenant killing his landlord, argument going too far— you name it. If a nasty wound made it look like the victim did not die a natural death, the police called it a homicide. Someone was killed by somebody. It was up to the DA to figure out which variety of murder or manslaughter the somebody was charged with.

No matter which crime he was charged with at arraignment, it had a habit of morphing into any of a number of others as the case made its way through the courts. Murder down to man one, murder two upgraded to murder one, ten years upstate reduced to five years probation due to some inane technicality or other. Watching the legal jousting from the back of the courtroom she did not really care what crime the guy was found guilty of, as long as he was guilty and did not walk. *While the courts may let bad actors off easy, I can't. I live here.*

She always tried her damnedest not to let bias creep into her reporting, yet with all the violence she had witnessed, it was inevitable her neutral observer side lost to her outraged citizen side. It had to.

Civilians picked Barbieri's brain all the time about crimes and criminals, and she was not at all shy about sharing what she knew. It was an occupational hazard, and reporters like her learned to deal with it. People thought her job was exciting, dealing with cops and criminals for a living, and she rarely tried to correct them. *Let them have their vicarious thrills. What's the harm?* The fact that she was not a lawyer and could be way off base never stopped her, though. Civilians accepted it as gospel when she said it.

Based on what I know from the killings I myself have covered, it's pretty clear John Doe is planning on committing murder one, murder in the first degree. Life without parole if convicted. There's no death penalty in New York State.

The bring-back-the-chair crowd was very much alive and kicking in New York. While Barbieri was personally against it, some cold-blooded murders she had covered made even her sympathetic to their cause. As this one was shaping up to be. This killing was totally different from any other she knew of, if only because the crime was developing in real time. *I'm following a guy planning an assassination, not covering it after the fact. Am I right it's murder one?*

She knew a few minutes with a lawyer would save her the effort of trying to decipher law books herself, so she called on someone in the Brooklyn District Attorney's office she had interviewed a thousand times for the *Daily News*.

The ADA, Eric Danziger, tried his best not to read any news articles about his own cases, although he often could not help himself. Barbieri was one reporter he could count on to get his side right, so he felt he owed her a few minutes of his expertise on the subject, and told her as much.

They met in Eric's office on Joralemon Street near the Criminal Court building, a labyrinth of soul-crushing cubicles as drab and dingy as the day it opened in the early Christian era: tall gray file cabinets against the walls, spewing loose tan file folders; glue traps underfoot; and flickering flourescent lights above. ADAs doing time there were as far as they could get from the Emerald City of private practice.

Short and round, with salt-and-pepper hair and a pencil mustache, ADA Danziger was a Fernando Botero fat figure drawn to human scale. Wearing a gray pinstriped suit, a white shirt and a dark tie, he seemed to be doing his best to fade into the drab background.

Barbieri took a seat across from him and placed a new notepad on her lap. She was not doing research for a piece she was writing and would not be taking down everything he said, yet taking out her notepad for an interview was simply second nature. Barbieri was a little hesitant about sharing the reasons for this friendly interrogation, in part because she did not want Eric to think she was wasting her time on some fool's errand. Or some pretty outrageous practical joke being played on her. She also did not think she would be able to come up with an excuse for picking his brain; Eric would see right through it in a second. Prosecutors pounced on lame excuses.

Barbieri did not lie if she could avoid it. Telling the truth was always easier. So she told Eric she would tell him nothing now, and promised him the full story later.

The ADA sat back a moment, then started giving Barbieri a tutorial on legal definitions, starting with murder in the first. He gave her the official definition from the New York State penal code, which had four elements he would have to prove to a jury beyond a reasonable doubt in order to convict. He held up four fingers on his left hand and proceeded to fold each one down in order.

"First, the perpetrator has to kill the victim unlawfully."

"You can kill someone lawfully?"

"In certain situations, maybe. To tell the truth, this element of murder one has never been an issue in my cases. I think it refers to killing by a police officer, or maybe 'stand your ground' if a civilian takes a life. It's never come up."

"Makes sense."

"Second, he has to have malice aforethought, which simply means he intends to do the victim harm."

"Gun went off by accident, Officer. I swear."

"Like hell, asshole. There's a witness who says you pointed it right at his head. Third, the murder is premeditated, meaning the killer thought about committing the crime before he actually did it."

"I wrote about an arrest in Queens a few years ago. He came home a couple of hours early from work and found a guy there shtupping his wife. Grabbed a gun and killed him. Murder one, right?"

"Or maybe murder two, or even man one," the ADA responds. "Heat of passion. He didn't plan on killing Romeo. He was provoked and let his emotions take over. Total rage, in that case. Now if he goes to Romeo's house a day later and kills him, it's murder one. I could sell murder one to the grand jury, easy. Difference is intent. Premeditated."

"Meaning he had time to think it over and decided to shoot him anyway."

"Precisely. Four, the murder has to take place at a specified location." Eric folded down the fourth finger. "A known scene of the crime. It's the official definition we work with, Barbieri, although lots of homicides fall outside the lines. Start with intent."

"Intent. I did a story about an older Polish guy working in a factory in Greenpoint who had a beef with his boss. Which is hard since he spoke not a word of English. He drove over to Dick's Sporting Goods in Long Island somewhere, bought a rifle and ammo, drove back to the factory, and blasted his boss to smithereens. Murder in the first degree."

"Correct, Barbieri. Even though the result is the same—a dead body—the difference between murder one or two is only a matter of what the killer was thinking at the time. If you meant to kill the guy, it's murder one. If you didn't, it's not. Which explains why, if you commit murder, we also often charge you with *intending* to commit murder. The intent itself is a big-time felony that could land you in Sing Sing for a decade or two, even if you managed to screw up and the victim walks away unharmed."

"That much I know," Barbieri replied. *The guy writing to me has certainly made his intent clear. He's already guilty on this charge alone, even if his plot goes nowhere.* She had decided before meeting Eric she would abide his mansplaining. He knew more than she did, and it was his brain she had chosen to pick. *If he wants to show off his legal chops, I'll act like a lady and let him.* "ME reads the lab reports and examines the stiff, says the corpse on the table didn't die a natural death. It was a homicide. Then it's up to the detectives and you guys to decide if he was murdered."

"It is, but even this distinction about intent isn't cut and dried. If you *meant* to kill someone and you're acting in self-defense, like some nutjob is attacking your kids, you might get a lesser charge like justifiable homicide. Hard to keep straight."

Barbieri understood that as well, and described another case she had reported on. "An abused wife stabbed her old man in his sleep. Judge found her guilty of man one because her life had been in danger. Not *was* in imminent danger. *Had been* in danger long before." Athough she had covered maybe hundreds of bad guys, she was able to remember nearly everything about every single one of them. Some memories were not meant to fade.

"Manslaughter's not clear-cut either, it turns out," Eric continued. "It can be voluntary, like you find some drug dealer piece of shit trying to sell meth to your son, and you grab a gun in a rage. You were *provoked.* It can also be involuntary. You get totally wasted and run over someone with your car. You weren't provoked: it was only an accident."

"So I slaughtered some poor shmuck without thinking, but it's not murder one or two. It's manslaughter."

"If only it was that simple, Barbieri. You can commit murder even if there's no intent, which is where my job gets a little complicated. Asswipe starts a fire, which kills a couple of firemen who took a wrong step and fell through the floor to the basement. They died of smoke inhalation. "

"I covered the case."

"We both did, Barbieri. I was the ADA who caught it. He intended to burn the place down, not commit murder—"

"Firebug's sent away for felony murder anyway. He committed a crime, without any intent to kill anyone on his part, and a couple of fire fighters end up dead."

She believed the ADA had answered all her questions about the killer she was dealing with, but she let Eric continue his seminar on the classification of homicides anyway. He was obviously enjoying the chance to show off.

"Then you have to factor in cruelty, Barbieri. If you went out of your way to be cruel, the judge could send you away for life without parole if he's having a bad day. If the murder's not cruel, it's second degree. In which case you'll be celebrating your seventieth birthday behind bars. Good defense lawyers make a nice living threading that needle."

"How do you know if the defendant was trying to be cruel? He's not going to tell you." Her killer had not told Barbieri—yet—whether he was going to be cruel in any way or intended to make the death as quick and painless as possible.

"He doesn't have to. Cruelty is in the eyes of the prosecutor, not the killer. It's a little complicated, but what it boils down to is the perpetrator goes overboard in some way, acts like a sadistic motherfucker who seems to enjoy what he's doing. Beat someone's brains out with a hammer and it can elevate the charge from murder two to murder one. Sadism tends to piss off judges and DAs—and jurors."

Barbieri had not seen much cruelty to speak of. The murderers she wrote about tended to be much more considerate of their murderees, dispatching them with a kinder, gentler weapon such as a gun or a knife. If their deaths were agonizing, it was not intentional.

"Of course, intent doesn't mean squat if the defendant's insane. Diminished mental capacity, to us."

"Guy's too crazy or stupid to know what he's doing," Barbieri volunteered.

"Correct. It doesn't matter what mental illness he has. Could be psychotic, schizo, retarded. Or he could be perfectly sane until the moment he committed the act. The guy of yours who killed Romeo? We could've let him plead not guilty due to temporary insanity, maybe."

"I get the feeling you're not losing any sleep over any of this."

"When I started, sure. First couple of homicides were tough. Not since then. Once in a while, it's the jury keeping me up at night. The facts could point straight to murder one, no question, but the jury's not buying it."

"OJ?"

"OJ."

"Jury nullification."

Barbieri had covered deaths all along the spectrum, which in a way explained how what looked like clear cases of murder at the crime scene were pled down to manslaughter, if not dismissed entirely, in the courtroom.

Law school introductory class over, Barbieri thanked Eric for his time and let him get back to his case folders. She retraced her route out of the cube farm, convinced that, due to the mystery letter writer's planning and clear intent, he was about to commit murder one. Maybe murder two if he had a good defense lawyer or a bad ADA. One definition of the crime in question seemed to morph into another based on what the bad guy was thinking at the time. State of mind.

Despite her attempt at being on top of the situation, cool, calm and collected, Barbieri felt her interview with the ADA only exacerbated her sense of helplessness. *This is murder one, not jaywalking. I could ignore the letters and get my life back. If I do, though, a murder will be committed I maybe could've prevented.* She could neither ignore the letters he sent, nor stop him from sending new ones. Yet stubborn pride kept her from dumping the whole damn thing in Brennan's lap. *A woman with a brain versus a cop with a gun? I'll take the woman with a brain.*

She was feeling compelled to play a dangerous game, one where she knew next to nothing about the killer, yet he seemed to know everything about her. *I'm walking into a deadly trap with a blindfold on.* It was a feeling, not a fact, and she was fully aware of the difference between the two. She was overreacting and she knew it, yet she could not help herself. *How can I be complicit in a crime a guy I never even met is committing? Get a grip, Barbieri!*

Her fear was slowly completing its migration from her mind to her gut, and it was beginning to hurt.

Chapter Twenty-eight

Death isn't simple. The deceased may not even be dead, for that matter.

I go to our local public library, find myself a quiet table with no room for a busybody to look over my shoulder, and pore over reference books on anatomy, medicine, and forensics, of which there are plenty. I read them all right there, rather than check any out with my library card, in case the detectives start poking around later.

My do-it-yourself forensics education tells me there's dead, as in "call the undertaker" dead, where there's no chance of an EMT bringing the guy back to life. What lawyers and doctors call "legally dead." And there's dead as in, "He's not breathing at the moment, and he certainly looks dead, and he's not moving, but perhaps we should try to resuscitate him. What do you say?" This is "clinically dead."

And if you want someone not to come back, it's preferable to go with the former. You don't want sorta, kinda dead. You want dead dead. Legally dead.

What makes a guy clinically dead versus legally dead? The only expert I could consult is my family doctor, a woman Helen and I have used for years, and I couldn't possibly speak with her about it. Our circle of friends doesn't include any morticians or EMTs. I'd have to come up with some phantom illness as an excuse to schedule an appointment with our doctor, which she'd see right through in no time. Besides, her waiting room is always pretty full, so her day at the office doesn't allow much room for personal tutoring in mortality. Not if she wants to give each patient more than a minute or two of her time.

All the information about clinical and legal death is at the library anyway, if you could wade through all the medical jargon, which I've done. I was never good in science, to be honest, so some of this is tough to follow, but I think I got the gist of it right. The first thing is when you're murdered, it's not the weapon that kills you. Not directly, anyway. The knife wound or the bullet hole isn't the cause of death. What really ends your life is the lack of oxygen the knife or bullet brings about. It's pretty logical, if you think about it.

See, all the cells in your body need oxygen to live. Without a steady supply, your cells die, whether they're in your brain, your liver, wherever. It's the blood's job, bringing oxygen to your cells. All your blood is, when you come right down to it, is an oxygen delivery system. You take oxygen in with every breath, and blood picks it up in your lungs and brings it back to the heart for shipment all over the body, to each and every cell from head to toe. While it's delivering oxygen, blood's also carrying waste away from cells. This is true, but in terms of moving up your victim's departure date, the lack of oxygen is key.

An adult male has maybe five, five and a half quarts of blood. Female, three, three and a half. For all your cells to get the oxygen they need, every drop of this blood has to stay inside your arteries and veins. As long as all your vessels are intact, with no holes for blood to leak out of, everything's hunky-dory. However, if blood leaks outside your arteries, like in internal bleeding, it means there's a lot less blood going to the cells.

No blood, no oxygen, no cell life, no human life. Death by domino effect.

So when you have internal bleeding from being cut with a knife or shot with a bullet, you're cutting off oxygen to your cells. That's the real cause of death right there. It explains why when you're bleeding to death, you hyperventilate. You're trying to breathe in more oxygen to make up for all the oxygen you lose due to internal bleeding. Your heart goes a mile a minute for the same reason.

How fast you die is all a matter of which organ is struck. If it's your heart or your aorta, you lose a lot of blood really fast, and death comes pretty quickly. If it's your liver or stomach, where bleeding is more gradual, death could take hours.

When you're *clinically* dead, your heart stops. You're not breathing, and your brain seems to stop working. Your eyes get glassy and dull, and your face turns pale and seems to flatten out. Even with all that, you can still be brought back to life if EMTs get there fast enough. They have maybe four minutes, tops, to do CPR, get the heart pumping, get the lungs breathing in and out, and get you doing the Lindy again.

When you're *legally* dead, it ain't gonna happen. The doctor's only job is to sign your death certificate and wait on the next customer. There's no brain function. Zero. No reflexes, no electrical signals for hours. You've lost so much blood, not enough oxygen's reaching your brain cells to keep them alive. Your cerebral cortex, the outside with all the ridges, goes first. After, your brain stem goes. Reach this point and you're not coming back no matter how hard the EMTs work their magic.

End of lesson. You might get a few more details from a medical school textbook, but this is all you need to know to understand what I'm dealing with. What it all boils down to is this. When I attack my victim, I want to hit a part of his anatomy that would bleed fast enough, and heavily enough, to cause death in seconds, not minutes. Or one that would cut off his oxygen so completely and so rapidly death is inevitable.

I want my guy legally dead. I don't want him to suffer needlessly, and I don't want the medics to have any chance of reviving him no matter how hard they try.

I have the end figured out, so the next task is choosing the means to this end. The weapon. For the time being, at least, I'm focusing on the murder weapons that seem the most doable, at least in my mind. Gun or knife. Poison. Car. Or my own hands, by smothering him, suffocating him, or breaking his neck. If those don't pan out, I'll have to expand my list.

Chapter Twenty-nine

I'm no lawyer. The fine points of the law have always meant diddly to me, and my least favorite thing in the world is lawyers battling it out in a hair-splitting contest.

I know from my old job words have consequences. They mean something. Using the wrong term like *must* instead of *should*, or *through* when you mean *to*, can cost a company millions. Which is why corporate attorneys get paid the big bucks. There's a lot of money at stake in good grammar.

I'm also perfectly aware, even if the law's clear, and a man's guilt or innocence is unmistakable, a bad lawyer can really screw up a case.

From watching enough cop shows on TV all the time, *Law and Order, CSI* wherever, I'm well aware of the damage one human can inflict on another, and I believe what I'm about to do would be murder in the first degree. Murder one, as ADA McCaughey puts it. I don't think it would be man one or man two, or reckless endangerment, or anything short of murder in its purest form. Deliberate, planned, unprovoked, and certainly undeserved. 'Course this is only my opinion, not a lawyer's.

I still want to know for sure what kind of criminal act I'd be committing, legally speaking, and what kind of penalty I'd be facing if I screwed up. I'm pretty sure no prosecutor's going to let me plea bargain my way out of this. Make it damn sure. Knowing that isn't going to change my date with destiny, though. Some poor bastard is going to be killed regardless of how the police and the DA define it, and what kind of punishment I'd face if I got caught.

I'm making damn sure I won't be.

By the time weapon meets victim, I'd know for certain a man is about to lose his life, and I'd know for certain I'd be the one taking it. Clear-cut as this seems to me, I decide to seek a second opinion from someone with a little more expertise in the field than I have.

A friend of ours happens to be a lawyer, Cherie. Not criminal, civil. Trusts and divorces, mostly. She's kept up on criminal law, though, especially the juicy cases the tabloids feast on. They're always a good topic of conversation among friends, sensational crimes right in the neighborhood, only a couple of degrees of separation between the killer or victim and ourselves.

Cherie and her husband, Mike, joined Helen and me for dinner one evening at a tiny Japanese place we really liked. Momoya, on Fifth Avenue. We look like we really don't belong together, the two couples. Helen and I are both pretty tall and look like we take care of ourselves. Cherie's just over five feet and her husband's just under six, and they clearly never look in the mirror before they leave the house. Not arm candy, if you know what I mean, but they're smart and funny, and we love them both.

Momoya has no atmosphere at all, kinda grungy actually, except the food's worth going out of your way for. The place is packed, as usual, and we're clearly the oldest people there, as usual. I mean, this is Park Slope, where people our age have to go through security. While we're waiting for our table, we're having two separate conversations: Mike and me, and Cherie and Helen. All I want to do is pick Cherie's brain without raising her suspicions, but right as I turn my attention to her, the waiter shows us to our table.

After we order, I manage to bring up legal terms that had come up in another criminal case recently making its way into the news. "Guy who killed his neighbor's kid for throwing rocks at his house, over in Canarsie?" I ask. "Why was he only charged with manslaughter? He shot the kid on purpose."

"Indeed he did," Cherie explains. "But it wasn't premeditated. He didn't plan on taking the child's life. He was caught up in the moment. He was enraged and lost control."

"The boy's still dead," Helen says. "The neighbor meant to kill him, didn't he? He didn't grab a gun to have a little target practice."

"Killed, yes. Murdered, no," Cherie replies, pausing to gather her thoughts. Law school was a long time ago. "Before the night in question, he bore no ill will toward the child. He had no reason to. The victim was just another kid in a neighborhood full of them, who had never even met the shooter before. No deliberate intent, in my language. He didn't think about hurting the boy until a few seconds before he killed him."

"What difference does it make?" I ask, not understanding the fine point Cherie was making. "He still got the gun, aimed it at the kid, and pulled the trigger. The gun didn't go off by accident."

"It makes a big difference, David," Cherie answers patiently, as if she were trying to help a client understand why his ex can get away with emptying his bank accounts.

Before she can elaborate, though, the waiter comes with our meals. While we're stuffing ourselves on California rolls, edamame, and sashimi, Cherie finishes making her point.

"He didn't have time to consider what he was doing and decide with his own free will to kill the boy. There was no *malice aforethought*. Harming the boy wasn't on his mind at all before things got out of hand and he went ballistic. Therein lies the difference between manslaughter and murder. Much higher bar."

"He snapped. Lord knows I have once in a while," Mike says.

"I have, too. Only not with a gun in my hand. Fortunately," Cherie replies.

I try to get her to talk a little more about malice aforethought. I'd assumed—incorrectly, it turns out—malice meant some kind of ill will or bad intentions between killer and victim, but Cherie clears it up for me.

"Separate out the malice part from the aforethought part," she explains. "The way the term is used, at least in New York State, malice simply means when you killed your victim, you meant to hurt him. It wasn't an accident, but totally intentional. You thought about harming him, and you harmed him."

"I see." I don't.

"Malice isn't the same as malicious."

What makes murder murder and manslaughter manslaughter still escapes me, to be honest. Seems to be a big gray area, where a lawyer could really earn his keep if he could limit his client to a charge of man one or man two rather than murder one. Maybe get him ten years instead of life. Regardless, I know for sure in this case, the criminal act I'm planning will be committed with aforethought aplenty, but with no malice to speak of. I have no feelings at all for the victim, no hatred or anything, to be honest. Why would I? Don't know him, never met him. At least, it's what my self-imposed education taught me. I could be interpreting this stuff all wrong, and I know as with all things legal, civil, or criminal, God is in the details.

I've obviously given myself plenty of time to consider the enormity of this undertaking, as well as its consequences. I'm in no hurry. I have to get it right the first time, and this means weeks and weeks of planning—and premeditation.

Chapter Thirty

I've done nothing except open a few letters. Big deal. I'm not about to go out and kill anybody. Yet there was something the ADA told Barbieri that made her want to go back and double-check her assertion. Maybe she was wrong about being totally innocent.

The next morning, she walked over to Eric's office downtown without calling first. It was one of the benefits of living where she did: just about everywhere she needed to be, outside of Aunt Estelle's, was in walking distance. Especially when the weather was nice, which it definitely was that morning. When she was not out on assignment, she could go for days without having to take a train or bus or Uber.

She took a chance Eric would be in his office, rather than a courtroom, and would not mind the interruption from the onslaught of documents he had to read and prepare. She was right. The rotund ADA was at his desk, surrounded by case files. Like the defendants themselves, the files looked like clones of one another.

He had shoved a few case records aside to make room for his Chinese takeout, and was manhandling the chopsticks from the container to his mouth. Not altogether successfully, given the fresh stains on his otherwise white shirt.

"Hey, Barbieri. What can I do for you? Haven't had enough of homicide?"

"I need five minutes."

"Sure." Eric looked at the timer on his display. "Clock's ticking."

"Talk to me about misprision."

"Concealing a crime someone else committed. Never charged

anyone with it myself." As Eric spoke, he put down his container of kung pao chicken and went online to look up the term in a legal dictionary. "Don't know of any ADA who has. Okay, two elements. Failure to notify the authorities about a felony. Active concealment of the felony."

"A felony someone's already committed."

"Yep. Misprisionment means you had full knowledge an individual committed a crime. You not only didn't tell the police—you actively concealed the crime from them. Actively is key. If you don't make any effort to conceal what you know, then it's not a felony. Could be charged with a misdemeanor, maybe. Obstruction of justice."

"Actively. Got it."

"You know something you're not sharing, Barbieri?"

"I didn't hear what you just asked, Eric. What if there's some guy who knows a crime is about to happen yet does nothing to stop it?" Barbieri made it sound like she was throwing the question in almost as an afterthought, rather than it being the one she really needed an answer to.

"Now we're entering territory between unwitting acccomplice and aiding and abetting. Somewhere on the spectrum, I'd think. If the DA's got a real hard-on for him, he could try to indict."

"Help me out here. You can go to jail for knowing someone's going to kill somebody?"

"Depends. Say you know someone angry enough to kill the next guy he bumps into on the street. Probably no legal liability to worry about. You can't prevent it."

"It may not even be a crime. Cop I know told me there's nothing they can do about a man threatening to kill no none in particular." This was all anybody needed to know about Brennan. He was a cop she knew.

"Nothing? That's what he said? I'd have to look it up. Now if you know he's out to kill a specific individual—"

"Business partner."

"—or wife's boyfriend, that's where you may be liable. May. I've charged accomplices with accessory after the fact, except it was *after* the crime was committed. Plus it was for hiding information from the investigators. I can see where a prosecutor could apply it to keeping information from the police department that could've prevented a crime. There's always a first time. There are guys here who live to set a precedent, get their name in the paper."

"*New York Law Journal.*"

"Your paper. The *News*. Nobody reads the *Law Journal*."

This talk with the ADA was the last thing she needed to have, as far as misprisionment went. She had no idea who the killer was, other than he was possibly, maybe, living in Brooklyn. She did not know whom he intended to kill, yet she could definitely be in a legal jam if the grand jury decided she had withheld evidence. That was a big-league no-no. She decided not to press her luck with Eric by revealing the plot she was being sucked into.

She had another reason to keep him in the dark. She hated lying to him, even by omission, on the chance it could ruin their relationship if he found out what was really going on. Her job was built on relationships, starting them and cementing them, with contacts in the judicial system like Eric. Their relationship would crumble lickety-split if he found out she had misled him in any way. At the moment, though, she felt she had no choice.

"I owe you one, Eric," Barbieri said as she left his cube, without noticing the quizzical expression on the ADA's face.

"Anytime, Barbieri. Stay out of trouble." The ADA went back to confiscating his defendants' "Get Out of Jail Free" cards.

The conversation with Danziger was all the motivation she needed to tell Brennan about the letters without delay. Later, in bed, she slept maybe an hour, tops.

Chapter Thirty-one

Friday, April 7
11:00 PM

By the time Barbieri received the third ominous note, again on a Friday, she did not have to open the envelope to know what the topic of the day was. She was nevertheless unprepared for her reaction to it. *This monster is definitely trying to make me his accomplice!*

She could feel her heart beating a little faster, tiny beads of sweat forming on her brow. The fear was almost as intense as she had felt the day at the post office, when she had sensed the killer was just a few feet away. She knew she had to contain it before it overwhelmed her.

She carefully put the envelope and letter in their own plastic sleeves, then put them in a binder. It had dawned on her a few days before, they should all be protected in case they were ever needed as evidence. *Maybe he's not as smart as he thinks he is and licked the envelope. The strongest alibi in the world can be demolished by a single DNA match.*

Scanning the latest message, she understood at once her involvement had been ratcheted up a notch:

The victim's gender and age range now set. My next decision is choosing the murder weapon. Thoughts?

She was startled, wigged out even, by the question at the end. *Thoughts? Why the fuck do you care what I think?* She was now having a dialogue with the killer—more like a one-sided conversation—as if he were right there. He was becoming real to her, someone she knew. *Are you actually getting me involved in this hit? Or are you only trying to keep me hooked?*

This last letter confirmed the suspicion she had had from day one: The killer was definitely a male. *Typical toxic relationship. Insecure, immature, narcissistic male playing on a female's feelings to get his way. But I am no "yes, master" female. I'm not his plaything.*

Do-as-I-say controlling men were topic number one whenever she got together with her girlfriends, and at work she was adept at letting them know who was boss. She stood her ground and he backed off. This typical man, however, was not typical in one crucial way. He was a ghost she could not control back.

This letter came exactly one week after the second. Which had come exactly one week after the first. All three had been mailed from Bay Ridge two days before. Would the pattern continue? *If it does, when is the execution scheduled for? Is it in week four? Week six?*

She was a little unnerved about her talent for reading the killer's mind. *It could be luck. Or it could be I'm beginning to identify with this demented fuck.* It seemed he was getting under her skin way too deep for her to comfortably accept.

She also knew anticipating the killer's next decision would be a whole lot harder than before. Either way, she realized she was now at a crossroads.

I could call 911 myself and wash my hands of the whole thing. Without involving Brennan. How could threatening to commit murder not be a crime? Does thinking about a weapon mean intent? When does intent become attempted murder? That would dump it into the lap of the NYPD, but could spell trouble for herself. Or Brennan. Why had she done nothing knowing a murder was being planned?

I could continue this one-way correspondence and keep it to myself, and maybe Delaney too, yet that would only drag me deeper into the quagmire the killer's preparing for me.

I could wait till it's over and maybe turn the attempted murder into a series of articles for the Daily News. *A scoop this big could help me get hired by another paper looking to throw money at a good reporter.* Washington Post *or* Wall Street Journal *territory. I could write some kind of true crime book, about the true crime, about to happen. Lots of readers out there would eat this stuff up.*

The downside to waiting, though, was someone would get killed if the bad guy did not come to his senses and call off the execution. Or the killer could get cold feet and stop writing to her at all. Her guy would commit the crime, but without any more letters leading her on.

If she had any reluctance to call in the cavalry—Captain Timothy Brennan—the third letter ended it right there. *Drop the feminist martyrdom control bullshit and tell him!* She promised herself—no, swore to herself on a mile-high stack of Bibles—he would see all three letters as soon as she figured out the murder weapon the killer would be using.

~ * ~

Torturous as all these internal debates were, she could not keep herself from having them. Each letter triggered a whole new round of self-doubt she struggled to prevent. Was something else going on? Self-aware as she was, Barbieri understood her own defense mechanisms. She deployed them from time to time like every other human being on the planet.

Am I masking a part of me I'd rather not see, a part of me actually enjoying this? So what if I am?

She did love mysteries, and she was smack in the middle of a riveting one. If there was a smidgen of enjoyment here, let it be. Self-awareness addressed, she did what she did after the other letters came and called Delaney. He knew as much as she did about the tools men used to end other men's lives—maybe more. He told her he would swing by her home as soon as he could.

Until he arrived, she attempted to ease the chaos ricocheting inside her head the best way she knew how: opera therapy. It was her go-to choice whenever all she wanted to do was hide under a rock for a few days.

She turned on her dad's old stereo and put one of his favorites, *La fanciulla del West,* on the stereo. Puccini, and most critics, thought it was the best opera he ever wrote. Barbieri gave it a slightly less enthusiastic review. *Meh.* She listened to it from time to time only because she was drawn to strong women characters, and Minnie was one tough broad.

~ * ~

Delaney had the good sense to arrive just as one of her favorite arias, *oh! se sapeste,* was ending. She reluctantly lifted the arm off the LP and turned the stereo off so they could focus solely on the latest message.

She and the photographer took their usual places in the living room, him on the sofa, her on a wooden chair she took from the kitchen. Barbieri turned the chair around so the back faced Delaney, then straddled the seat so she could rest her arms on the back and face him.

"Another one, I gather."

"Yep. He's choosing his weapon." She handed him the letter, already in its plastic sleeve, which he read to himself several times.

"He cares what you think?"

"So it appears."

"Weapon could be almost anything."

"Gun. Knife."

"Poison. Car crash."

"Never killed before. It's his first murder."

"He's got no relationship to the victim."

"No bad blood between them."

Barbieri and Delaney focused on the homicides they had covered where the killer and victim did not know each other beforehand. Never met. No fights. No motive. Two guys bumping into each other crossing the street. She had reported often on the other kind of homicide, where the killer hated the victim's guts enough to kill him, except this was a whole other category. Those killers grabbed anything within reach, like a golf club or a broken bottle, and turned it into a lethal weapon. Concentrating on killings of strangers by strangers, they thought back to the kinds of weapons used to hasten their departures. Ninety-nine times out a hundred, the weapon was pretty common.

"Weapon he already had."

"Or he could get his hands on without too much trouble."

If there was any mystery in these homicides, it was who did it, not how. Based on probability alone, their list of likely weapons was fairly short. It was made even shorter if, as they assumed, the guy had never killed before and wanted to be certain to get it right the first time.

"We covered a couple of strangulations."

"No weapon needed. Only their bare hands."

"He wouldn't use brute force."

"Where would he strangle him?"

"Break into his house?"

"Too slow. Victim breaks his stranglehold and gets away."

"Same with vehicular homicide. Victim's only injured."

"Lives to tell the tale."

"And ID the driver."

"Poison's out. Too dangerous to himself."

"Couldn't get close enough to a stranger to use it."

"He'd need a relationship. Wife. Landlord."

"Gun or knife. They're the only weapons left."

"Kitchen knife. Everybody has one."

"Disposable. Toss in the trash."

"Gun's easy to get."

"For sale everywhere."

"No questions asked. Fuckin' NRA."

"Point and shoot and go home."

"Lot of noise, though. Evidence, too."

"GSR. Shells. Lead right back to him."

"Paper trail. Background check. Registration."

"He's figured this out already. Probably. Mucho downside."

While they could be way off, she knew their intuition had paid off so far.

"Ever been to a gun show?"

"Don't reckon' I have, Tex."

"There's always one in darkest New Jersey. Pennsylvania."

"Lovely way to spend the day, I hear."

"Maybe we'll get lucky."

"Find a dealer who saw a nervous guy who looked completely out of place."

Chapter Thirty-two

Is this what paranoia feels like? I mean, this guy is making my skin crawl twenty-four/seven.

Barbieri's eyes snapped open, and she found herself staring at her bedroom ceiling. Again. It was just before four. Too early to get up and start the day, yet too late to try to fall back to sleep. Insomniac's sweet spot. The room was still totally dark and the apartment totally silent, save for the rumble of the occasional van driving down her block. Even at this ungodly hour, deliveries had to be made.

He's here. I feel it... him. Just outside the door. How the hell did he get into my apartment? What do I do now? Call 911? Call Brennan. Phone's in the kitchen. Shit. Why'd I leave it there? Too late. Maybe I should move in with him? Creep wouldn't dare come there, to a cop's place. Would he? I'm not living in fucking Staten Island! Can I get Delaney to move in with me? He'd do it. I know he would. We've always had each other's back. I should have a gun. I'm not getting a gun. Don't be ridiculous....

She knew it was all in her head. No one was in her apartment. Her mystery man was not going to kill her, simply because he needed her. *I'm no good to him dead. He chose me because I'm a reporter. He wants his story told—by me—but only after the murder is committed. I've interviewed bad actors desperate to give their side of the story. Is he any different? What do I ask him? Would he open up to me?*

The perps she wrote about every day were not exactly complex creatures. Their motives were never a mystery. There was the occasional gentleman bandit or lovable rogue she truly enjoyed interviewing, but they were far outnumbered by thugs little more evolved than primordial ooze.

The phantom lurking outside her bedroom door was waiting. *Am I safe with him? Let's say I am. I'm going to interview him sooner or later. Might as well get a head start. I'm never going back to sleep anyway.*

Me: You want to kill for no reason, correct?

Him: Correct. If it makes you happy, say the reason is I want to take a life. Hard stop.

Me: You're a bit self-centered. Domineering, even. You have control issues you need to resolve, friend.

Him: Where do you get off diagnosing me?

Me: I'm not diagnosing you. I'm diagnosing your relationship with me. Trust me, you have issues there.

Him: We're in a relationship?

Me: A really bad one.

Despite knowing she had just totally made herself part of the story, Barbieri continued the interview—journalist objectivity be damned.

Me: You're insane. How can you not see this?

Him: Nobody I know thinks I am. They would've told me.

As she was conducting the interview, Barbieri tried to imagine what the killer looked like, what he sounded like. She was in the dark about both. If he was in fact stalking her, as she feared, he was doing a good job of not letting her see his face. Certainly not at the post office.

Me: Never killed before?

Him: First time.

Me: Any idea how traumatic it'll be? For you, I mean.

Him: I'll deal with it. Man is murdered, and I disappear. Adios.

Me: You'll make his wife a widow.

Him: So? People lose loved ones all the time. Time passes, they get on with their lives.

Me: You assume you'll kill the guy quickly and walk away, like nothing happened.

Him: That's the plan.

Me: What if he doesn't cooperate? He takes his sweet time dying, long enough to tell the cops your height, hair color.

Him: He won't tell them anything. Trust me.

Me: You've been telling yourself this bullshit so often you believe it.

Him: I believe it. I don't give a shit if you do.

Me: Then why recruit me for your mission?

Him: You're a reporter, Kim.

Me: Lost me there, pal.

Him: I'm creating a masterpiece, a perfect crime—and you're planning it right along with me. I'm bringing you close enough to see what a thing of beauty it is. You'll show everyone how I did it. How we did it.

Me: How can I ever thank you?

Him: You're having too much fun to end this game we're having, Kim. It's exciting, planning a homicide. I know it is for me.

Me: Interview over. Get the fuck out before I call the cops!

With the last response, the killer, or her imaginary version of him, had brought the discussion to a sudden halt. Had she just admitted to herself there might be criminal tendencies incubating inside her own mind as well? *Maybe I've got inner demons. Maybe everyone does. Do I have an inner killer he's releasing?*

If she had been in any kind of dream state before, this frightening thought was a real wake-up call. She got out of bed, walked to the kitchen, and turned on the coffee machine. If this was a game, she wanted no part of it. She had no desire to be this monster's publicist, either. She had just been conjuring a man who was a complete enigma. He was a specter, unnamed and unknown, and he was never going to leave her alone.

~ * ~

Barbieri was feeling besieged. It was not just that he was stalking her, at least in her imagination. She was still unable to say for sure if he was actually at Starlight and the post office. Something else was eating at her— the fear she was putting herself and Delaney in danger. *We're becoming co-conspirators, Delaney and me, aiding and abetting a capital offense.* The fear was irrational. Baseless. She understood it completely, yet it did not keep the fear from bouncing all around, out of control, inside her head.

What if I'm wrong? What if he comes after me once he's done? I'm not being paranoid here. He knows where I live.

The fear, paradoxical as it was, that she was turning into a secret admirer was even more alarming. *Am I becoming this wacko's cheerleader? Really? Is this what Stockholm syndrome feels like?* That she might be more interested in seeing how his plan played out than in stopping it in its tracks terrified her about as much as feeling vulnerable. *This is not normal.*

Of course, Barbieri knew Brennan would be there for her... as soon as she could tell him which weapon the killer would use. She had no idea right then, so her knight in shining armor would have to wait.

Once again she summoned her consiglieri, Delaney, for guidance. He joined her for drinks at one of their regular hangouts on the Lower East Side, near his place on Avenue A. The evenings were becoming steadily more pleasant by then, flirting with balmy, so much so people were starting to eat outdoors again. All the tables were taken, but the bar itself had room for a few more patrons. They carved out a space for themselves at the end and ordered drinks. By facing each other with their backs to the room, and keeping their voices down, they managed to hear each other without being overheard by anyone nearby.

"We in over our heads?"

"Legally, you mean?"

"I think we're about to commit a crime."

"Come again?"

"I can't stop thinking we're involved."

"We are. He's given us no choice."

"In a murder?"

"If we don't stop this hit."

"Point taken. Letters implicate us."

"Like we're planning it with him."

"That's insane, Kim. We're not."

"I know, but he's got me almost convinced we are."

"You're not. We're not."

"I'm feeling like I can't get away from him. Anywhere."

"Paranoid, are we?"

"Hallucinating, probably. He invaded my bedroom last night."

"Succumbed to your charms."

"As any man would."

"Not me."

"You're not known for your taste."

"Perhaps if you learned how to accessorize…."

"He gave me a full confession."

"You got a good look at him, I hope."

"Too dark. We talked for a while and I kicked him out."

"You got it all on tape, right?"

"No, but I keep playing it back in my head anyway."

"He say anything useful?"

"Yes. He's a cold-blooded killer who needs a publicist."

"Which explains the letters to you. Still want to keep them coming?"

"I do. This is nuts what we're doing, but I do."

"Let the plot unfold, then."

Putting their heads together, Barbieri and Delaney suspected they might need to lawyer up. They had no idea where or when the victim would be killed; true, yet they feared the cops would think they were hiding evidence. Was it a crime, not stopping a murder that was still a long way away?

There were too many loose ends. One thing was clear, though. She would not be telling her editor about all this. This was all her problem, not her employer's.

Chapter Thirty-three

Okay. One decision under my belt. Now that the victim's gender and age are checked off—he'll be an adult male, a stranger to me, of whatever race and sexual orientation happens to show up to the party—the next logical decision to make is figuring out *how* he's going to die.

Murder victims, I knew from years of watching the news, are killed by guns, by knives, by strangulation, and by poison every day. They're run over by cars, bludgeoned with baseball bats, thrown off roofs, mauled by pit bulls, and pushed in front of trains.

Killers can get very creative.

So I asked myself, what is the best weapon for me, a homicide virgin, to use if I want to drive an otherwise healthy guy I've never met before to an early grave? I do what I usually did when I was handed an assignment. I take out a pad and pencil, and list all the criteria my murder weapon would have to meet. To make sure said victim stays dead, the weapon I choose will be the one meeting all or most of them.

The weapon has to be easy to get.

Easy to learn.

Easy to use.

Fast.

Quiet.

Reliable.

Easily hidden.

Untraceable.

Most critical, it has to work without fail. Guaranteed. If it malfunctions in any way in the middle of trying to kill someone, it's game over. Go right to jail and do not pass go.

Beyond all these, the weapon I choose must not make the victim suffer. Dead is enough. I want the death to be as quick and painless as possible. I'm pretty sure it could be done. There are stories from time to time of sudden deaths where the victim, the papers said, hadn't felt a thing. Dead before he hit the ground.

The poor bastard I'm about to put in the out box hasn't done anything wrong, after all. He doesn't need to suffer, or wonder what he's done to deserve being punished, or be given the illusion he could survive. He is simply in the wrong place, at the wrong time, and he has to go.

For obvious reasons, I also don't want any weapon where I'd end up killing myself by accident, like a bomb of some kind. My luck, I'd only wind up blowing myself to bits. The other thing is, and this is really important to me, I don't want the murder to be gruesome. No wood chipper, no axe, nothing that would cause needless suffering. Or give me nightmares. I know this sounds weird coming from me, but I want this to be a clean killing, or as clean a killing as possible. I don't know if it's to preserve my sanity or my dignity, but this demand is nonnegotiable.

Another sticking point for me is the weapon would have to allow me to literally get away with murder. It can't draw attention from anybody before or during the murder, or leave any clues the police could follow back to me after. Anonymity is critical.

This isn't a complete list of criteria for my weapon, I'm pretty sure. I'm making it up as I think it through. It's not like I'm going to Home Depot to figure out how to put up a toolshed, but it has to do for now. If I need to add criteria later on, after I do some research, I'll add them. No big deal.

Perfectionist that I am, I know I have to get smart real quick about the topic. I've never had much experience with lethal weapons, save maybe a box cutter I sometimes use around the house. The goal I've set for myself is to become a self-taught weapons expert. The most important factor to consider, I figure, is what the weapon needs to do. Kill the victim quickly and make him stay dead. It's not as easy as it sounds.

The one thing I'm sure of, is this is strictly top-secret stuff. Doing research at work, I'd usually ask an eager beaver junior associate assistant whatever to dig into the subject, analyze strengths against weaknesses, yadda yadda. It's a nice perk, having somebody I can dump the grunt work on. One of the few things I miss about my job.

Here, now, it's all me. I have nobody. I know I'd have a hard time explaining to Helen why I'm all of a sudden so interested in human anatomy and the destruction thereof, so I can't pick up books from the bookstore. I could only read them when she's out working, except being self-employed, she can pretty much set her own hours, so there's always the chance she'd come back unexpectedly. Women are like that.

I can't check books out of the library and leave a record there the cops could find. I also don't want to leave any search history on my laptop. If I forget to erase it, I know my wife would find it somehow. Even if I do erase it, the computer geeks the police use could probably find it buried somewhere.

So it seems wise to do research on fatality studies, a field in which I've developed a rather morbid interest, only at the bookstore, where I can take notes without leaving a record of what I've been reading. Nobody there seems to mind if you grab a book off the shelf and sit and read it a while. Makes the place look busy, my guess.

Chapter Thirty-four

A few minutes at the gun show, chatting up gun dealers, convinced Barbieri and Delaney there was no way in hell their guy would use a gun. At least not one bought from a legitimate dealer who did background checks. They had already ruled out the killer buying one illegally, which would require him to commit a felony even before he made it to the big-time, capital murder.

New York City was not NRA-friendly, to put it mildly, so the closest gun show they found was a two-hour drive away, outside Lehigh, Pennsylvania, where deer play and deer hunters abound. Even though hunting season was months away, gun season had no beginning and no end. So the two intrepid journalists were not surprised when they pulled into the parking lot at ten the following morning and it was already almost full—and not only with the late-model SUVs usually congregating at the mall.

"Old fuckin' cars."

"Older pickups."

"Think these guys have ever set foot in Bed, Bath & Beyond?"

"Not unless the store's started carrying ammo."

"Check out the bumper stickers."

"Rebel flags. NRA."

"New York City's a million miles from here."

"He might show up anyway."

"Might. We'll never know."

"I'll know."

"Sixth sense?"

"Can't explain it. But if you see me having a panic attack…."

"We've got him."

They made their way into the hall, not knowing exactly what to expect. Walking around, trying not to be too conspicuous, they passed row after row of booths displaying their wares, with customers either window-shopping or actually ready to walk out with a new piece.

"Holy…."

"Fuckin' airplane hangar."

"Expecting a crowd."

"Not gun nuts. Regular guys."

"This a PTA meeting or an NRA convention?"

"Need an AR-15?"

"Get the urge to kill hundreds of people in a second or two, you're good to go."

Whatever a man might need to fantasize about killing the enemy alongside GI Joe, Barbieri and Delaney found it. The vendors were offering antique guns, knives, swords, Civil War rifles, canteens from Korea, and T-shirts with two main themes—either something along the lines of "I'm packing. Now, what were you saying about the Second Amendment?" or "Infringe THIS!"

The first thing to strike them was dealers seemed to be advertising their wares either for hunting or for personal protection. Kill the bastard before he kills you. Not surprising, given the paranoia about home invasion driving gun sales. The second thing was some dealers seemed more legitimate than others, more professional. These were the licensed dealers, and they were not going to sell even a bullet without doing a full-out background check with the federales. Buyer had to declare he had no criminal record, and was neither a meth addict nor insane. Other vendors, guys who did not bother with paperwork, could not care less. *Here's your new Smith & Wesson 9 mm semiautomatic, holster and ammo. You go have a nice day.*

Each booth had a couple of guys in front, ready to engage. While there were a few tough-looking women here and there, guns were clearly a guy thing. In terms of getting accurate information they knew they could rely on, they zeroed in on a licensed dealer.

The one they approached was busy filling out what they took to be ATF forms. Guy was straight out of central casting, almost a caricature of what a red-blooded, all-American right-to-bear-arms worshipper should look like. Maybe forty, a little shy of six feet tall, solidly built, gray ponytail and goatee, wearing camo cargo pants, a black Carhartt work shirt, and a black baseball cap with the insignia of his unit in Iraq.

"He's not the type I'd have over to dinner, necessarily," Barbieri whispered to Delaney, "but I'd definitely want him on my side in a gunfight."

"Hi. Ask you a few questions for an article we're doing?" They showed the dealer their photo IDs, hoping he would think they were actually legit. Real reporters on a real assignment for a real newspaper.

He did.

"Sure. Gun owners?"

"No. City slickers. I'm Kim, and my partner here is Pete. Neither of us knows anything about guns, actually."

"Johnny Graham. Nice to meet you." the dealer said, shaking her hand, then his.

"Editor's idea, not ours. He assigned us to a story on responsible gun ownership."

"Always use more of that."

Barbieri took out her notepad and pen and began jotting down notes while Delaney fiddled with his camera equipment to look busy. Both would also take mental notes, expecting to compare them later.

"Buyer will have to take a few lessons."

"Where? Shooting range?"

"Yep. Not legally required. Should be, in my opinion. Can't hit shit if they don't learn to aim right. Or grip the firearm right. Kick'll make you miss the target if you let it."

"Loud too, I imagine."

"Deafening. Damage your eardrums if you're not careful. Learning how to fire a gun is number two. Gun safety's number one."

"Going off accidentally, you mean?"

"And keeping it locked away. Every bit as important. You don't want it in the hands of anyone else. Someone could get killed."

"Young children. Criminals. Crazies."

"Had a customer one time, I think bought a Glock pistol. Strictly to protect his family. Gun'd never leave the house, he swore up and down. Took lessons. Kept it in a safe. Totally responsible. Left his safe open for a minute while he went out to get the mail, and the daughter's curiosity got the better of her."

"She shot herself?"

"Father. Got his blood all over her."

"Jeez. But you did exactly what you're supposed to."

"Not on me. I did everything by the book."

"Ever screen buyers yourself? Besides the ATF forms?"

"Not my job." The dealer took some umbrage, clearly. He was used to arguing with abolitionists and had his position nailed. "Customers I get are regulars. Buying a new firearm for their collection. For their kids sometimes. They know as much about firearms as I do. I can tell pretty quick if they never bought before, though, in which case I direct them to the gun range. After I make the sale."

"Due diligence."

"Common sense. Now, guy looks unstable, on drugs, that's another story. I won't sell to him. Legally I can't refuse, but I will. Let's say me and the NRA don't agree on that point. Gotta live with myself."

"He can try other dealers here."

"Sure. Couple of dealers here'll look the other way. No friggin' conscience."

Barbieri changed the subject. "Which kind of gun would our responsible owner have? Revolver? Automatic?"

"Depends on what he's looking for. Revolver's more reliable." He took a revolver out of its holster and aimed it at nothing in particular. "More accurate. No problem learning how to shoot. No safety, though. It could go off by accident. Happens."

He put the revolver aside and took a semiautomatic from the display case. A Luger.

"Now if he's keeping the gun on his person, semiautomatic's the way to go. Lot thinner. Loads faster. A little too complicated for beginners, maybe. Harder to learn."

"Ever steer them one way or another?"

"Whatever direction they're already going is where I steer 'em. They want a revolver, I convince them it's the right call. They want a semiautomatic, same thing. As long as they don't leave empty-handed, I'm good."

"See any first-time buyers today? City slickers like us?" Barbieri was not sure she wanted to ask this question, because she was afraid of the answer. Deathly afraid, in fact, because the answer could confirm her suspicion the killer was stalking her.

"One man. It's early yet. He chickened out anyway, left same way he came in. Empty-handed. You guys just missed him."

"Where was he from? Around here?" Delaney asked.

"Didn't ask. Not my business. All I can tell you is I never saw him before."

"About covers it for us. Thanks for your time." Barbieri put away her notepad, and Delaney took a couple of photos of the dealer in his booth. They were keeping up their journalist appearances.

"Glad to help." He took two business cards from the countertop and handed one to each of them. "Case you ever grow a pair," he called out as they walked away.

Suddenly she pulled her partner off to the side, where they could not be overheard.

"He followed us here! Shit!"

"Where?"

There was outright dread in her eyes. Viper-slithering-under-your-bed fear that gripped her even more tightly than it had in the post office. Like the last time, her body gave her away. Goose bumps suddenly appeared, and shuddering escalated into trembling. Her breathing got faster.

"He's over there." She gestured with her head down the aisle. "I'm sure."

"There are at least a dozen men there. Which one?"

"Can't see him now. Must've walked away. I'm sure it's him. Positive."

"Let's say he is. Could be a coincidence."

"Not a chance."

"He came out here for the same reason we did. There's a first time for everyone, Kim. Even people out buying guns."

"I'm telling you, he's here because I'm here. Maybe it was a coincidence in Bay Ridge, but not now. It's him. I feel it. I still feel it. He's pretty close."

He looked up and down the aisles with her. If the killer was still there, he blended in perfectly.

"Anything?"

"Nope."

"What if he comes after me? After us?"

"At a gun show? Seriously? He'd be nuts to try. Good guys would like nothing more than to use a bad guy for target practice."

"Right. Too smart for that."

"Probably gone by now. Saw us first and took off."

"My pulse is returning to normal."

"There's your proof. He's gone."

"I'll take your word for it. Think he bought a gun? Think he'd use it? "

"Not on his victim. Or yourself."

"None."

"ATF form. Paper trail."

"Serial number."

"He'd be recognized at the gun range."

"Gunshot heard far and wide."

"Blood and splatter if he's too close."

"From a distance, he only wounds the victim."

"Or misses entirely."

"Knife's looking good."

"Agreed, but it's not going to help us find him."

~ * ~

Gun seemed a logical place to start my search. Seems damn near everyone in America has one, 'cept me.

Never fired one, don't know how to use one. I'm not anti-guns or anything. I'm not. Long as folks don't use them to commit crimes, I have no quarrel with the right to bear arms, yet my research into guns gave me a ton of reasons to cross this weapon off the list first.

Buying a piece legally, from a dealer, would leave a paper trail back to my front door. And I'm not going to file off the serial number. While buying off the street from some guy I don't know from Adam could lead to my arrest before this plot of mine gets a chance to thicken. There goes my plan, shot to hell.

Either way, I'd have to take a few lessons. I'd have to sign up for them, show some ID. I'd have to become friendly, or at least a nodding acquaintance, with other shooters there. Which would raise red flags galore to detectives investigating a murder.

A gun would also make a rather loud noise when it's fired, making it a little hard for me to slip away unnoticed. I couldn't do the deed outdoors unless the victim and I happened to be the only people around in the middle of nowhere. Not much chance there. Instead, I'd have to shoot him indoors, me alone with the victim. Also highly unlikely.

Something I also knew from all the cop shows I saw was when you shoot a guy at close range, there's a good chance his blood and tissues could wind up on the gun itself. A gift for the forensics guys if the gun is ever found, which is likely considering how hard it is to make one disappear for good. Also a gun would leave gunshot residue on my hands and clothing. Telltale proof I had indeed fired said weapon. Like a tar baby you can't shake off.

Despite these obvious drawbacks, I decided to learn as much as possible about firearms. There could be a way to work around them. 'Course, the idea a possible nutjob like myself is allowed anywhere near a firearm gave me more than a little pause, let me tell you.

I went where NRA gun junkies congregated to share the latest gun control conspiracies, a gun show. Those shows are everywhere, all year round, so without looking too hard, you can find one almost every weekend, if you're willing to drive a few hours away. That's where I found the one I went to, out in Pennsylvania. Being so far out of town was fine by me. It meant I'd be less likely to run into a gunslinger I knew there.

I was wrong on that point, turns out.

If you want to go where guys love to talk shop, let me tell you, a gun show is the place to be. Glance in a dealer's direction, make just a second of eye contact, and his can't-shut-up switch flips on and stays on. If there were no paying customers coming his way, he'd be only too glad to talk shop with the guys in the next booth. They live for that stuff.

I walk around, getting my bearings. I have to remind myself I'm not really interested in joining this particular fraternity. I'm preparing for a single mission and need the one right weapon to assure my victim ends up dead and I end up safely at home.

"Take your rifle," the first dealer I approach says to me. Big, tough-looking dude. Iraq veteran.

I stop him right there. Gun dealers and gun buyers are brothers in arms, almost literally, and I tell him what he probably already knows by looking at me. "I'm no hunter."

"Okay, handguns." The dealer is clearly enjoying this teachable moment. He takes out a revolver and spins the cylinder. "Your revolvers are the kind cowboys and gunfighters shoot in Westerns. Think Wyatt Earp. They haven't changed a whole lot since then. Bullet goes where you tell it to."

I'm hanging on his every word. For my purposes, of course, accuracy is critical. I gotta hit what I'm aiming at, because where the guy is hit determines if he lives or dies. A bullet in his heart or lungs would kill him in seconds. Death is less likely if it goes into his guts. Last thing I need is to only wound the guy so he lives long enough to point a finger in my direction.

My distinguished professor puts the revolver back and takes out another gun. "Then there's your semiautomatic, gun 007 packs. Bullets are kept in a clip, like so." He pulls out the clip, making sure it's empty, then shoves it back in with a loud solid click before handing it to me. Thing is heavy, a lot heavier than I expected. "First thing you gotta do before you fire is turn the safety off. Then rack the slide. Like so."

I rack the slide. I didn't know I have an inner Navy Seal waiting to get out, but I do, bearing a major woody. I notice racking the slide itself makes noise, because it's all metal hitting metal. What I need is silence.

He pointed to the semiautomatic in his holster. "Most guys here carry semiautomatics. They're a lot thinner, so they're easier to conceal."

That's the one major selling point for me, yet one feature is a deal-breaker as far as I'm concerned. I'm not sure what evidence police can pick up from a shell casing, maybe fingerprints or DNA, but I don't want to risk leaving one behind at the crime scene.

I thank the gun dealer for his time and continue walking around the arena. If he thought he converted me to a brother-in-arms it's fine by me. Based on this limited tutorial, I think I'd have a better chance of a clean kill with a revolver. I'd only have to figure out the caliber of the bullet I'd need—the size, in plain English—and you'd have to be a rocket scientist to figure that out.

Rather than stop by another dealer at the gun show and create a second chance for someone to identify me to the police, I decide to head back to the library and do more research the old-fashioned way. On my way out, though, I spot a familiar face. Reporter again, with the same guy she was with at the post office. He's a photographer, taking one shot after another nonstop, as if he's working. They're talking to the same gun dealer I was. I'm maybe fifty feet away from them, hiding in plain sight, going from dealer to dealer. Perfectly camouflaged. Then just like before, they stop what they're doing and look at everyone around them. I guess I have an aura or something. I don't want to spook her any more than she already is, so I leave the arena in a hurry, resisting the urge to go up to her and scream, "You're getting warmer!" I don't know about the man she's with, the photographer. He wasn't part of my plan at all, but I've clearly chosen the right person to write to. She's good.

Here's the bottom line, as far as I'm concerned. There are a lot of pluses to making a gun my murder weapon, but even more cons. Too many. I rule out shooting the victim and start looking into other options.

Why don't I strangle the guy? I've always been the hands-on type.

Chapter Thirty-five

"I thought I'd seen everything, Kim. I was mistaken."

"Glad to expand your experience, Counselor. What clients are for."

She was sitting across the desk from Gerald L. Simon, Counselor at Law, in his offices near Rockefeller Center, in a glass-encased building identical to the others up and down the avenue. While his firm's reception area had absolutely no character, his personal office had plenty. A fitness freak who looked a lot younger than his actual age, sixty-seven, Simon was a licensed pilot. He owned a vintage Cessna 150 he flew every chance he got, and his office was a wall-to-wall shrine to aviation. Old Constellation posters, a model of his own big boy toy suspended from the ceiling, and selfies of him climbing into and out of his holiest of holies.

Ignoring the air show around her, Barbieri got right down to business. She gave Simon the binder with the three letters, and as he leafed through them, she looped him in on the assumptions she had made about their author and his likely victim, as well as her what-if discussions with Timothy Brennan, Commander of Brooklyn South Homicide. Without revealing his name, she described the conversation she had had with the ADA about her potential legal risk. She omitted any mention of Delaney's role. Lie or no lie, this escapade was all on her.

"Have I done anything illegal here? Do I need you to keep me out of jail?"

"Depends on what happens next, Kim. What were you thinking?"

"When?"

"When you kept getting these letters."

"Not clearly, apparently. Brennan told me there's nothing the police could do." *Telling my attorney I've been relying on my boyfriend for legal advice? Not a great idea.*

"There's failure to report a crime, for starters. You know the guy's attempting to commit murder. Conversations with your cop friend and the ADA may not qualify."

"What would I tell the police? They wouldn't know anything about him."

"Not your decision, I'm afraid."

"I believe his victim's going to be a man. That's it. If a murder is going to take place, that wouldn't help them at all."

"You don't know that. You're a damn civilian. I think they could try to get you on accessory. I could see the prosecution argue by not reporting him, you were egging him on. I don't think they would, but they could try."

"Accessory? For a couple of letters?"

"Three. I could argue these messages are just blue sky. I'd argue they could be interpreted as thinking out loud, which isn't a crime that I can see. Attempted murder is only a crime when it's attempted. Buying a gun is not a crime. Pointing it is."

"Okay. What if he writes to tell me *when* he's going to commit murder? He hasn't yet, although he might."

"This makes your legal jeopardy even worse, potentially. The more information the police have, the more likely they could track him down and stop him."

"If the guy does commit murder, what then?"

"Think about it. Say the guy actually kills someone, *and* he gets arrested, *and* he confesses. He tells the police he's been warning someone, meaning you, and they find out that someone is in fact you, you're in really deep shit."

"Crap."

"Indeed. The authorities won't look kindly on you. This I can guarantee. My advice is go to the police. Today. Not Tomorrow."

"Okay."

"One more point. If you do get another letter, send it to me."

"Got it."

"Unopened."

"Unopened. Got it."

She took back the binder and got up to leave, prompting her attorney to walk with her out of his office. On the way out, she thanked Simon for his wise counsel and asked him to send her the bill for his services. As the elevator doors opened, he offered her one final thought, an appeal to her vanity.

"Get this resolved, Miss Barbieri. People are getting killed left and right out there, and your devoted readers need you."

Simon's opinion about her legal jeopardy was not the same as the ADA's, yet it was his opinion, and he was her attorney. She believed what he had told her and fully understood what she needed to do to stay out of jail. Whether she would go ahead and do what she needed to do was another matter. She could not bring herself to go to the NYPD, but maybe it was time to cave and tell one member of it.

Chapter Thirty-six

Turns out strangulation is also a nonstarter. I simply don't have it in me to strangle a guy with my bare hands. I know I'm strong enough physically speaking, but psychologically? Sorry, no.

Deep down, believe me, I'm nonviolent. Really. I don't think I've ever hurt anyone on purpose, ever. What you're doing when you squeeze his neck real hard is pressing down on his airways so he can't breathe air into his lungs. No oxygen, no life. Very simple, very effective. While you're at it, you're also squeezing the carotid artery carrying blood to his brain. Cerebral hypoxia, technically speaking. No oxygen to feed the brain, which keeps you alive.

So strangulation's a two-for-one killer. Still, this means to a lethal end isn't very fast. You have to keep on squeezing really tight for what seems like an eternity. If you're careful, you could leave no bruises, making it hard for the ME to say what killed him. Remember, I want the world to know this was no accident.

Maybe it's the fact that strangling someone, killing with my bare hands, my skin touching his, is a lot more intimate than killing with a gun or a baseball bat. Can't do it. Even if I wore gloves, strangling someone is hard. It's an agonizing, slow death, and I don't want my guy to suffer. I know I couldn't keep the pressure on his throat for the minutes it would take him to die. It would give me time to think about what I'm doing, decide to abort the mission, let go of his neck, and run like hell.

Besides, what if the guy fights back and breaks free? When a guy is fighting for his life, he gains almost superhuman strength.

Strangulation is out. What about its close relative, snapping his neck? If you're looking to send someone to an early grave, the neck's a target-rich environment if there ever was one. This little piece of real estate is like a superhighway jammed with your nervous system, your blood supply, and your air supply between your head and your body. Cut all of this life support at once and the victim doesn't have a chance. Call the mortician.

From the little I do know about it, you could break a man's neck by grabbing his head from behind and somehow twisting and jerking it so the bones at the top of the spine are broken or moved.

Those neck bones are like a shield of solid armor keeping the spinal cord safe from injury. Break through the shield and you're talking permanent injury or permanent death. Now, if you break only the bones, not the spinal cord itself, the attack wouldn't be fatal. If the bones heal, the guy would be okay. Damage the spinal cord itself, though, he's got problems. He'd probably end up paralyzed. Wheelchair for the rest of his life. I don't want him to go through all that. He could also die from lack of oxygen. Asphyxiation. He'd stop breathing, but he'd take his sweet time about it. Again, not what I want.

What I want is sudden death. Like in seconds, not minutes. The guaranteed way you accomplish it is to cut the nerves in the cord completely in half. Nerve cells can't heal themselves. Then there'd be no messages from the brain telling the heart and lungs to keep working. There'd be a fast, major drop in blood pressure, causing death in seconds.

In the end, though, as good as it is in causing sudden death, I eighty-sixed breaking the guy's neck. With my luck, I'd probably leave him paralyzed. Mission definitely not accomplished. He'd be stuck in a wheelchair, and I'd be living with a ton of guilt for the rest of my born days.

To be honest with myself, the real reason for rejecting this method is, I'm not going to break someone's neck. No way. It would say something about me, that I'm maybe subhuman, which I don't want to hear.

What if I smother the guy with a pillow? I wouldn't have to look him in the eye, at least.

~ * ~

Smothering I also rejected out of hand. If you can keep up the pressure and keep the oxygen from reaching his lungs, the victim's sure to die. Eventually, anyway. Sounds simple enough, yet there are way too many problems here, too many unknowns. In business terms, there are too many variables I have no control over.

How would I know where my victim lives? Would I have to stalk him? I'd probably have to break into his house, so would I go in through a door or a window? Either way, I'd have to commit another crime first, breaking and entering, before the main event. This would be a little hard to explain if he wakes up, or his wife's in the den watching Colbert.

The place could be alarmed—most houses seem to be—so I'd have to find a way to sneak in, stay in, and sneak out without tripping it and sending police cars racing over. Why would I risk going to jail without even getting close to the guy for Christ's sake? All my hard work, only to end up doing time for breaking and entering.

Also, I'd have to be certain which bedroom is his, what time he goes to bed, and whether he's alone. No way would I learn all that. He'd also already have to be lying down and sleeping, rather than sitting up reading or watching TV, in order for him to be pillow-ready.

All smothering has going for it is it's quiet and takes no special skill. The weapon would be courteously supplied by the victim himself. Also on the plus side, smothering causes tiny hemorrhages in the eyes. If the EMT guys happen to notice, the police would know they had a homicide on their hands.

That aside, there isn't much else going for smothering the victim; with all the unknowns, my chances of being caught are too high for my taste. Adios, smothering.

What about poison? Tons of people are killed by it, and there's no violence at all. How hard could it be?

Chapter Thirty-seven

To my naïve mind, poison is a gimme. Pretty common MO among the homicidally inclined, far as I could tell. People are killed with it, or kill themselves with it, every day. Sometimes on purpose, sometimes not.

There was the Russian spook in England nearly killed by some toxin no one can pronounce. A few years ago, some lunatics dumped sarin gas in the Tokyo subway in the middle of rush hour. Killed a lot of people who were only trying to get home in time for dinner. Even the government uses poison to kill, only they call it execution by lethal injection or in the gas chamber. Either way, it's poison.

And some stuff that's absolutely fine for ninety-nine percent of humanity, like shrimp, is lethal to people who are allergic. Dead before they know it. You don't even have to eat it yourself. I remember there was this one girl who was allergic to nuts. She was kissed to death by a guy who'd had a peanut butter sandwich moments before. Death by tonsil hockey.

If you think about it, poison is anything you take enough of to kill you. Still, if I was out of my league with a gun, mastering this particular murder weapon is even more challenging. A few hours of research showed me exactly how lousy it was as an instrument of death.

If I start looking up poisons online, it could well be the end of my project. It's one of the search words known to cause conniptions at the NSA, since poison could be turned into a WMD pretty easily. I'd be threading a very, very fine needle, investigating poisons without raising their alarm. In the library, though, I'm not connected to the universe, or the federal government.

There is a whole vocabulary I'd have to get up to speed on, for one thing. Now I'm no dummy. You want to discuss market share or supply chain management? I'm with you. Absorption, excretion, and pharmacokinetics—not so much. It's all a little above my pay grade. The CliffsNotes version is this: Don't use poison if you want to kill one victim quickly.

For one thing, there's an incredible variety of poisons out there, beginning with controlled substances like anthrax. I mean, they're controlled for a very good reason. They're made for one purpose—death. You don't want your average jihadist anywhere near them.

Though I figure if the federales are working hard to control it, then someone is trying to sell it. Trying to get my hands on it would cause alarms to go off all over the place and leave a brightly colored paper trail right back to me. I crossed controlled poisons off my list.

Then there's the prescription drugs like oxy, which suicidal types swallow by the fistful. Take the right dose and the pain goes away; take too much and there's a table for one at the Medical Examiner's office. What with all the records drug stores and insurance companies keep, I can't get any prescription drug without triggering alarms.

Nothing's simple, is it? And also, how would I be sure no innocent bystander would take it? I have a very limited goal, one dead body. It seems everywhere I turn, no matter what poison I think of, problems like those come up and make my head spin.

Complication numero dos is some poisons cause a slow, agonizing death. Vomiting and pain for hours. If my guy takes too long to go belly up, it would give EMTs time to give him a reprieve. Not what I have in mind. So, if I make poison my weapon du jour, it would have to be one made to kill in seconds, maybe a minute or two at most.

Number three, poisons can be gas, powder, or liquid, so they enter the body in different ways. Give the guy a shot or mix it in his food. Either way, he's toast. Some are inhaled. Some poisons, like cyanide, are multitalented; whether you inhale it, swallow it or touch it, you're dead before you know it. Too many issues to deal with, too many opportunities to screw up. Another headache for math-challenged wretches like me is figuring out how much of the stuff I'd need. Bigger bodies need more poison. Since I haven't had the pleasure of meeting my victim, I'm at a loss here. The amount also depends on how long your guy's exposed to it. If he breathes in a gas for a long time, a small dose'll do. If he takes only a whiff, you'll need a bigger dose. Lots of room for error.

Using poison gas also runs the risk of what the military types call collateral damage. Innocent victims in the wrong place, at the wrong time, who happen to make a habit of breathing. I'm prepared for a body count of one. One innocent life. Singular. Call me what you will, but I'm no Jeffrey Dahmer or what's-his-name, the other nutjob from Chicago who buried twenty or so boys in the basement. I'm no mass murderer.

Of course, one possible other victim would be me, and I'm not about to wear a gas mask. I'm not on a suicide mission. If I get careless, I'd only wind up killing myself. How would I explain that to Helen?

All in all, poison sucks big-time. Enough to make my head explode. Going back to my list of criteria, poison has very few check marks going for it. I have only one person on my to-kill list, so gas is out. It has to be someone I don't know, so a pill is out. I don't want to leave a paper trail, so controlled poisons are out. The list goes on.

What if I run over the guy with a car? Driving's something I do every day.

Chapter Thirty-eight

Curious term, vehicular homicide. It's the car's fault somebody gets runs over, not the driver's.

When a guy's hit by a car going maybe forty, it's basically a fatal case of blunt force trauma. Like what happens when you jump from a ten-story building. Dead on impact.

There is one big difference between this and the other means of execution I've been looking into. If I stay at the scene and the police come, I could always claim it was an accident. *It's dark, Officer, and the idiot walked right into the street without looking*. Cop wouldn't think twice. The chance to change intentional to accidental is about the only thing going for it, but it's an option I don't really want. I want it known a murder was committed and the murderer is out there. Somewhere.

A guy who sometimes joined our poker game is a claims adjuster. State Farm, I think. Steve something. Always on the road investigating accidents, mostly run-of-the-mill fender benders. He's one of those guys who loves to talk about his work. No off switch.

"First thing I look at when a pedestrian's run over is the damage to the bumper," he explains. "Hit a human body at twenty-five, thirty miles an hour, the front end's wrecked. All I care about's the damage to the car. The poor guy got hit's the responsibility of the EMTs." Which tells me after the murder, I'd have to abandon the car and hope it's sent to a chop shop. I could buy a used piece of junk I won't mind getting rid of, except that would leave a paper trail right back to me.

"When a pedestrian is hit," he continues, "both he and the vehicle pick up traces of each other. Paint chips wind up in his hair, giving the cops a good idea of what color car to look for. Look hard enough, you'll also find traces of his skin, hair, and blood on the car. Stuff's almost impossible to get off." Which means even if I clean the car thoroughly, scrubbing down every inch, I'd leave evidence for the detectives to find.

This conversation is pretty much a turn-off, far as this weapon goes. If I go this route, I'd have to commit the crime on the street or in a parking lot, probably lit up by streetlights, which means there'd probably be witnesses. I definitely don't want to have to eliminate them, too. There's always the chance I'd hit the wrong man. Or hit the right one but only hard enough to injure him. Again, not the desired outcome.

When I perpetrate this hit-and-run, chances are pretty good I'll leave tire tracks that could at least tell the cops what kind of car they should look for. If the tracks also show a wear pattern only my car has, it could be even more trouble for me. Or, my luck, I could be pulled over by the police and charged with leaving the scene of an accident. Who knows if I'd cry like a baby if they decided to interrogate me? I don't think I would, and I don't want to find out, either.

Adios, hit-and-run.

I'm quickly running out of options. Every weapon I look at gives me less control than I need if I'm to bring my project to a successful end. The only one left I could see is a knife, which is clearly not my first choice. Killing with it is so personal. I mean, it's pretty close to killing someone with your bare hands.

I decide to head to the Barnes & Noble to see if there's a way to make killing with a knife more acceptable to me. They really don't seem to mind if you sit and read a while, which I do.

Chapter Thirty-nine

"We're going about this all wrong, Delaney."

"Meaning…?"

"We should work backward."

"Focus on the damage he needs to inflict."

"Tell us his weapon."

To a man as methodical as the killer seemed to be, she reasoned, this kind of reverse engineering could point to the ideal murder weapon. It would do no good if the weapon was easy to use but could not be counted on to cause a lethal injury. Or if it was certain to cause a quick death, and was too difficult for a novice to use.

"Has to cause serious trauma."

"Major hemorrhaging."

"No oxygen to the brain."

"No time for EMTs."

"Lost cause."

Barbieri and Delaney were playing verbal badminton on her patio, sitting across from each other with their feet on the table. Neither happened to be out on assignment then, as the criminal population apparently decided they had fulfilled their quota of mayhem for the month and took some time off from the swift completion of their appointed felonies. Only possible explanation.

After a drab, overcast morning, a gentle breeze started coming in off the harbor right down the block, and by afternoon the clouds were politely staying out of the sun's way. They were both in off-duty mode, dressed way down in their spring collection: T-shirts, jeans, and sandals.

When it was only the two of them, off the clock and with nobody important around, appearances were not kept up. Delaney had even taken off his camera vest, an unthinkable act simply not done in public.

"Go online, Kim. Look up emergency medical care."

"Counterintuitive. Like it."

"See which wounds are treatable."

"And beyond treating."

She took out her laptop, booted it up, and put it between them so they could both look directly at the screen. They hit the jackpot with the first article she came across, about the treatment of lacerations. It gave them a pretty good idea about the damage a knife causes when it cuts through the skin, what kinds of stab wounds can be successfully treated, and more important, what kinds are too severe to even try treating. Their search ended right there. They heard hoofbeats and thought horses, not zebras.

The murderer's goal was for his victim was to bleed out quickly, so the only logical choice giving him the control and accuracy he needed was a knife. The murderer could not be as sure other weapons would cause the massive blood loss that leads to a quick death. A knife could practically guarantee a quick death, if the killer was sure to pierce the body part that bleeds out the most.

"Knife."

"One hundred percent."

"Any garden-variety kitchen knife would do."

"It can cause major hemorrhage."

"Bleeds out quickly."

"If it severs an artery."

"Hemorrhaging ends only when the victim dies."

"Corpses don't bleed."

"Victims die from stab wounds all the time."

"Probably already has his sharp instrument hidden in plain sight, right in the kitchen drawer."

"Garage. Basement."

"Shed out back."

Morgues have had a lot of stiffs whose last moments alive were spent impaled on a sharp instrument, terminology Barbieri sometimes resorted to when she was quoting technicians from the ME's office.

Search over, she put away her laptop while Delaney put his vest back on, grabbed his car keys, and headed out to his Subaru. After seeing him off, she returned to the patio, plunked herself back down on her chair, put her feet back on the table, and thought about the irony of what they had learned. The emergency medical care article helped them in a way its authors may not have intended. What they wrote was how to save a stabbing victim's life. What the duo took away was how to make sure the victim was beyond saving.

I can now inform my personal police force the weapon will be a knife, and show him all the mail my homicidal apprentice has been sending me. What I should've done from day one. Idiot.

~ * ~

"He's using a knife."

"I assume we're talking about a certain hypothetical individual. You know this how? Wild guess, Barbieri?"

"More than that, Cap'n. Logic."

"Whose?"

"Mine. Knife's the one weapon clearly idiot-proof, easy to get, and able to kill in seconds. Assuming he can get close enough to his victim. Other weapons have too many problems."

"Okay, I'll accept your hypothesis. What are we supposed to do about it? All we still have is an unidentified individual, could be male or female—"

"I'm sure it's a male. Definitely."

"An unidentified male attempting to take the life of another unidentified male with a weapon everyone has a dozen of."

"And he may be insane. Let's not forget that." *Tell him everything. If it helps get this bastard put away, tell him everything.*

"Well, that narrows it down to a few hundred thousand suspects.

Give or take."

The lovebirds were at Aroma Trattoria, a new Italian place off Gramercy Park. Together they had feasted on just about every ethnic cuisine the city had to offer, and she was always ready to try out new *ristorantes*. For those she changed from crime reporter to restaurant critic—and she was especially critical when it came to northern Italian places. The highest compliment she could give was coming back.

"At some point you're going to tell me how you're involved in this, Kim. And with whom. Sooner rather than later. Before a man gets killed, preferably."

"I don't know who. I really don't. All I'll tell you is some weirdo has been in contact with me." She had promised herself she would wait until the end of the meal to tell him about her pen pal, yet her resolve was no match for his. Strong-willed as she was, she went down without a fight. *I hate how he gets his way all the time. I have to find someone new. As soon as I'm done with him. It'll be a while.*

"Contacting you how? Phone calls? Texts?"

"Mail. Snail mail. He's sent me three letters, unsigned."

"Was that so hard? I'm going to have to see them, Barbieri. And we'll have to bring in investigators from the postal service, too."

"Why them?"

"Evidence. Mail tells postal inspectors a lot more than it's telling you or our forensics lab. Fibers, DNA. Language patterns. Anything to help us ID the sender."

"They're good at that? Analyzing words he uses?"

"Exceptional. It's sort of like profiling, but based on his writing style. Idioms, typos. NYPD works with them all the time, mostly to catch meth addicts stealing checks from mailboxes. Get-rich-quick scams. Occasional mail bomb. If mail's involved, postal inspectors are involved. Standard operating procedure. Criminal investigation is about the only thing the post office doesn't suck at."

"Any chance you can accept them not in your official capacity? As a cop-slash-friend?"

"Sorry. I have to keep my boss at Police Plaza in the loop. At least tell him what this bozo's up to. Postal inspector I used to work with owes me a favor. He may cut me some slack if I ask nicely. I'll explain about the letters you got and see if he can look the other way this once. Worth a try, anyway"

"I also think this guy's been following me. I can't swear to it, because I never got a good look at him. More like a sixth sense than anything else. I ain't imagining it, Timothy."

"This isn't good, Kim. Men I sent to protect you didn't see anything or they would've told me."

"I still think I'm not in any danger. I think he needs a writer of some kind to make him a star. Why he chose yours truly, I'm not really sure."

"Luck. You may be right, Kim, except there's something you're not seeing. If he ever gets his day in court, you'd be a witness for the prosecution. Maybe the only witness. I think he'd prefer you didn't testify."

"Why on Earth didn't I see this? Shit. Any idea how he found me, my assassin?"

"Saw your byline in the *News* and went from there, my guess. Another nutjob coming out of the woodwork. Half of your paper's readers are borderline. The other half are cops."

"You do know how to sweet-talk a girl, Cap'n."

Official business over, Brennan changed the subject back to safe territory.

"Verdict?"

"Worth a second visit. Order the branzino next time."

~ * ~

A knife's the one weapon I already used every day. Slicing bagels, opening boxes. Except now it would be used for something a little more sinister. "Repurposed," if you're conversant in corporate-speak.

Knife is a silent killer. No moving parts to click against each other or blasts to muffle. So if you can somehow stifle any protest from the victim, no one within earshot would know what's going on. If a bystander is really close, a few feet away maybe, he might hear deep, rapid breathing as the victim bleeds out and gasps for air, which you could muffle by putting your hand over his mouth and nose. That's about it. Anal as I am, I want to know as much as I can about what makes one knife better than another for my purposes.

There are a lot more knives out there than you'd imagine. Hundreds, in a bewildering variety of shapes and sizes and uses. No question I wouldn't get any kind of military knife, like a ka-bar, since I'm sure the cops would check all the army-navy stores. That leaves going to a kitchen supply store, of which there seems to be one on every corner CVS hasn't claimed. Which is exactly where I find myself early one afternoon, since I have nothing but time on my hands.

Happens to be one Helen and I have gone to a few times, Williams Sonoma. Store's loaded to the rafters with every kind of pot and pan and gadget imaginable. I go in, and the first thing I notice is the aroma. Something really good. They're giving a cooking lesson in the kitchen in back, where customers are learning how to use utensils the store happens to have in stock. Pretty good sales tool, if you ask me. All in all, it's Disneyland for cooks, where everything is designed to make you believe you're one tortellini maker away from making the best damn Italian dinner of your life.

Here, asking the experts about cutlery isn't a problem in terms of arousing suspicion. The saleswoman who intercepts me the moment I enter is only too glad to give me a guided tour. Maybe she's taken pity on me, being a sorry-ass man in a woman's domain. She's a little younger than I am, maybe forty or forty-two, a little on the heavy side, short brown hair, terrific smile. I could tell right away she loves her job. Nametag says her name is Tricia, and Tricia, as luck would have it, knows her way around the knife drawer.

I tell her I'm thinking of learning to cook, which sounds credible enough, given all the male chefs on the cooking shows, and need a Kitchen Knives 101 course. Her eyes light up because I've given her a chance to show off.

"We'll start here," she begins, directing me to a set of knives in one display rack. "If you're serious, first thing to know is there's a specific knife for everything you need to cut. You don't want to use a bread knife for steak, et cetera, et cetera." That much I understand from watching my wife make dinner a thousand times.

"Your most basic one is this, a chef's knife, sort of a knife of all trades for chopping and slicing. The smaller version, the paring knife, is for smaller items or peeling fruit." I notice the blade looks maybe four inches long and make a mental note.

"Now, these two are a carving knife to slice a roast, and your trailing point knife for trimming meat from bone," she continued. Maybe a chef knew it, but I sure didn't. No knife she's shown me seems to be made for stabbing someone to death, far as I can tell.

"You recognize this one, right?" Tricia asks me, picking up a cleaver. Talk about overkill. I know I'm not going to need anything like it for my project, so I rule out this baby. Tricia, poor thing, has no idea she's abetting a murder she'll soon be reading about in the paper. I pretend to study the two knives she's given me to hold.

"It's all kind of intimidating for novices, I know," Tricia tries to reassure me. "Start out with one or two for the next meal you're cooking and go from there."

Everything's complicated if you look too closely. I thanked her for her time and her cutlery lesson by buying a generic chef's knife. Before I left, I had one last question for Tricia.

"Know what they're cooking back there?"

She checked her computer. "Coq au vin."

I knew right then where Helen and I were going for dinner.

Within a block or so of leaving the store, I tossed the knife I'd bought minutes before. Helen would spot it in her kitchen drawer in a nanosecond. I still had a few questions about knives I couldn't ask Tricia, so on the way home, I stopped at the library to dig a little deeper into cutlery studies.

When you knife someone, the stab wound can be pretty deep, and the forensics guys can figure out how long the blade is by sticking a kind of ruler into the wound. They can also tell if it had a serrated edge or not, and whether it was double-edged or single-edged, which would tell the detectives to look for a dagger rather than a plain knife. All of which made me dead certain when I got rid of it, I'd have to dump it miles away from the scene of the crime, never to be seen again.

The deeper I dug, the more I realized I was doing this search for the perfect knife all wrong. I couldn't possibly choose the ideal knife until I chose the ideal target first. Not the victim, but the organ in his body. I didn't want to leave the guy undead by penetrating something that wasn't guaranteed fatal.

Once I nailed the organ I was aiming for, I'd call on my newfound expertise to find the one knife designed to penetrate at precisely the right spot to induce the earliest possible expiration date. I don't want to have to stab him more than once, which would give him a chance to fight back, and if I choose the right organ, I won't have to. I'm not interested in reenacting the shower scene from *Psycho*. Remember *Psycho*? The original—not the remake? I had nightmares for months.

Going back to my list of criteria, a knife has a check mark next to every item. I may already have the one I need. It's easy to use. It's fast, only a matter of plunging it in. It's reliable, since there's nothing to break or malfunction. It doesn't make a sound. It's proven to kill, as long as it hits a critical organ. It can't be traced back to me, as long as I wipe off my prints and make it disappear for all eternity.

A knife also, at least I hope it does, causes less suffering than the other weapons. When you're stabbed, you only feel pain right on your skin, where your pain nerves are. Once the knife makes it past this barrier, your internal organs feel nothing. No pain nerves. Getting stabbed hurts like hell, but only on the outside.

So I'm making progress. Good progress. I have my victim, a healthy adult male, and his undoing, some kind of knife wound. Now, what part of my victim's body should I pierce with the knife?

Chapter Forty

Looking into weapons first, before knowing what task I need them to perform, was my bad, but not too bad. Chalk it up to a learning experience in my new field of endeavor. A teachable moment.

As far as which part of the gentleman's body would be most likely to have massive and rapid internal bleeding, I have no idea. Which would be most vulnerable? Again, no clue[1]. How would I know? What I do know is I'll have to be really close when I plunge the knife in, if not actually touching him.

If I don't hit a critical organ, like the heart, the victim could certainly bleed to death, but he'd take his sweet time. He'd suffer for hours, needlessly, before he breathes his last. He'd also leave a lot of blood to clean up, which would no doubt slow down my getaway.

The library again. Only this time one a few towns away, where I'm a total nobody. This research has to be done on the QT, as far away from my neighbors as possible. I choose the library out in Mineola, about eight miles from home, where my wife and I have no friends I know of.

This branch has a ton of anatomy textbooks with all kinds of fancy overlays showing you where each body part is located, and takes you inside it for a closer look. Turns out your neck and leg are likely candidates for cutting, because both the carotid artery and jugular vein in your neck and the femoral artery in your thigh, gush out blood when they're cut. Cutting the neck means the crime could be noticed by a passerby, while cutting the guy's thigh is less likely to be noticed by others, as it's not in anyone's line of vision. When the victim is sitting down, that is. An attack there, however, is more likely to be blocked by the victim himself.

He'd be sure to see the movement of the knife toward his thigh and take exception. Another thing, femoral's not a vulnerable target. It's well-defended by a thick layer of muscles, all of which the knife would have to pass through in order to get to the good stuff.

Take these two prime candidates off the hit list.

I'm not going to stab the guy in the brain. What am I, an animal? The only organ left is the heart itself, which bleeds a lot faster than its torso mates like the stomach and lungs. If you cut a hole in it, blood will spew out, causing almost instant death, especially if you twist the knife to open the wound up. Injury to the other organs would kill the guy, of course, only not as quickly, giving EMTs enough time to keep him alive till they get to the ER and eventually make our guy good as new—and an excellent witness for the prosecution.

Heart is definitely doable. Still, there's room for error. Are all parts of the heart equally critical? It's a complex little bugger with many different parts, notably the two chambers taking blood in and the two pumping it back out. I need to figure out if I should aim for a specific point. Once I identify the sweet spot, what's the best point of entry to reach it? Head on? From underneath? And is it better to leave the weapon in or pull it right out? If I leave the weapon in, the victim might live. Especially if the EMTs get there in time to stop the bleeding. Pull the weapon out and blood fills the space around the heart. The pericardium. That puts pressure on the heart, keeping it from filling with the blood it's supposed to pump out. This can kill the victim pretty quickly.

I have to get it right, and I'm trying real hard to find the one target that reduces my chance of making an error to zero. After a little more time with the anatomy books, one structure has made me sit up and pay attention. It's not in the heart exactly, but right on top of it.

The thoracic aorta is the artery that carries all the blood the heart pumps to the rest of your body. It's a pretty small target, about two inches long and one inch wide. Ever puncture a high-pressure hose by mistake? Water gushes out of the hole instead of going out the nozzle. Well, the aorta is a high-pressure hose for your blood. If you slice it open, blood will spew out and bad things tend to happen. We're talking heart attack and death, with a written guarantee. It's ideal for my purposes because it's right on top, like a gift for the homicidally inclined that says "open me first."

Now, the heart itself is really hard to get to. Nature went out of its way to make sure nothing bad happens to it. It's protected by your spine in back, your breastbone in front, and your collarbone on top, and it sits behind some pretty thick chest muscles the knife has to cut through first. Looking through the graphics, I did find one weak spot in its defense. Someone left the upstairs window open, right on top of the aorta. It sits right below the gap between the top two ribs on your left side, so there's nothing to protect it from attack. It's a small window, to be sure, but if you aim the knife right between those two ribs and point it down, you have a clear shot at the aorta.

There it is. My target. Even if I'm off by an inch or two, I figure I'll slice open the heart itself. Either way the victim is a goner.

Before I leave the library, I make sure all the books on human anatomy are back on the shelves, exactly where their call numbers say they belong. If any book is out of place, it could be the first step in a chain reaction of detective work that wouldn't end happily for me.

Now that my target's IDed, I can go back to answer the previous question on my list. Of all the kinds of knives I can pick up at the mall, which would be most likely to reach this most vulnerable, most mission-critical part of my victim's anatomy?

Chapter Forty-one

Out in cyberspace, I had a lot of company in terms of being curious about human bodies and the mangling thereof. Everyone has a jones for violence and death. Go online and without having to search too hard, you'll find clips of people falling off roofs, getting creamed in car accidents, shooting themselves by accident. All kinds of mayhem. I have to remind myself what I'm doing is work, not fun and games; I need to limit my research to things that would help me graduate from cutting open cartons to taking a life.

I go back to my clandestine research on the aorta and the severing thereof. I discover it isn't particularly hard to find the weapon able to reach the heart, sever the artery in question, and get the blood flowing. It's pretty easy, in fact. I found a lot of articles about injuries to the aorta, and attackers have cut it open with icepicks, scissors, knives—whatever sharp instrument they had handy.

What I concluded was most any kitchen knife will do, as long as the blade is sharp enough and long enough. Make sure to strike right between the first and second ribs on the left side, pointing down rather than straight on, and some poor schmuck's aorta is ripped open. You can't miss.

All that work, only to end with the weapon of choice of your average mugger or angry spouse. Kitchen knife.

Based on my newfound expertise in cutlery, I settle on a basic paring knife, figuring it fits the bill nicely. Still, even this decision isn't so simple.

I know I need a blade long enough to reach the aorta, and sharp enough to slice through his skin and chest muscles without a lot of pushing from me. Also, the handle has to allow me to keep a firm grip on it, so my hand won't slip onto the blade when I push it in, or slip off entirely when I pull it out of his body. Blood can mess things up.

I choose a three-and-a-half-inch blade, thinking it's easily long enough to penetrate to the aorta. The artery is only maybe an inch or so under the skin, so a blade of this length can reach the poor bastard's aorta with room to spare. A knife with a small blade would also be a little easier to hide on my way to and from the crime scene.

All I have to do is sharpen the blade myself right before I use it, and it'll go straight in nice and smooth. Then straight to the dumpster, never to cut again.

As far as the handle goes, all I'm concerned about is how firm a grip it would let me have. On this basis alone, I've chosen a plastic handle with sort of a textured surface. A little rough rather than smooth. I tried all the handles on the knives in our kitchen drawer, and a textured surface has the surest grip by far.

The only decision left is what brand. I can't very well take a knife from my kitchen drawer, use it to kill someone, and put it back afterward. Use it for murder on Monday and a steak dinner on Tuesday. That'd be too gruesome even for me. I can't tell one brand from another, so I go back to the kitchen store to consult with my mentor, Tricia.

"Can't go wrong with Global," she tells me. "Nobody's ever returned one, not in this store anyway." Which is how a Global three-and-a-half-inch paring knife with a textured handle became my murder weapon.

I buy a complete knife set and pay with cash, if only to frustrate any investigators checking recent knife purchases after the deed is done. I keep two knives for myself and donate the rest to a soup kitchen out in East New York somewhere. I figure why not use this opportunity to help out a worthy cause, feeding the homeless. I'm not a totally evil monster.

First chance I get, when I know Helen will be away for an hour or so, I sharpen the edge of the knife I'm going to use to stab my victim. I use the sharpening steel we've had forever, running the blade down it again and again until the edge is as sharp as a razor. I've never seen a scalpel up close, yet I can't imagine it's any sharper than my trusty knife after I'm done with it. You could bleed out looking at it too close.

It's going to require some kind of sheath, I reason, or else I'd probably cut myself to death the first time I carry it. Suicide by stupidity. Some thick cardboard, an old piece of cloth I had lying around, and some duct tape do the trick. Instant sheath. I then hide it in my closet until I'm ready to use it.

The knife I actually use will never be seen again. I'll make sure of it after the murder. I'll keep the second one, sort of as a surrogate trophy of my homicidal accomplishment. I know for a fact it'll never be used, and there'll be no blood or DNA on it for the police to find, so that's not an issue. Nobody's ever going to see it besides me anyway.

I now have the actual murder weapon, which alone gives me a growing feeling of confidence my project will end in success. The more I've learned about weapons of targeted destruction, the more confident I've become. This feeling is self-fulfilling. So much so that I believe I can actually pull this caper off, and there's nothing to hold me back. There's something inevitable about it, so my job is more a matter of keeping it from failing than making sure it succeeds.

Preparation is everything in my line of work. *Ex*-line of work. It's as if the criminal enterprise of which I am the founder and CEO is on autopilot, and I'm just along for the ride. Sound like a cop-out? It sure does to me, yet that's how I feel. Understand, I believe we're all adults, and as adults we're responsible for what we do. If you're not ready to own it, don't even try.

Next up on the agenda, I have to figure out where I'll execute my plan.

Chapter Forty-two

Friday, April 14
5:00 PM

The fourth letter came right on schedule, seven days after the third. By then, Barbieri and her journalistic BFF had already concluded—with almost no real evidence other than intuition about crimes and the criminal mind—an unknown, possibly insane man would be using a knife to murder an as-yet-unidentified able-bodied man.

That was what logic had told them, and she would let it drive her thinking until proven otherwise.

It still would not be enough for the cops, as Brennan had explained to her at Aroma. The one break he expected would be from the postal inspector friend of his he had given the first three letters to, after getting them from Barbieri. Until Brennan heard from him, there was nothing to investigate.

Barbieri was not surprised at all this last letter confirmed her conclusions. She knew they were on solid ground, although they sometimes merely guessed right, yet she was startled by it nonetheless. Like the first three, the fourth letter was postmarked with the Bay Ridge zip code, 11209. With this one, though, the control freak was trying to ratchet up his control of her to a whole new level. On the top third of the folded piece of stationery there were two questions.

Now that we've concluded I intend to stab an adult male to death, where should the crime take place? Will you and I, separately, come to the same decision?

The writer was transforming himself into the killer he wanted to be, step by step. This much was clear. Now it was also clear he believed he was successfully transforming her into his partner in crime.

"We've concluded." "Will you and I come to the same decision?" What should I make of his assumption that I concluded, as he had, the murder weapon would be a knife? He's right, but how the hell would he know? He's profiling me as much as I'm profiling him.

And then there was the question about the location of the crime. It was not so much a question about him, she believed, but a question about herself. *Where would I commit murder? Is he succeeding at letting my own inner demons out as well?*

This was the important question. *He thinks he won't be committing the crime alone but with an accomplice. He thinks he's changing me from passive observer to active participant in his nefarious plot, with my permission.* He seemed to be repurposing her logical mind into a criminal mind, and if she was not careful, he might well succeed.

Or did he think nothing of the sort and was only being a macho shithead? He's continuing to manipulate me. Men do this only to women who let them.

After she and Delaney finished working on a story on their latest stiff, a sixty-five-year-old Elmhurst man killed by his wife of thirty years during an argument about their marriage counselor, they debated the issue over a beer. They went to one of their usual haunts, an old, and old-fashioned bar on the far West Side called Hell's Kitchenette, which seemed oblivious to the gentrification going on around it. Its customers were almost all construction workers putting up the high-rise fortresses nearby that, ironically, would have no room for them when their work was done. Luxury condos priced well out of their reach, and luxury stores they would not be seen dead in. Their wives dragged them kicking and screaming to Macy's or Target, not Nordstrom or Saks.

Barbieri and Delaney claimed a table for two off to the side and sat across from each other. They did not want to be overheard by any of the hard hats nearby, who were too busy nursing their beers and labor grievances to bother them anyway. When the waitress came over, they ordered a couple of Amstels. Barbieri knew her body language and tone of voice gave away what she was feeling. More often than not, the message her nonverbal cues sent out was, "I got this." While others may not have recognized the change, she knew Delaney did. She was in distress and was doing a lousy job of hiding it.

"What's he up to?"

"Crime scene. That's what he wrote."

"No, the questions. Will I choose the same place?"

"Fuckin' with your head."

"Right. You don't exist."

They were interrupted mid-conversation by the waitress, who set their bottles of beer on their table and asked if they needed anything else. They did not. She walked back to the bar, but before they restarted their rapid-fire back-and-forth, Delaney changed the topic.

"Why are you letting him get to you, Kim? You look like you got hit by a truck."

"What a girl wants to hear, Pete. Thing is, I'm not letting him. I stopped letting him, yet he doesn't know or care. That's on him, not me. He's still managing to get me—"

"Us," Delaney corrected her.

"—involved in his fuckin' assassination. Fuckin' madman. God, I despise him. He's trying to change me from a person with nothing to hide, which I've been my whole life, into a person with something to hide. This isn't me."

"Take your feelings out of it. Look, what are you two doing? He's provoking you, Kim, and you're taking the bait. That's the wrong move on your part. Imagine you two are playing a weird game or something."

"Crime in Progress: Home Edition?" Barbieri just could not help herself sometimes. Sarcasm was a defense mechanism she deployed when she was about to be confronted with an unpleasant truth.

"Cute. No. You play chess, right? Opponent makes his move, and you make your countermove. You don't get pissed. Worst thing you can do. You keep your cool."

"I do. I am. I stopped letting him play me a while ago, but it looks like I was too late. By now he thinks he's got me right where he wants me, aiding and abetting him. He's got me thinking like a killer, following along as he snuffs out someone's life. I'm good at it, too. We both are. I had no idea I had it in me until he came along. God, I hate him."

"I'm not a fan, either. I'll buy he's trying to make you complicit in a murder, except that's a mental game he's really playing on himself. Look at it this way, Kim. He's active, you're passive. You're never passive about anything. You hate being played. He's acting, and you're reacting. You're also reacting emotionally, not intellectually. If we don't get our act together, Kim, someone's going to die."

"Okay, Peter. You're right. This time." Barbieri dropped the subject, an almost instinctive reaction whenever she felt the walls she had put up were being breached. She trusted him to talk her down, and he did. "Where, then? Must be sitting down."

"Right next to the victim."

"Sneak attack. Stealth."

"No witnesses. No one sees anything."

"No prints."

"Escape in a hurry."

"No posse chasing him."

"Clean getaway."

"Park bench? Office?"

"Store?"

"Warehouse? Train?"

"Church? Movie?"

"Not a movie. Train. Two strangers together."

"Killer and victim."

"No witnesses."

"Disappears into the crowd."

"Perfect."

"Night or day?"

"Day is my guess."

"We'd make great detectives."

"Or criminal masterminds."

They finished their drinks, paid the tab, and took the subway back to their respective homes, confident their crime scene would match the killer's.

They were wrong.

Chapter Forty-three

Early the next morning, Barbieri walked over to the Atlantic Avenue terminal, maybe fifteen minutes away from her home. The walk was not a pleasant one, with a steady, heavy rain coming back to town after a brief dry spell. Inside the terminal she dried herself off the best she could, grabbed a cup of coffee from Starbucks, and took the 8:11 LIRR outbound to Manhasset, where she got off, crossed to the inbound platform and took the next train heading back in. On the inbound ride, she noticed the lights went off when the car entered one of the tunnels—why, she never knew—and it got totally dark. She could not see her hand in front of her face. It lasted maybe ten seconds, more than enough time for the killer's purposes.

Seats were usually in pairs, facing forward or back depending on which direction the train was going. If there was any place where a guy would not give a second thought to some stranger sitting right next to him, it was on his commute to the city. At the last stop, Atlantic Avenue, everybody got up and piled off at once. *If he wants to escape in a hurry, it's almost too easy for him to get lost in the crowd and disappear.*

If their logic about the crime scene was as airtight as their logic on the killer and his weapon, she was sure they were closer to preventing the killing. Just not close enough to notify the police. Or Brennan. Besides, she had been avoiding him because she knew he would demand the last letter. It was more a matter of control than anything else. By handing it over to him, she would be giving him the okay to take over the hunt for the killer from now on. By holding onto it, she would be keeping at least some control with herself.

He's always getting his way. Not this time.

This fourth message, like the one before, could have again triggered the thought she had had about enjoying this deadly game too much to stop. If she had been getting even a little kick out of it before, she certainly was not now. *There's absolutely nothing enjoyable in taking the train back and forth and back again, like an unending journey on a Möbius strip.*

~ * ~

Is there anything better for getting close to a complete stranger than a commuter train at rush hour?

Of all the possible places I considered to kill my victim, it's one I already have a comfort level with. Commuter train into the city seems ideal, actually.

It's maybe the one place, besides an airplane, where you have no choice but to sit for an hour or so right next to someone you never met before and may never see again. No alarm bells going off, which is a good thing. You usually sit in a pair of seats together, with no one facing you to see what you're up to. The seatback also blocks the view of passengers sitting behind you. They're too busy sleeping or texting to notice anything unusual anyway.

Like me taking a knife from the inside pocket of my coat and grasping it firmly in the hand hidden by my body.

I know the commute from New Jersey backward and forward from when I used to live in the suburbs. Before we moved out there, Helen and I lived in Brooklyn, Prospect Heights. When the neighborhood went south, we went west, out to Jersey. When the old neighborhood changed back, we joined the exodus back in. Boy, did I hate the commute!

I decided to take a test run, see if there were any holes to patch up. The next day, I got up at five in the morning, showered and shaved, and got dressed. Helen was still sound asleep, so she didn't notice me putting on the kind of clothes I used to wear before I retired. The goal for me is to blend into the background, be a nobody, and I don't want to appear out of uniform.

I finish getting dressed without waking my wife, go down to the kitchen, and down some coffee. I write her a note telling her I had to leave early, then drive out to my old station in Edison, like the old days. My usual spot close to the platform is taken, of course. I haven't parked there in years. How soon they forget. I find a spot much farther away, practically in the next county, and walk to the station. I buy a round trip ticket to the city, pick up a coffee to go at the Dunkin' Donuts and go up to the platform. I see a few familiar faces: men and women who used to take the 7:49 with me, and a few new ones, yet otherwise the commute hasn't changed a bit since the last time I took the train. I fit right in.

The train pulls in on time, and everyone semi-jostles to their customary seats, making a minimum of small talk. Code of conduct requires almost no verbal communication.

I take a seat next to another man about my age, in a row with only two seats facing forward. I don't recognize my seatmate, maybe because he doesn't lift his face out of the paper the whole ride in as I take in my surroundings. Nobody seems to notice me, not even my pretend victim. I'm the invisible man.

Everything seems to go according to plan: the location of the target, the anonymity, the train going dark in the tunnel, until the train pulls into the final stop in midtown, Penn Station, and passengers shuffle off into their weekday cesspools.

I glance up at the ceiling and spot security cameras fuckin' everywhere. Escalators, waiting areas, street entrances. I'd forgotten all about them. They get you from every angle, everywhere you go. Where there aren't cameras, there are armed guards; cops and soldiers in uniform carrying assault rifles, or patrolling alongside their German shepherds. This is the new post-9/11 normal, and security is really intense. Like in Rome and Paris. There's way too much chance of being identified, or worse, getting caught.

I know in my gut if I really want to commit murder without getting caught, or even recognized, I'll have to figure out a way to defeat the cameras and avoid the soldiers and their dogs.

Or choose another crime scene.

Chapter Forty-four

Unable to let the commuter-train-as-crime-scene go, the next day Barbieri took a number of morning and evening commutes, yet noticed exactly nothing suspicious. Zilch. Average, totally unremarkable men and women got on at their stations on the way in. Average, totally unremarkable men and women got off at their stations on the way back. Inbound, they read their papers or wrote on their laptops. Outbound, they slept or texted or read. Rhythm of life in the big city.

If the plainclothes officers Brennan had sent to protect her were among them, she could not tell them apart from the other commuters. She really did not mind if they were in the same car, though. While Barbieri was not feeling the eerie, spine-chilling sensation the killer-in-waiting had induced in her before, she did not want to take any chances. He could show up anytime, anywhere.

All these train rides to nowhere gave Barbieri ample opportunity to second-guess the conclusion she and Delaney had come to about the scene of the crime. The first reason was the laws of chance. There were different lines connecting the city to all the suburbs in all directions, each with any number of trains heading inbound each morning and back to the suburbs each night. *The likelihood of one of us being in the right car, on the right train, at the right time, and sitting close enough to the killer and victim to intervene, is pretty damn close to zero. Brennan was right, dammit.*

Then there was the role the killer-to-be had given her. *If this man is trying to string me along, why would he lead me to even consider a crime scene so impossible to nail down? Why torture me like this?* She believed he wanted her to have a fighting chance and would lead her to a location where she would at least have a shot at intervening.

The third reason came to her when she got off at Grand Central. The overwhelming and very visible security might actually dissuade the killer from making a train car his crime scene. If the police did not catch him, the cameras definitely would. Though the killer could probably cancel out all the cameras by walking out of the train and into the station wearing a disguise, or walking where the cameras were not. If he did not wear a disguise, he could still easily hide in plain sight, blending so well into the mass of humanity no cop would even notice him.

Why would he even take the risk? Even if the uniforms ignored him, an undercover cop might not. Who knows how many of them there were blanketing the station? If the killer was as smart as Barbieri thought he was, he would choose a location with none of the downsides the train presented.

There had to be another crime scene, one she and Delaney might have dismissed, which had the same pros as the train: the opportunity to get right next to the victim, the likelihood nobody else would see or hear the crime; and the ability to leave the scene quickly, well before the murder was discovered.

Barbieri had no clue what this location could be, yet she was perfectly well aware the killer did. Reluctantly, she allowed herself to consider the other options she and Delaney had thought of earlier and tossed.

Chapter Forty-five

"Hey, Cavanaugh."

"Kim, come in. Sit."

Barbieri had overcome her reluctance to tell her editor about the potential jeopardy she was potentially exposed to due to her being in potential cahoots with a potential murderer. Even though he had given hundreds of assignments to her, and she had sent hundreds of completed stories to him, they had never met in person. Freelancers never had to show up for staff meetings or office schmoozing. Cavanaugh was a far cry from the Perry White she had expected. He was way younger than she was—maybe twenty-eight, tops—and had fully embraced the hipster look she avoided. He sported a crew cut and an unruly red beard, and was in full Williamsburg uniform—oversized black glasses, loose-fitting, washed-out T-shirt that had seen better days, jeans that clearly had not seen the inside of a washing machine for a while, and retro sneakers like she used to wear as a kid. *They don't make newspaper editors like they used to, Lois Lane.*

Cavanaugh was not technically her boss, as she was an independent contractor. Still, if she fell out of favor, or worse, had a serious lapse of judgment that made him look like an idiot for using her, she could easily stop getting assignments and become persona non grata on the tabloid metro desk circuit. Every newsperson was fodder for the next gossip column.

She had called him earlier to let him know she needed to speak with him in person. Once past security at the *Daily News* offices on East Forty-second Street, a couple of blocks from Grand Central, she headed up to the metro desk on the third floor. There was none of the manic frenzy that used to take place in days of yore, before newspaper offices switched from typewriters and typesetting to computers and file sharing. She rapped on the wall outside Cavanaugh's cube, a bare-bones space revealing absolutely zilch about the tenant. Only a laptop on a built-in desk, included at no extra charge with the Acme cubicle kit, and a whiteboard listing the day's stories, what time they were due, and who they were assigned to. Not a flowerpot or picture frame to say it was an environment hospitable to life.

"We finally meet, Kim! I have to tell you, you make my job pretty easy."

"I try." Barbieri always had a hard time accepting praise for doing what she was supposed to. Fishing for compliments was not in her DNA.

"It shows. Floor's yours."

Saying nothing, Barbieri handed over the binder with the four anonymous notes she had received so far. Cavanaugh read all four, in chronological order, and said nothing. He then went back and read them again.

"When did you get these?"

"First one was four weeks ago. The others every week after. Last one came yesterday."

"At home?"

"Yep. No other contact."

"This individual serious?"

"I think so. No reason not to. Looks to me like he's already decided to kill some stranger, and he's about to figure out when the crime will take place."

Barbieri was faced with a tough choice. Tell Cavanaugh everything she knew, which was next to nothing, and leave it at that. Or add everything she and Delaney had hypothesized about the killer, which was a lot. She decided to leave Delaney out of it, mostly so he did not get in trouble due to her stupidity.

"That's pretty clear. You write back?"

"I couldn't. There was no return address or anything else to identify the sender."

"So all you did was read them. Nothing more. Anybody else know? Police?"

"Officer I know. I haven't called 911. Nothing they could do so far."

"Your attorney? You may be doing something illegal, like failing to report a crime."

"I'm already in touch with him."

"You write anything down?"

"Nope. No notes or anything."

Cavanaugh abruptly stopped the conversation and said nothing for what seemed like a full minute, at least, before restarting it. "I think you may have stepped in it, Kim. If this man actually goes ahead and kills someone...."

"I know. It could get the paper in hot water. You guys would be implicated in a crime. Serious stuff."

"Like felony murder? Yeah, that's serious. I'll contact Marty in Legal." Cavanaugh paused for a second more before continuing. "And my boss, the executive editor. Last thing they need is for us to be indicted. We'll both be out of a job."

"Or the paper itself. Leave my name out of it, okay?"

"I don't know if I can, Kim. All this is a little scary."

"If you don't?"

"Don't know. I'm afraid they may ask me to fire you. Or order me to."

"Crap."

"They don't give a damn about you, Kim. No matter how good you are, the minute you're a liability, you're gone. They don't really give a damn about me, either. Only the paper."

Barbieri said nothing as she gathered her stuff and prepared to leave. She was mystified by how she had wound up in so much trouble with no clue how to get out of it. Now she might have a second adversary to deal with besides the killer. The laws of the State of New York. Plus a third, the possibility of not getting any more assignments from

Cavanaugh.

"Heads-up if you get another one," he said as he stood up to see her out.

"You got it."

"And let me know if you hear from your lawyer again. Please."

Chapter Forty-six

Exhausted from way too many commutes to Nowheresville, Barbieri found herself at home, pretty much alone with her thoughts. *When all else fails, use logic. Think things through until there's nowhere else to go.*

The reporter made herself a cup of tea, took her favorite spot on the sofa without the usual distraction of cable news or Italian opera, put on her thinking cap, and racked her brain for another location that made sense. One she could identify before it made the transition from not worth a second thought to crime scene.

Where else could the killer and victim be in close contact by mutual agreement? Park bench, in line at the bank, at a street fair, at a gym, or at the movies?

Where would nobody notice his presence or remember anything about him? That pretty much ruled out any outdoor area people used in the daytime, like a public park, or an indoor place where he would be surrounded by shoppers, like at the supermarket. He could not approach his victim on a deserted street at night without causing suspicion, yet he could sit next to a stranger in a darkened theater. It would have to be a place where the killer knew his victim, or at least someone who fit his profile, would show up when the killer was there lying in wait. So it would have to be some kind of scheduled occurrence, like when you go to the gym three days a week at the same time. Or take a class the same night every week at the Y. Or go to a movie you have been meaning to see.

Where would a victim, an adult male, most likely go by himself, with no friends nearby to witness the crime or come to his aid? A museum, maybe, or the hardware store. Or the movies, if he could not get anyone to go with him.

And where would the killer be able to leave quickly, and anonymously, with no one the wiser a killing had taken place moments before?

Of all the possible locations, each was ruled out save one. The only one that seemed to meet every need the killer had. *Movie theater. Delaney would approve.* She still had a lot more to figure out, and she certainly could not go to Brennan until she could ID the scene of the upcoming crime. While there were a lot of theaters in New York— hundreds, maybe—and she still had no idea when he would attack, she was convinced she was back on track.

With her logical mind prevailing over the forces of darkness, Barbieri pried herself off the sofa, walked over to the kitchen, and poured a glass of wine. As exhausting as riding the rails all day was, she felt a small celebration was in order.

Chapter Forty-seven

Just do it already! I want this jerk off the streets and out of my life.

Barbieri was sitting on a bench in Fort Greene Park, not far from her home, at five fifteen the next evening. She had been a regular there from the day she moved to the neighborhood, and this was the first night warm enough to spend outdoors. Around her, lilacs and lilies were beginning to bloom, the grass was a brilliant green she had not seen since Halloween, and moms and dads and children, their designer dogs in tow, came out to play. Even the background music was worth being outdoors for: A Mister Softee truck had emerged from hibernation and was parked right outside the entrance, luring kids with the same Pied Piper jingle she had heard every summer of when she was growing up. Staying indoors was no match against all this.

Taking her cell phone out of her pocket, she dialed Brennan's number before she could talk herself out of it. He answered on the first ring, and she skipped the pleasantries and got right down to business.

"You hear from your contact at the post office? The inspector?"

"This morning. Nothing. No prints, no fibers. Could've come from a million printers. Nothing. Total dead end."

"I suspected as much. Any point in them intercepting the next love letter?"

"I asked. He didn't think so."

"Okay. Because I just got it. I think it's going to be a movie theater."

"What is?"

"The murder."

"Oh. I see. The hypothetical crime you brought up is now the real deal."

"Don't make this any harder, Timothy."

"Okay, Kim. Which one?"

"The theater? Haven't worked it out yet. Probably in Brooklyn."

"Probably. Big borough. When?"

"That either. Next day or two, my guess."

"I can't assign officers to every movie in the borough, all day and all night, Kim. My boss would crucify me. What I will do is keep sending men to protect you. Otherwise…."

"Ever the optimist. I'll try to pretend I don't see them."

"They're that obvious?"

"Like floats in the Macy's parade."

"It's good you called. I know how hard it's been."

"Thanks, Timothy. I'll call you as soon as I know more." Barbieri pressed the red "end call" icon on her phone and went back to people-watching. At the moment, she found observing her neighbors living perfectly normal lives was a pretty good way to pass the time.

Chapter Forty-eight

"Dave, it's seven fifteen." Helen had glanced at her watch just as the waiter came with our desserts.

"Oh crap. I'll get the check."

"I'll bring the car around."

The wife and I are having what passes as date night for us. Meaning dinner and a movie in the middle of the week. Just the two of us, no other couples allowed. It's a little "us time" we'd insisted on having when we were both working, and now that I'm not, we still enjoy it. I can't say it's kept us together, although it's certainly better than staring past each other like other married couples do.

All we do is talk about this and that, nothing important, but at least we're communicating. That's the important thing. Who even bothers going to the movies, anyway? Netflix, Hulu, Amazon Prime—nobody has any reason to get off their damn couch anymore.

During this particular evening out, though, while we're discussing the state of the world, my mind's hard at work trying to find a better crime scene than a commuter car. So far, I'm coming up empty. Nothing.

Luckily, Helen finds a good spot right around the corner from the theater we're going to, the Kent, and we speed-walk over. Kent's a battered old relic that's somehow managed to survive the onslaught of multiplexes that ate Brooklyn. As we enter the lobby, our "this and that" conversation picks up where it left off, about some student who was giving her a hard time.

"If you're not getting through to her, speak to her mom and dad. Tell them they're wasting their money."

"Admit failure? I can't."

"She's the one failing, not you."

"You've never dealt with parents. Buy the tickets. I have to run to the ladies'."

I buy two tickets and get a popcorn big enough for us to share, and when Helen comes back from the john, we look for a couple of seats with nobody nearby to ruin the movie for us. The theater's half empty, so it feels like we have the place to ourselves.

As soon as we sit down, I realize my prayers are answered. I'm in the middle of a crime scene.

The coming attractions start, and Helen goes into full escape mode. While she's busy eating popcorn and staring at the screen, I'm focused everywhere else, gears spinning.

I notice the exit signs at the corners of the theater. My eyes follow the tiny dim lights framing the aisle floor. Compared with the grand movie palaces I went to back in the day, these renovated theaters have all the charm of big box stores that happen to sell one item—an hour or so of escape.

I notice the isolation. We're in a crowd of maybe a hundred, give or take, yet we're alone. Nobody notices us in the not-totally-dark theater. Nobody talks to us. Nobody recognizes us, certainly. Anonymous as can be. All the seats have high backs, so anyone sitting one row behind us sees only the tops of our heads, maybe. Perfect.

If I were so inclined, I could see myself sitting to the left of a stranger, or to the right, or one row back. No one else would give it a second thought. Unlike everyday co-existence, where people stake out their personal territory and insist it was their space, not yours, theaters allow complete strangers to invade another's space with impunity. To come within inches of each other, even share an armrest. Anonymously.

People going to the movies don't want to know. They want to be ignored, invisible. They're trained all their lives to focus forward and upward, to the screen, not to their left or right. God forbid they should have any human interaction at all.

And I notice how dark it is once the movie starts. Every so often, the theater can get almost totally dark, depending on the action on the screen. If the movie has a pitch-black scene, the theater becomes close to pitch black itself. You can see the exit signs, and that's about it. The darkness lasts at least for a moment or two, sometimes longer.

A moment is all the time I need.

Once the movie's over, people return to the normal rules of good citizenship, of giving one another their own private space. If the lights go up and a moviegoer's asleep, the patron sitting one seat over to his right or to his left wouldn't give it a second thought. He'd simply squeeze past the sleeping person on the way out and try to not wake him.

Nobody would give a darn until the next showing, and even then it would only be the morons who clean up everything the earlier audience left behind. If a sleeper is in their way, they'd maybe give him a nudge. The theater makes for a perfect scene of the crime—as long as it isn't my neighborhood Rialto. Anonymity, again.

I'll have to find a movie appealing to the male demographic, in the age range of my male victim. It would also have to be one with scenes at night, or in dark rooms, to keep the light low in the theater. Or scenes loud enough to drown out any noises my guy makes as he slips this mortal coil.

I'd have to go when it isn't so crowded I can't find a seat, or so empty it would be suspicious, or creepy, to sit too close to someone. So Friday and Saturday nights are out, rainy or overcast weeknights and weekend afternoons in.

Once I enter the theater, I'll have to find a guy sitting alone. This doomed fellow would have to be sitting in an aisle seat, with only the next two seats not taken. This way I can sit one seat in without creeping him out. Even better for my purposes, he could also be sitting one seat in, with me taking the aisle seat. It wouldn't do for a guy who killed someone only seconds before to have to say "excuse me" over and over again as he squeezed past everyone else sitting in his row on the way out.

Before the movie starts, I ignore him. No small talk or anything. I don't want to know him as the ordinary man he is, even for a second.

Do I do the deed and simply get up and walk out of the theater?

Would it draw unwanted attention from the more curious members of the audience sitting nearby? I could wait till the end, although the idea of sitting next to a corpse for an hour or so isn't at all attractive. Either way, I'd have to remind myself to buy surgical gloves, the kind nurses use when they take blood, so I won't leave fingerprints behind on the seat or the armrest. They should be flesh-colored, preferably, which I'm sure all drug stores carry. Do you think CVS would mind if they aid and abet a capital crime? I have no idea if the police would be able to tell my print apart from the thousands of prints left by the thousands of people who sat in that particular seat over the years, but why take chances?

Finally, it would be most helpful on the part of the victim if he'd already taken off his coat. Forcing a knife through layers of material before hitting the skin makes it a little less likely it would penetrate fully enough, or accurately enough, to pierce his aorta.

This movie theater idea just might work out, I'm thinking. There are a lot of variables to watch out for, yet I feel they're all manageable, not critical issues. I would think on my feet, as it were, and deal with them when the time came. It's merely a matter of waiting for the right moment when all the stars align.

"This could work," I whisper to myself as the credits come on and the lights come up. Helen and I grab our things and start walking up the aisle.

"What could?" I'd been whispering loud enough for her to overhear, apparently.

"What could what?" Now I'm buying time, since I can't think of an answer that'll make any sense.

"Why are you talking to yourself? I'm a much better listener. What did you think?" Lucky for me, her attention shifts away from what exactly I'd whispered.

"About the movie? Not bad." It's the best I can come up with at the moment. She saw the movie. I didn't.

"That's it? Not bad? I thought it was fantastic."

Date night almost over, we continue talking about everything and nothing as we make our way out of the Kent and into the real world. Anybody listening in would probably think we're having empty conversation, but I disagree.

How do people live alone?

Chapter Forty-nine

Friday April 21
8:45 PM

"Talk about a deadline."

"Double entendre. Who *are* you?"

"You may have to rethink our relationship."

"The next topic is when."

"Only thing left. Gotta be."

"We'll know soon enough."

Expecting letter number five to come on schedule, Delaney had made sure to be at his partner's apartment early on Friday, well before the mail arrived. They had agreed he would take a picture of her opening the envelope, in case this whole matter ended in a book or article by them. Delaney had the good sense not to mention the topic he had brought up over beers at Hell's Kitchenette, about how she was letting this guy get to her. He had made his point, and she had made hers. He knew she would not give an inch if he reopened the debate.

They were waiting outside, in front of her building, watching the mail carrier slowly, steadily making her way down the block. Painfully slowly. Ten minutes at one address, fifteen minutes at the next. The piece of mail they were expecting was the only one whose delivery was a matter of life and death, yet that did not make the completion of her appointed rounds any swifter.

"Taking her time, the mail lady."

"Mail carrier." *Delaney's a work in progress, but he'll get there.*

There's a gentiluomo in there somewhere.

When the carrier reached her building, finally, she handed Barbieri her mail before going to the mailboxes in the lobby. It included the envelope they were expecting. *The man's consistent.* Opening it right then and there, on the sidewalk, captured on Delaney's Nikon, they found the message to be as unsettling as it was predictable. Especially its first word.

Our next decision concerns timing. When shall this man's life end by my hands?

"*Our* decision?"

"He and I are soul mates."

"Thought you and I were."

"Should've mentioned it. Sorry."

"Wait. I'm not the one with control issues."

"Maybe your only good point, Delaney."

"I'm heartbroken."

They had guessed right about the victim, and right about the weapon. Her thinking about the crime scene had led her to conclude it would be a movie theater, of which there were plenty. She had not filled in Delaney yet, and she wanted his buy-in on that.

The latest letter and envelope now safely in their sleeves, Barbieri and Delaney continued talking conspiratorially on the front stoop of her building. They were both anxious to answer the killer's question, while trying not to be overheard by neighbors passing by or her fellow tenants climbing up and down the stairs beside them.

"You start."

"Two issues."

"How soon?"

"And what time of day?"

"Only he knows."

"Ideas?"

"Planning's all done."

"No reason to wait."

"This week? Today?"

"Unlikely. We just got the letter."
"Gives us time to think it through."
"This week, then."
"Or next. Where? Train still?"
"Been thinking. A movie."
"Gotta be better than the damn train."
"Dark. Sits right next to the victim."
"Matinee?"
"If the victim has no day job."
"Could work nights."
"Like us. Contractor."
"Days free."
"People with time on their hands. Seniors."
"Not necessarily. Self-employed. Keeps his own hours."
"Matinee, then."
"Better chance of empty seats."
"More opportunity."
"Here? Brooklyn?"
"Good a place as any."
"Home in time for supper."
"It's never wise to doubt me."

Chapter Fifty

"You've never been suspended or anything by the department, have you, Timothy?"

"Never had the pleasure. No warnings, no reprimands. None of the usual slaps on the wrist. I've never given them a single reason not to keep promoting me, proud to say."

"Good career growth strategy. Show up and don't screw up."

"Secret of my success, Kim. I now have a whole squad of detectives who don't ignore me when I tell them what to do. You should try it. I was just fired by my doctor, though. By email. That count?"

"Cold. Failure to follow doctor's orders?"

"I do. Every time. He just started making you pay an annual fee to see him. Everyone else, his nurse sees, like me. Email said to pay the fee or find another doctor. Yours any good?"

"I'll tell her you'll be calling."

The reporter and the detective were engaging in their typical romantic shoptalk in her apartment, in bed, under the covers, waiting for the coffeemaker to finish brewing the first pot of the day. It had been four days since her meeting at the *News*. They both understood it was way too early to turn on her dad's stereo and incur the wrath of the neighbor on the other side of the bedroom wall. It took a few mornings of him banging on the wall and her banging right back, until they eventually signed a peace treaty. No music before ten.

The sun had come up hours earlier, completely obscured by threatening clouds. Heavy showers and strong winds were predicted for later in the morning, and they were in no hurry to get dressed and brave the elements if there was no need to. There was none, at least for the time being. No texts had come in requiring either of them to report for duty.

As far as Kim Barbieri knew, Brennan had no idea she had been reamed by her editor. The way he worked, gossip and rumor were only worth repeating if they helped clear homicides. If they did not, they were noise, auditory clutter best filtered out.

Barbieri knew a man with his connections would find out, sooner or later, about her hiccup at the *News*. Yet as a reporter who made a living digging up dirt ne'er-do-wells desperately wanted to stay buried, she knew all about spin control. Right before her story would come out, the about-to-be-embarrassed A-lister would minimize the damage by getting his side of the story out first. *Better he should hear it from me.*

"Something I need to tell you, Timothy. My editor's pissed at me."

"He didn't fire you, did he?"

"No. I'm still with the paper. I think he's going to stop giving me assignments. For a while, anyway."

"Hence your question about whether I was ever suspended. How'd you mess up, Kim? You show him the letters?"

"Copies. I had to. He said I could be putting the paper in legal jeopardy. Him, too. From his point of view, I'm getting the *News* involved in a murder plot. Another thing I didn't think of."

"He's looking out for his interests, not yours. I would've done the same thing. Sorry."

"Don't be. I haven't taken my suspension, or whatever they call it, very well. I haven't been sleeping. I've felt like shit—useless and helpless. Testy. Being excommunicated by the paper was sort of a tipping point for me. I've had nightmares." She did not dare tell him those nightmares were actually about the letters. Each one involved a man she did not know hunting down another man she did not know. They were in the subway, or at a ballpark, and she woke up right as the hunter was going in for the kill. "I thought they were over, the nightmares, but I woke up in the middle of the night. Been up since three."

"I didn't know, Kim. I'm sorry. Why'd you keep this from me?"

"Not our deal, Cap'n. You know that."

"Do you think you should see someone? A psychologist you could talk to?" The conversation was entering relationship territory, boy-girl feelings stuff they never bothered with. "Maybe take some kind of drug for anxiety. I'm not sure I'm doing you a lot of good here."

"I'm not pushing you away, am I? That's the last thing I need right now." She felt as uncomfortable as he obviously did.

"You're not, Kim. At least think about getting help, okay? I'm no therapist, but there's clearly something you need to take care of."

"I'll think on it…after I get up. Right now, I'm going to try to go back to sleep."

This was a lie. Barbieri withdrew from the conversation right after they overstepped the boundaries she had set for the thing she had with Brennan. She had let him see something she wanted kept from him: weakness. He reacted as a boyfriend-slash-lover should, which was the problem. If she were not careful, she would allow their relationship to make the transition from friends with benefits to true intimacy. From the physical to the emotional. This was a no-go, to be avoided at all costs. Barbieri wanted the companionship, the comfort, and yes, the feeling of being protected Brennan offered. He was Mr. Right Now, and he played the part perfectly. She wanted to leave it at that.

I don't love Timothy now. I'm not at all sure I want to let myself love him. Do I set boundaries, or do I move on?

Chapter Fifty-one

No assignment. Again.

Barbieri was not surprised Cavanaugh had stopped sending her out. He had made it clear he might be ordered to fire her, or do whatever contractors did to get rid of contractees. She had seen stories in the paper over the last few days that should have had her byline, yet did not. Street crime and lawsuits went on without her.

I always knew I could be replaced, and maybe I have been. Is my exile permanent or temporary? Will I work again for the News, *or am I also on the do-not-hire list of all the other papers and online news sites in New York?*

She did not know. What she did know was Eric, the ADA, had warned her about getting involved. Her editor had warned her. Her attorney had warned her. Brennan had warned her. *I heeded none of their warnings, and now I'm paying for it big-time.*

With nothing better to do, she walked a couple of miles over to a bar in Chinatown, a few blocks from One Police Plaza, NYPD Headquarters. Force of habit. Ale and Farewell was the official clubhouse for all the crime reporters who had to spend time at 1PP prying information they needed for their stories from the higher-ups. She had no reason to be at the bar, having been sent to the corner for a time-out, other than wanting to see if her colleagues knew anything about her situation with the *News* she did not. They fed on scuttlebutt. *Has Cavanaugh actually fired me? Am I suspended? Blackballed?*

They apparently had not heard anything. The reporters there from the other local papers, televisions, radio stations and websites interacted with her like they always did: with a combination of brotherly love and bitter rivalry. "How you doing, Barbieri?" "Any big stories coming up?" "Hey, you know who I just interviewed?" "I heard CNN is looking."

For people trained to dig up dirt, they seem to be clueless. I have to thank Cavanaugh for keeping his mouth shut—if he ever talks to me again.

Barbieri made a quick exit from the bar, glancing around to see if the bodyguards Brennan sent were nearby. If they were, she could not see them. On the walk back to her home in Fort Greene, she thought about confiding in her girlfriends. Her misery would love a little of their company. Maybe they could listen to her whine or talk some sense into her, but she could not bring herself to call even one. They would have heard her out and cheered her up if she had.

The whole thing, the whole messy quagmire she had found herself firmly embedded in, was way too embarrassing. If Delaney was right, she had only herself to blame for giving the killer permission to torment her.

The only solution she could think of at the moment was an hour or two of grand old opera. She was unsure which to go with, a tragic opera to indulge her foul mood or a comic one to overcome it, so she took the easy way out and settled on a record she had not played in a while. As soon as she closed the door behind her, she took off her shoes, put the LP in question on the turntable, plopped down on the sofa, and leaned back with her eyes closed. By the middle of the first act of Donizetti's *Lucia de Lammermoor,* Barbieri was fast asleep.

Chapter Fifty-two

Barbieri was on her sofa, catching up on her reading while listening to *The Marriage of Figaro* on the stereo. It was the one LP she owned that she had not inherited from her father. Like him, Barbieri normally had no use for works by non-Italian composers, but she was confident he would not have disowned her over it. The librettist was Italian, even if Mozart was not. *Perdonami, Papa.*

She was suddenly brought back to the here and now by the loud, shrill sound of the buzzer. It was her building's security system yelling at her that someone standing outside wanted to be let in. She walked over to her front door to check the security camera, and saw her visitor was not the police, who she always feared would come for her. Neither was it the man she had caught only glimpses of before, whom she also always expected—him, the murderer.

She buzzed Delaney into the building and left her apartment door open. After letting himself into her apartment, the photographer shut the door behind him and joined her in the living room.

She was not looking forward to the conversation. There was risk in all this, a risk that could put them both in a ton of legal trouble, and she knew it was only a matter of time before it became too much for her co-conspirator to bear.

"Hey, Pete."

"I'm out, Kim. I can't do this. We've got no business getting involved in aiding and abetting this… assassination."

"Or any other crime that could ruin our lives. I understand." *Simon thinks I'm an idiot. I can't blame him. Cavanaugh's pissed. I can't blame him, either. Now even Delaney wants nothing to do with me. Good going, girl.* "We're journalists trying to earn a living wage, not some kind of undercover cops."

"Told Cavanaugh about me?"

"No, Pete. He doesn't know you're involved—were involved. If anyone gets into trouble over this, it'll be me. Not you."

"Thank you for that."

"All we discussed were the letters. Far as he knows, I'm the only person who's seen them."

"You lied to him? A little out of character, Kim."

"I did, but only by omission. To keep you out of it."

"What'd he say about them? The letters?"

"He wasn't pleased, to say the least. He's speaking with legal and the higher-ups about what this could mean for the paper."

"We could be getting the *News* in trouble. I hadn't thought of that. He firing you? No more assignments?"

"Not yet, but he might. I think it depends on what legal says about all this. The worst thing that can happen for you is they pair you with another reporter. At least till this ends."

"I'm not finished bending you to my will."

"You'll survive. I did speak with my attorney, by the way. I thought it was about time he found out what a bad girl his client's been. He's not pleased."

"Perhaps not, but it was the right thing to do. I'm sorry, Kim. I really am."

"Feeling guilty, are we? Trust me, Peter. I feel as bad as you do about all this. I'll keep you posted."

Relieved that he had dodged a high-caliber bullet, Delaney got up off the sofa and made his way to the front door. On his way out he turned back to his partner and gave her a small nod, then left her apartment, carefully closing the door behind him.

Alone again, she went back to the sofa and turned up the volume on the stereo. Her position in this tug-of-war with Mr. John Doe had now gotten a little more untenable. She always held her own against even the toughest of hombres, yet this adversary was different. She had been counting on Delaney to help her pin down a shadow. He was a danger, a lethal operator, and a complete mystery. Undercover cops were protecting her, but were they enough against a man as determined to kill as he was?

Chapter Fifty-three

Now that I know I'll be spending an afternoon at the movies, waiting for the right moment to stab a man in the heart, the next logical step in my journey to the dark side is to rehearse. Strictly from a businessman's point of view, this may be the most critical part of any plan.

Again, this is where my project management skills kick in. The more you prep before show-and-tell, the less you risk screwing up when it really counts. Business 101.

It takes practice, practice, and more practice. Only this time, I have no one looking over my shoulder to critique my work. If I lose my way during the crime, I won't have anyone waiting in the wings to come to my rescue.

First thing I need is a body to practice on. So I drive over to the garment district and talk a guy there into giving me a male mannequin, the kind department stores use to display the fashions they bought way too much of and really want to unload each season.

There are a million stores selling dresses and shirts to the stores selling them to the great undressed. Rack after rack of the same identical items retailers buy by the truckload, hoping their own customers will snap them up. There's a sign in all their windows saying "wholesale only," but I walk into one selling men's clothing anyway. I'm not sure the salesman there actually cares one way or the other if you're a wholesaler, as long as he helps get rid of some inventory that's not moving. If I happen to be wrong and he does get pissed, I'll claim ignorance and try another store down the block. Maybe get lucky next time.

I browse around, hoping to find a mannequin in about the size I'd expect my victim to be. Pretty tough, because while living and breathing adult men come in all manner of odd body types and sizes, mostly out of shape, male mannequins in Macy's window seem to come in only one ideal physique. Tall, trim, chiseled cheekbones, perfect posture, six-pack abs. Average man? Maybe in Stockholm, not here.

It's all about flattery. Stores sell to the manly man a guy thinks he looks like, rather than the portly schlub staring back at him in the mirror.

After a few minutes of pretending to browse shirts I'd never wear on mannequins with a physique I'll never have again, I approach a salesman, an older gentleman wearing a three-piece suit that's seen better days and a toupee that's impossible not to stare at. He has the weariness of an old pro who knows his next sale will be identical to every one he's ever made.

"The mannequin here. Any idea where I can buy one? It's perfect for a science lesson I'm giving." I make up the excuse on the spot. Who wouldn't want to help out a teacher trying to educate our youth? Sort of like the opening move in a negotiation, which I happen to know a little about.

The salesman perks up at my question. "One? You gotta buy them wholesale, like we do. Dozen at a time."

"It's eleven more than I need," I tell him. "Any chance of helping me out here, selling me only one?"

Salesman hesitates a second, unsure of what to do. Selling anything besides men's outerwear clearly throws him off. Then he gives me a look like a brilliant idea's popped into his head.

"Even better, I'll save you a few bucks. Once in a while, a mannequin gets a crack or chip, and we have to toss it. If you can live with that, go around back to the loading dock and help yourself. Anybody stops you, tell them Max says it's okay."

Piece of cake.

I thank Max and his hairpiece for their excellent customer service, walk back to the loading dock behind the store, choose my new supersized Ken doll from the discard pile and put him in the trunk of my car. I don't want to attract attention by letting him sit up front with me. When we get home, I leave him in the trunk a few hours, till Helen leaves the house to go the mall, then pull the car into the garage and carry Ken to the basement. Knowing Helen, I have maybe four solid hours of rehearsal time before she comes back with her trophies.

First thing I do after I get him down in the basement is draw a rib cage on his torso. It has to be anatomically correct. The mannequin is some kind of hard plastic a regular knife can't penetrate at all, no matter how hard I try. So right over Ken's heart, I glue on what I think is a pretty good substitute for human skin, a piece of steak about an inch thick I found sitting in the back of the refrigerator. Helen probably forgot it was there. That's the toughest barrier I have to get through. Once the knife makes it past the slab of meat, I know it'll be clear sailing the rest of the way. On a real flesh-and-blood human being, it would cut straight through skin and muscle into the aorta like... well, like a hot knife through butter.

Next, I scrounge through my closet for a decent shirt I stopped wearing and dress the dummy up so he looks presentable. He'd be sitting down, so a shirt is all he needs to dress for success. At this party, pants are totally optional.

I happen to have a couple of chairs in the basement that pretty much match the seats attached to each other in a movie theater, so I sit him down in one of them as if he's watching a movie. Relaxed position, facing forward, leaning slightly back. Or as relaxed as Ken can be. Now, I'm a lefty, which means I'd prefer to sit to his left and attack across my body, as the hand next to him would be too close to do me much good. Grabbing the second knife I'd bought—not the one I'll actually be using to kill my victim, since I don't want to damage the blade—I take the seat to Ken's left, face forward like him, and slouch a little like him so we're more or less at the same height. I put a glove on my left hand, grip the knife handle firmly, and start swinging. Believe me, swinging blind and trying to hit a small target not in front of you but at your side is a lot harder than I thought.

First few tries, I'm several inches off the mark. Way wide. I miss the left side of his rib cage completely, let alone the space between his first two ribs I'm going for. After a few more minutes of trial and error, though, I start hitting the sweet spot, thrusting downward between rib one and rib two without fail. Every time I pierce the skin substitute and hit the plastic body, I swear I can hear my new BFF wince in pain.

That's muscle memory. Some experts call it implicit memory, although I don't see anything implicit about it.

Once I master the left-handed attack, I do the reverse. On the chance I'd be sitting to his right, I practice sitting on that side and become equally adept at hitting the sweet spot with my right hand. A pretty good switch-stabber, if you will.

It takes maybe three hours of practice to get it right and give myself complete confidence I would hit the target when it mattered. Having outlived his usefulness, Ken has to go. I undress him, dismember him the best I can, put him back in the trunk of my car, drive to a construction site, and toss his remains in a dumpster.

Helen never knew we had company.

Chapter Fifty-four

Friday April 28
9:45 AM

Barbieri could not count on her loyal sidekick when the sixth letter came.

I'm ready, Kim. Let's do this!

Question time was now over. This last letter triggered something in her the first five had not, a view of herself she had refused to let herself see before. The lightbulb Delaney had given her came on. Her relationship with the killer, such as it was, where he sent her pieces of a puzzle whose dimensions she could only guess at, had been keeping her in a passive position. She had learned long ago it was a position she never wanted to be in. It was a fast track to losing, and she did not like losing.

She was now ready emotionally, viscerally, to concede Delaney had a point. She could see it, and she could feel it in her gut.

Sancho Panza is right. I may be back in control, but I'm still knee-deep in his plot to commit murder. He's still manipulating me only because I gave him permission to make me his victim. Well, my permission is hereby withdrawn. Done.

Crap! Simon.

In the middle of feeling like a superhero coming to the rescue, she remembered her attorney's request to bring him any more letters without even opening them. She had already broken the "unopened" part. *Is there even time to bring it to him? If I stop the murder, he'll forget about it anyway. Won't he? Screw it. I'll do what I have to do and figure out Simon later.*

She had deduced he would commit the crime in a movie theater somewhere in Brooklyn, yet the odds of her being in the right theater at the right time were not in her favor. Until she could ID the theater, the police would not know where to go, either.

There were ten popular movie houses spread throughout the borough, all multiplexes. She looked up each one online and learned one had fourteen screens, one had twelve, two had ten, one had eight, one had seven, two had five, one had four, and one had three. Seventy-eight screens total. Most of them had maybe four or five daily showings for each screen, depending on how long the movie was.

She had to narrow down the list of cinemas about to be a crime scene. *Assuming the victim is going to be an adult male, then I can eliminate all screens showing movies likely to appeal to women and children.* The irony of making such a sexist decision did not escape her, but she had to start somewhere. Half of the screens down.

Assuming the victim will be going in the afternoon, eliminate screens showing movies targeted at adult males that don't have matinees. Another quarter off the list.

Assuming the killer makes a decent living, a safe bet given his language skill, he probably lives in one of the gentrified neighborhoods like Cobble Hill or one of the older ones like Midwood near Brooklyn College. After the crime, he'd want to get back home as fast as possible. Where would he feel safer than in his own home?

Her fingers firmly crossed, she narrowed the list of possible theaters to three: the Court downtown, the Kent on Coney Island Avenue, and the Albion on Flatbush. Barbieri knew she was playing a game of movie theater darts here. The guy could have another Brooklyn theater in mind, or any other theater from New Jersey to Montauk. There were hundreds in the city and suburbs he could have chosen, yet her intuition had successfully taken her this far, so she stuck with it. Or was stuck with it.

Three theaters. Two too many to stake out by one person. Delaney isn't here to split the workload. I'll do the only logical thing—pick one theater at random.

Court, Kent, or Albion? Eeny meeny miney mo. She chose the Albion, if only because the theater itself had recently come back from the dead, having been rebuilt and restored after being shuttered for years. Besides, she used to go there as a kid, and that counted for something. Good a reason as any.

She was confident enough to call Brennan.

"Albion."

"You sure, Kim? City must have hundreds or theaters."

"Ninety-eight percent positive. Demographics and target audience all point right there."

"Any other theaters they point to? Round you up to one hundred percent?"

"Court and Kent."

"I'll send men out to all three, to at least keep an eye out."

Without a specific time, or any information about the perp, she knew that was about all he could do. He would not be able to tell them anything more than to watch for suspicious activity by a suspicious-looking man.

"Thanks, Cap'n. I'll be at the Albion."

"Say hello for me when you see them."

Barbieri's transition from doormat to avenging angel was off to a promising start, and she allowed herself to feel pretty close to triumphant. *I should've tried this whole epiphany thing before. I've been stuck in this abusive relationship, where I did as I was told. No longer. Sicko's not going to know what hit him.*

Chapter Fifty-five

By now, it's clear the thought of cold-blooded assassination has become my upstairs tenant and shows no signs of leaving. I've found myself going back to the one question I can't seem to make go away. *Am I fuckin' nuts?*

Yes or no? Crazy or normal? Choose one. What's so hard about that?

Now, I'm well aware I'm beating a dead horse here. No question. The idea that I'm bananas keeps eating away at me. I can't shake the fear I've been some demented lunatic masquerading as a decent husband and brother. Here I am, a straight-laced, law-abiding citizen, turning into a homicidal maniac. Real Ted Bundy, *Bates Motel* territory.

I do feel pretty bad about the prospect of taking the life of a good person, though. Kind of sad, I admit, yet I'm taking this bit of empathy as a sign of good mental health, not bad.

Does anyone know exactly when their sanity has vacated the premises? I'm planning to kill someone and don't really give a shit. Is that it? I'm about to take a life with no sign of remorse, not a smidgen. If this isn't sick, what is?

If I am some kind of sicko, I'm not in full control of my actions. I'm not totally rational. This is simply not acceptable to me. I've spent my whole career dealing in certainty, on absolute facts and crystal-clear language. The plan I'm about to execute depends on logic, on mental discipline, on keeping focused. And the upshot of the whole debate? If I am insane and end up getting caught, I'd be too incompetent to go on trial or have my confession accepted.

~ * ~

This question of my mental health, or lack of it, has become one for which I demand only one answer. I am sane, definitely. Who knows me better than me? I'm either in complete denial, or I have a form of illness I've never heard of. Believe me, from what I'm reading, there's craziness out there that could leave any shrink just scratching his head.

I've ruled out all of the common illnesses. The ones I could understand anyway, like depression and anxiety. Each one has a handful of symptoms you have to have together, like a lunatic package deal, and I don't have the complete set for any of them. If I'm right, it isn't full-blown craziness, but normal, whatever-gets-you-through-the-day neurosis.

Want to drive yourself to the insane asylum? Try to figure out the difference between a psychopath and a sociopath. From what I can tell, I have symptoms of both, and symptoms of neither. I'm extremely organized and deliberate, which makes me a psychopath. I also come across as completely normal, which makes me a world-class one. I'm taking a huge risk here, though, and would never harm anyone I cared about. Both symptoms of a sociopath, not a psychopath.

The difference between the two comes down to shades of gray. I mean, how the fuck can anyone tell them apart? Absolutely maddening. One thing I've learned is, whether you're a psychopath or sociopath, you've been one for years, decades. They both seem to show up in your teens, starting with torturing puppies, before graduating to human lives later on.

Again, not me. If I'm mentally ill, I caught the disease maybe a few weeks before I accepted the project. I'm not committing this breach of basic human society till my fifties.

That's it. My out. I know I'm clutching at straws, and I find the exact straw I need. The fact that this obsession I have with ending a life is maybe weeks old, not years old. While I may be fooling no one except myself, it's how I've convinced myself I'm sane.

Truth is, it doesn't even matter. If I'm wrong, I won't let my lunacy keep me from achieving the one goal I've set for my latest project.

Chapter Fifty-six

Bobby Merriman was in the real estate business. To a disinterested observer, however, he specialized in just one side of that business—the seamy underside.

Bobby was in the flipping houses business. He bought homes that were falling apart for a few cents on the dollar. He would fix what was broken, paint only what he had to, and then sell at a hefty profit.

By all outward appearances, Bobby was a success. Still, there was a side to him he kept pretty much to himself. He was an addict. He had an addictive personality. Whenever he felt stressed, or bored, he would turn to his supplier—an escort service. It was a secret he kept to himself, away from his wife and away from his girlfriend. He felt bad about himself after every hookup, so much so he decided to replace his sex addiction with an innocent hobby.

Whenever he needed to escape, he would find a movie he thought he would like and spend a few hours sitting in the dark at the local cinema. Today, Bobby felt like it. He scoured the listings and found one he had been meaning to see, a crime drama set in 1950s LA. It was playing nearby, at the Albion.

He found an aisle seat in the middle of the theater, with the next two seats unclaimed. This was good, as it meant he could stretch out a little and not bother anyone if he had to go to the john. The seats in front of him were empty as well, so there was no chance his view of the screen would be blocked.

He took off his raincoat and put it on the seat next to him, hoping against hope it would stay empty.

It didn't.

"That seat taken?"

"Uh, no."

Bobby removed his raincoat from the next seat and stood up to let the man by. The man squeezed past, took his seat, and settled in. The house lights, dimmed for the coming attractions, were turned completely off when the movie started.

As inconspicuously as he could, the man sharing his armrest shot a glance at Bobby to confirm it was nobody he knew. He also confirmed his neighbor was shorter and thinner than himself. He slipped a surgical glove on his left hand, undetected, and carefully took the knife from his jacket pocket. Without thinking, or looking, he knew the trajectory the hand holding the knife would follow.

Right as the movie started, everyone in the audience stopped talking and texting, put their phones on mute, and stared at the screen in silence. It was the first time Bobby had seen this movie, but not the first time the man next to him had. The man knew it attracted the demographic he was looking for, males between twenty-five and fifty-four. The fact that people in the movie business called them the "target audience" was an irony not lost on him.

He knew there were three scenes coming up where the screen went pitch black and two scenes where there would be bullets flying. Loudly. He waited, absolutely still, his right hand on his lap and his left firmly on the knife handle.

One hour and forty-eight minutes later, the credits rolled and the house lights came back on. En masse, patrons started collecting their things and heading for the exits. The man in the next seat started to join them, standing up and squeezing past Bobby Merriman, still in his seat.

"Pardon me."

"No problem."

The other moviegoers moved up the aisle, followed by Bobby and the man who had been sitting next to him. It is a good bet of all the people heading toward the lobby doors, only one checked his coat pocket to see if his knife was still there.

As they reached the lobby a few seconds apart, Bobby and the other man both put on their coats, then exited the theater. Bobby turned left and began walking north; the other man turned right.

Bobby did not seem to notice the two police officers on duty just outside the theater, but the man who had been sitting next to him did. He kept walking casually away from the scene of the non-crime, careful not to draw their attention.

Bobby pulled his cell out of his pocket about halfway down the block, and stopped in his tracks. There was a message from a contractor working on his property. Repairs were done, it said, and you should come by to check everything out.

Playtime was over. Bobby Merriman had to get back to work.

~ * ~

Kim Barbieri bought a ticket in the lobby and stood off to the side, watching everyone as they entered. She was not sure if she was looking for a man who was about to have his life cut short or a man who was about to do the cutting. About all she knew was they were both adult males. Which did not help at all, as this described most of the people coming there.

She did not see anyone who sort of resembled the man she had gotten only glimpses of before. Nor did she have any kind of feeling he was nearby. *Doesn't mean he's not here, though. My radar could just be temporarily out of service.*

She waited until the last minute before abandoning her post. As the movie was about to start, she hurried into the theater and looked for a seat in the back—preferably one on the center aisle. She was more interested in observing the entire audience than the screen itself. She certainly was not going there to watch any action movie.

For one hour and forty-nine minutes, Barbieri switched back and forth between the screen and the audience. Neither kept her attention. She saw nothing. *Was I wrong? Was my logic that far off?* If there were plainclothes cops there sent by Brennan, they blended right in. As the credits rolled, she joined the exodus and noticed the officers posted outside. She happened to recognize one of them and gave him a tiny wave as she walked by. She could not recall where they had met, as she had interviewed countless cops for countless stories, yet she fully expected to run into him again.

As she headed toward the subway, she made a mental note to thank her boyfriend for sending them.

Chapter Fifty-seven

What can I say? First day of my metamorphosis into a stone-cold soulless killer, I blow it. Why did this guy leave the theater on his feet and not on a stretcher? He was right there. We were practically joined at the hip.

The project's been well managed from day one, so much so I was certain success would be a slam dunk. No one was sitting close enough to see anything. Nothing was left to chance, period.

So why on God's earth couldn't I execute this perfect plan of mine? I hate to admit it, but I got a bad case of cold feet. That's what it was. Though I'd planned everything to the nth degree, the one thing I thought I had under control got the better of me. My conscience. Maybe I'm not quite the sadistic fuck I've told myself I am.

Mere inches from my target, I just couldn't bring myself to take someone's life. It's like I was paralyzed. Sitting there in the dark, not even paying attention to the movie, I had plenty of time to think about the blowback. Why would I make a wife a widow, or a child an orphan? Why would a decent, law-abiding fellow like me do this?

To this very reasonable argument for aborting my mission, I make up my own counterargument I can sell myself on without much effort. I tell myself regular folks lose their lives all the time. Surgeon screws up a routine procedure. A patient dies slowly, over a few years, from heart disease, or in seconds from a heart attack. People drop dead for no reason at all.

Some die by their own hand. Some commit suicide by cop. So widows and orphans are created all the time, often unfairly. One minute they walk among us, the next they're history. If I man up and become an agent of death, I'm one more in a long line of them.

While the movie's playing on screen, this debate plays in my head for what seems like forever. I'm frozen. For the moment, at least, the debate I'm having with myself is declared a tie. I sit paralyzed, not paying attention to the movie, not even seeing it, really. The knife stays in my coat pocket, unbloodied, as I leave the theater and head home. I do notice a couple of cops on my way out, though, standing next to their police car in front of the theater. Were they there when I first got to the theater? I don't think so. I'm not sure what they're doing there, yet I'm sure it has nothing to do with me. They're way too far from the scene of the crime to do any good.

I get home later in the afternoon, tail between my legs, greet Helen as I was trained to do, sit in my easy chair, and proceed to relive the last couple of miserable hours.

"How was your day, hon?" she asks me, in a tone that says she's really interested in my answer. Which she naturally is. It isn't at all robotic, even though she's asked me the same question every evening for decades as soon as I walk in.

"Sucked. Yours?" At least that's what I murmur under my breath. What I say loud enough for her to hear is far more conventional.

"Good, actually. Coffee with the guys. A few errands to keep me out of trouble. Everything I needed to get done got done." The usual stuff I say to keep her from prying too deeply, and me from playing the day's tape over and over in my head. Only I add a postscript she didn't expect, then duck. "And I saw a movie."

I say it due to the fact that I really don't like lying to her, one, and two, there's always a chance someone we know, friend or a neighbor, might've seen me on my way into or out of the theater, alone, and would mention it to her the next time they bumped into her. Better she should hear it from me, I think.

She reacts exactly as I expect. "By yourself? Without me?" Sort of playfully indignant, not really pissed off. "It better be something I'd never go to."

"It was," I answer. *Gangster.* "Bloodiest thing I've seen in a while. Barbaric." Not her genre by a long shot. It isn't mine either, to tell the truth. Yet seeing all this gore happens to reinforce my desire to keep the murder I'm about to commit as quick and clean as possible. More stealth attack, less violent assault.

"Good decision." Thank God. "Why don't you go wash up? Dinner's almost ready."

Lucky for me, her suspicious-wife radar doesn't switch on, and I make a mental note to hide the knife deep in my closet, maybe in the pocket of an old jacket I stopped wearing ages ago.

I made two critical miscalculations that put my project on hold— I both underestimated the enormity of taking a life, and overestimated my ability to actually do the deed. Are these problems insurmountable? Will I let them dictate terms? The answer escapes me for what seems like an eternity.

I thought I'd erased all my doubts before setting foot in the theater and I was only fooling myself. I made the mistake of giving them time to regroup and attack me from all sides.

I'd planned for everything except what I neglected to plan for. A whole new set of questions keeps popping up, waiting for me to knock them back down, like a deadly serious version of whack-a-mole. What if I'm caught? Hit men get away with murder all the time. I don't know if there's some kind of apprenticeship they take, but they no doubt learn on the job. Any trade secrets they could share with me?

I imagine hearing the phrase "You're under arrest" and getting handcuffed in front of my wife and any friends or cousins or aunts or nephews who happened to be visiting us at the time. It's hard to think the "you" in this sentence would ever mean me, yet this time, in my mind, it does.

I imagine cops reciting my Miranda rights, which I've heard a thousand times before on cop shows. I'm taken down to the police station, put in a room with two-way mirrors, and given the third degree. I try to explain away the evidence against me the best I could. If my hosts don't buy it, I'm arraigned.

I picture myself being escorted by a flying wedge of officers to the courthouse, trying to keep my dignity after they've taken off my belt and shoelaces. Denied bail after being charged with a capital crime. Confined with thugs of all sizes, shapes, and colors far below my station.

I imagine the jurors trying to figure out if "beyond a reasonable doubt" applies to me… and going upstate for a long, long time when they decide it does.

Most critically, I think about what my crime would mean to Helen. What would she think, knowing her husband killed somebody? Not in an accident, nor in a crime of passion, but in cold blood. What would my mother and father think, if they were still around?

Then there's the fear I'd get careless, leave some notes I've taken or other evidence behind. Or forget to erase my search history and leave a record living forever in cyberspace, waiting for some tech whiz in Bangalore to stumble upon it. The result would be the same—hope you enjoy your three hots and a cot upstate for the rest of your damn life.

If I'm being honest with myself, any of these doubts is a deal-breaker. I should stay at home and watch *Jeopardy* with Helen. Yet I know I'm not being honest with myself. I tell myself, convince myself, next time everything will go according to plan.

I decide to press on. The next afternoon, Monday, I put the knife and glove back in my left front pocket and check the listings. I see I could make the two o'clock movie at the Albion. Helen's gone for the afternoon to tutor some imbecile in chemistry, so I don't have to get her permission. I just go. I don't want another opportunity to go to waste.

Chapter Fifty-eight

Gil Bauer was living large.

He was in the software business, developing mobile apps to help online mom-and-pop stores draw buyers inside and move merchandise out the door. Mobile apps controlled the universe, and Gil was a master of that particular one. He made sure Mom and Pop could not screw up no matter how hard they tried. All they had to do was log on and voila! They were geniuses who could do no wrong.

His bosses did not want him to even think about jumping ship, so they kept him on a really long leash. If he wanted to work from home, it was okay by them. If he wanted to come in late or leave early once in a while, fine. He was that good.

He was born Gilberto Bauer, the only child of immigrants from Panama. They came here when Gilberto was five, and when his new Anglo friends in elementary school started calling him "Gil," his mom and dad gave up trying to get him to accept the Spanish version of his name and began calling him Gil themselves.

Like a chameleon, Gil adapted perfectly to both his Anglo and Latin worlds. He spoke Spanish at home, English everywhere else, both without any accent at all. Tall and fair-skinned, he looked, talked and dressed like a true Anglo. Inside, though, he felt Hispanic, and he had no problem conforming to either culture at any time.

Whenever he needed his space, he got it, no questions asked. His wife, like his boss, understood completely. When his time was his own, Gil would take in a museum by himself, go for a walk by himself, or go to the movies by himself.

Poor bastard chose one lousy day to go to the movies alone.

Around one thirty, Gil walked a mile, give or take, to the Albion theater on Flatbush Avenue, bought a ticket, and looked for a decent seat. The Albion was one of those grand old movie palaces from the 1920s that had been rescued from demolition at the last minute and restored to its past glory. New plush seats, gold-trimmed sconces on burgundy-painted walls, spiffy uniforms for the ticket takers. No expense spared.

The Albion came back, the neighborhood around it came back, and the audiences came back. To Gil, going to the movies at restored retro palaces was like going back in time. He had not grown up in the neighborhood, true, yet the Albion made him nostalgic for the old days nonetheless.

Surprisingly for a Monday afternoon, there were not a lot of empty seats at the theater. Everybody seemed to be separated by one or two, at most. Bauer was hoping for more. Scanning the orchestra from the back, he spotted what he was looking for—three unclaimed seats on the right side of the theater, one on the aisle—and walked over to claim his. Before he could settle in, a man wearing a baseball cap came up and gestured about the next seat in, communicating in the unspoken language every moviegoer is fluent in. Gil stood up to make it easier for the man to squeeze past him. The man thanked Gil, glanced at his face for a split second as he made his way past him, and sat down.

The movie started at 2:13 p.m. As soon as the opening credits appeared, Gil knew he had made a good choice. The movie was based on a novel he had read last year, and the twists and turns on the screen were pretty much faithful to the book. For Gil, knowing what was coming up made the movie even more enjoyable, and he was ready to leave his world and enter another.

At precisely 3:06 p.m., halfway through the movie, in the middle of a scene that takes place inside an almost pitch-black room, Gil Bauer felt a sudden sharp jolt of pain below his neck, right between his first and second ribs on the left side of his chest. This pain, far more intense than any he had ever felt before, was followed almost instantaneously by the severing of his thoracic aorta.

Gil grasped at his chest with his right hand, desperate to pull the pain off him. He started gasping for air, which refused to be drawn into his lungs. It was a futile effort. Hopeless, Gil was unable to say or do anything except feel his life leaving his body.

Then nothing. Gil Bauer's transition from life to death felt like an eternity, and it was over in seconds.

Chapter Fifty-nine

Outside the theater, under the marquee, two uniformed officers stood guard. Inside, two plainclothes officers positioned themselves on opposite sides of the lobby, watching for anything or anyone suspicious. They were told by their CO, Captain Brennan, that he had received a tip about a murderer, identity unknown, planning to attack his victim, likewise unknown, at the Albion. Although the information was incomplete and unverified, he believed a police presence was warranted. Better safe than sorry.

The officers were observant and vigilant, profiling for anything hinky separating bad actors from good citizens. Neither cop could tell you exactly what hinky was, yet they knew it when they saw it. Hinkiness is in the eyes of the beholder.

They noticed nothing unusual. Men and women alone, couples, a few groups of three or four women. They all headed to the doors of the theater, some stopping to buy popcorn on the way.

The two plainclothes officers took it all in stride; observing, rather than doing, was always part of the job. When the last stragglers made their way inside, the officers joined them. One took an aisle seat in the last row of the left side of the orchestra, while his partner sat right across the aisle from him, in the last row of the right side. If anything happened, they had a clear view of the entire audience. If the killer tried to escape, he would have to run right through their gauntlet, then get past the two uniforms posted outside.

While the movie was playing, they noticed nothing unusual. From time to time, a man, usually on the old side, got up and left his seat only to come back a minute or so later. It was perfectly understandable, and nothing unusual. When angry prostate syndrome flares up, a trip to the restroom cannot be put off. When you gotta go, you gotta go.

At three fifteen, a man sitting about ten rows down from them, on the aisle, got up and walked past them. His pace was brisk but unremarkable, and the two plainclothes cops made no effort to stop him. Nature called again. They failed to notice the man never returned to his seat.

As he left the theater, he walked past the two uniforms standing just outside, making sure to face away from them. It had started raining, and the marquee at least kept them dry. They made no effort to stop him either, perhaps because they heard no commotion coming from inside the theater, or because people leave in the middle of the movie all the time. In other words, a complete and total lack of probable cause.

The man adjusted his cap, zipped up his jacket, left the protection of the marquee, and walked away from the theater.

~ * ~

About half a block from the Albion, I stop short. Two cops are standing outside. Why? Is it a coincidence? Has to be. What if it's not? Do I abort my mission and go home? I've planned for everything, except this. Definitely not this. You want to know how fixated I am on completing my project? I convince myself then and there I'll be so stealthy, nobody will have any idea a murder is taking place. Nobody's going to scream for help. The two cops will just stand there like bozos when I leave the scene of my capital crime. If I'm wrong, I'll just be one more innocent patron in a theater full of them.

I stand in back of the Albion, looking for an opportunity. I'm lying in wait, ready to strike. Sorta feel like a big cat hiding in the tall grass as his helpless, clueless prey comes within striking distance. Just about invisible. Death inevitable.

I tell myself, "I can do this." Maybe I couldn't have the last time I tried, yet at this moment, in this theater, I'm confident I'll actually pull it off. I'm beyond confident. Absolutely certain. "I can" morphs into "I must." I've turned from man to monster, helpless to suppress my monstrous urge, and it's okay.

As everyone finds their seat, I keep my eye out for Mr. Right. Alone. Not too old, not too young. Not obese, tall, or muscular. Middle of the coming attractions and how-to-escape-if-the-theater-catches-fire announcements, a guy walks past me and stops for a moment, giving me a few seconds to size him up as a run-of-the-mill middle-aged white male. To my eyes, he looks pretty fit, as if he could take care of himself in a fight. Late forties, early fifties, about my height, maybe a little taller. Five-eleven, give or take. His hair, brown with some gray where you'd expect it, is neatly trimmed and combed back. His clothes are also absolutely what you'd expect—pressed khakis, plaid shirt, deck shoes, like he's a model for LL Bean.

After a few seconds, my man heads straight for three empty seats on the right side of the orchestra, about halfway down the aisle. The closest people are three rows back. Perfect.

He's alone. I follow him to make sure if he does sit down in the aisle seat, no one else gets a chance to take the next one in. Right as he begins to settle into the aisle seat, I come closer and ask if I can take the one right next to him. He nods, then stands up to let me by. I murmur a thank you, glance at his face for a second to confirm he is a he and I've never seen him before, and sit down.

So far, so good.

Coming attractions end, and the feature begins precisely at 2:13 p.m. I know this is the moment. I know it. All the stars have finally fallen into place. I've done all my homework. I'm psychologically prepared. Crime scene is perfect. Victim fits all my specifications. No excuses like the last time opportunity knocked. Just do it, asshole.

I'm not nervous in the least. My heart isn't racing. My breathing is normal. The idea I'd had of becoming a robot, an unfeeling machine, has come true.

It is now 2:53 p.m.

My victim is sitting to my left, which means I'd be striking him with the knife held in my right hand, across my body. Keeping my right hand hidden from view, I slip on a surgical glove, take the sheath out of my coat pocket, carefully slide the knife out, and hide it in my palm. It's now a matter of waiting for a scene that leaves the theater totally dark, to hide any sudden movement on the poor guy's part in response to the pain. Or a really loud scene, to drown out any noise he'd make. Either would do.

At 3:05 p.m., the scene I'm waiting for begins. The screen and the theater go totally dark, and stay totally dark.

At 3:06 p.m., I seize the moment and strike.

At 3:07 p.m., a man's life ends.

~ * ~

When people go to a funeral, they feel like they have to walk over to the coffin and look at the body for a moment or two. They're creeped out, yet this doesn't stop them from doing it every time.

Well, sitting right next to a stiff, shoulder to shoulder, creeps me out big-time. A lot more than I expected it would. It sort of takes away whatever feeling of satisfaction I have for a job well done. I expected to be panicky, maybe, or afraid. I mean, a dead guy is sitting right next to me for Christ's sake. Instead I feel totally revolted, like being anywhere near the guy would make me sick to my stomach. I just wanted to get out of there posthaste.

I've done the deed, with my muscle memory taking over and doing its job perfectly. Knife goes into his chest right where I want it to, sliding smoothly between his ribs right into his aorta. He slumps over, I wait a few seconds for him to stop struggling and accept his fate, and pull the knife out. One, two, three. No bloody mess. No scream. No protest. It doesn't seem to register with him he's been stabbed right in the chest. Maybe he had no idea what this felt like.

John Doe goes quietly, sticking faithfully to my script. There's no sign the man sitting across the aisle from me notices anything. Same with the couple in the row behind us, their view blocked by the high seatbacks. They're all sitting there enjoying the drama on the screen. The blockbuster keeps playing, and the Albion stays dark.

I know I'm safe for the moment, but I also know I need to make my exit while the movie is still playing, well before anybody has a chance to discover the body and the crime. Certainly before anybody else notices the smell of blood seeping into his shirt. I certainly pick it up, sitting a few inches or so from the corpse.

Corpse. A minute ago he was one of God's creatures.

Quietly as I can, I wipe the blood off the blade with a tissue, then put both the tissue and the knife back into my coat pocket, right side. I take off my surgical glove, put it in the other coat pocket, and wipe off the armrests on both sides of my seat with another tissue. I stand up, sort of hunched over so as not to block anyone's view, like you're supposed to when you're leaving a theater mid-movie. I glance down under my seat one more time to make sure I'm leaving nothing behind—no candy wrapper, ticket stub, or napkin that could have my prints or DNA—and whisper "excuse me" and "thanks" to the newly departed in the next seat, like people sitting nearby would expect, as I squeeze by his knees. Then I walk up the aisle, patting my coat pocket to check for the knife, and my pants pockets to make sure I haven't lost my wallet and my keys.

The lady reporter I'd been writing? Barbieri? I think I spot her on my way out, sitting by herself in an aisle seat. No photographer with her I can see. I was expecting to see her, of course, and she didn't disappoint. Although she doesn't seem to notice me as I walk past her, I give her props anyway for following the crumbs I left her. Ace student, that one.

I walk out the orchestra door to the lobby. The few people waiting there and buying popcorn at the concession stand take no notice, nor do the ticket takers at the door. Nothing to see here.

I then walk out the lobby door to the street, slowly and calmly, so as not to draw the attention of two police officers checking their cell phones just outside the exit. Between the time I walked into the theater and walked out a changed man, it had started raining. Not really hard, just enough for less hardy folks to take cover under awnings and in doorways. It's a good omen, I feel, as it means people walking near me are concentrating on trying to stay dry rather than people-watching. Even bumping into them wouldn't get a reaction. Which means less chance the cops will find any kind of witness to identify me. I button up my coat, pull my baseball cap down a little, and start walking home. I find myself looking back over my shoulder every minute or so to make sure I'm not being chased. I'm not. I listen for sirens or shouting. There's neither.

So far, so good, I think. This is easier than I thought. The mental torture I'd put myself through was all for nothing.

Halfway home, in the middle of a quiet residential street, I take out the murder weapon and hide it in the palm of my hand. I wipe it again for prints and blood I might've missed the first time, then put it back in the sheath. My arts and crafts lessons from elementary school paid off apparently, in that I manage not to accidentally kill myself with it. I make a mental note to toss the knife in a dumpster miles away from the Albion and from my home in the next day or so. There's always a dumpster around, as there's no shortage of construction sites these days. There are new condos going up everywhere you turn, I swear. I then continue walking home, not a care in the world, and on the way find a garbage can to ditch the glove in. I get to my front door, dry myself off as best as I can, and waltz in like nothing happened.

Chapter Sixty

From what Barbieri could gather from the cops who caught the case, and from local news shows, which were hard to escape in the days after the unfortunate incident at the Albion Theater, the crime was not discovered until well after the killer made his exit. Avenging angel Kim Barbieri avenged absolutely nothing. Her fierce, single-minded resolve to end his bullying, his power over her, meant nothing. He was still out there somewhere, waiting to strike.

On the way into the theater, she noticed a couple of uniforms posted in front. She assumed Brennan had sent them, yet thought they would not do much good. Her goal was to prevent a murder inside the theater. If she failed, they would be useless out here.

She had taken an aisle seat toward the rear of the theater, with nobody in the next seat, and like everyone else merely taking in an afternoon movie, she saw nothing. Heard nothing. *The killer wasn't where I predicted he'd be. I did notice one man wearing a baseball cap a few rows down get up and leave in the middle, walking right by me. Otherwise it was another couple of hours of bad movie I'll never get back.*

She left the theater and, caught in a sudden downpour, race-walked to the McDonald's down the block in a vain effort to stay dry. She bought a cup of tea and took a stool by the counter facing the street, numbed by the idea she had chosen the wrong theater or signed up for a horrible movie marathon with no end in sight. Her self-pity was brought to a halt by the sirens and flashing lights racing past the McDonald's window. All she saw were police cars, not ambulances or fire trucks, and they all converged outside the theater she had left a few minutes earlier.

Dread does not begin to describe what I feel right at this moment.

She walked back to the Albion, in the rain, hoping she would recognize one of the cops running into the theater she had left minutes before. None of the faces rang a bell with her, until their commanding officer arrived. As soon as Captain Timothy Brennan arrived, the two uniforms and two other men began huddling with him. His expression revealed nothing, yet she could see he was clearly not happy with them.

She was not surprised in the least to see him there—he was CO of the Brooklyn South Homicide Squad, and this was definitely not your run-of-the-mill killing in his part of the borough—and did nothing to draw his attention away from the business at hand. As a reporter who had covered her share of homicides, Barbieri knew enough to stay out of his way and let his officers do their jobs; otherwise, she would risk pissing off the very guys she needed in order to get out a story and make a living. Barbieri knew it was a murder even without being able to see the victim amid all the police officers crowding around him. *I have a good idea who did it. The man who left in the middle. I could never positively ID him. Though if I'm right, we know the murderer is a white male. Crime scene's what we thought, too. Barbieri and Delaney, Ace Detective Agency.*

When the police arrived, they came in force. Unlike more routine burglaries or muggings, where maybe a couple of beat cops were all that was needed, murder demanded everyone up and down the chain of command make an appearance and look busy: lieutenants, captains, even the commissioner. Especially when the crime happened in a good neighborhood: the victim was white and middle-class, and the murder looked like it would make the tabloids. Crimes like those received NYPD's deluxe platinum investigation package.

All these higher-ups are here for the show, since they can't do anything the beat cops first on the scene and the detectives who caught the case can't. By showing up, all this shiny brass reassures the public the NYPD is going all out to protect and serve.

Seventeen minutes after the uniformed officers arrived, they were joined by investigators from the Crime Scene Unit. It was their job to figure out how the victim died, at least until the medical examiner got his crack at the body, and look for friction ridges and other evidence the killer left behind. There was none. The detectives had their work cut out for them with this particular murder victim.

She knew she had been beaten. Her anger and frustration, however, were accompanied by a tinge of admiration. The guy actually accomplished what he had set out to do. *Fuckin' work of art. He's a smart, skilled professional who planned the perfect murder while leading me to the crime scene—just not close enough to stop him.*

Only after the cops wrapped up and the EMTs took the body away did she go up and speak to Brennan, who was busy taking notes and directing his men.

"Hey, Captain." She had interviewed Brennan from time to time on high-profile murders, and they kept their interactions professional, if not cordial, at all of them. Even though they had this thing, they automatically assumed their assigned roles without question. It was not an act. It was what they expected of each other as professionals. It was what they did with their clothes on.

"You just happen to be here, Barbieri? Scoop of a lifetime?"

"Yep. My day off, would you believe it?" The list of people she did not take shit from included the big shots in the NYPD, even a big shot who doubled as her boy toy. Their One Police Plaza address impressed her not a whit. Barbieri replaced her crime reporter persona with crime witness persona, finding it a little uncomfortable to be answering questions instead of asking them.

"Can't help you much, though, Captain. I was sitting by myself in the back. Movie ends. Credits come on. Everyone stands up, grabs their coats and umbrellas, and walks out."

"That's it? Nothing unusual? No argument? No assault?"

"What I saw, Captain. Everyone leaves when the credits start. Nobody gives a shit who the second unit wrangler is. Some folks take their time leaving, taking a minute or two to complain about what a lousy piece of garbage they sat through."

"Jibes with what my men told me," Brennan confirms.

"I saw the two uniforms you were talking to. Who were the other two? "

"Plainclothes. Might as well have stayed home. They saw nothing."

"You sent plainclothes?"

"Had to. You finally gave me something we could act on. Uniforms saw one guy leave the theater, but they didn't get a good look at him. He gave them no reason to stop him."

"Just walked away."

"Seems so. Nobody inside paid much attention to the victim sitting there, who probably looked like he was sleeping. Name's Gilberto Bauer, B-A-U-E-R. Even people who had to squeeze by him to get out ignored him."

"Gilberto Bauer," Barbieri repeated, making a mental note to look him up online. "Can't blame them. People fall asleep at the movies all the time, especially when they go alone, in the daytime. Escape another day of utter boredom. Ushers don't seem to mind as long as there are plenty of other seats paying customers could take. Nobody cares, to be honest."

"The perpetrator who killed him was good, though. Stabbed him right in the heart, so quick and clean the victim died in seconds. Didn't make a sound. Blood gushing out stayed inside his body."

Barbieri finished the thought, as she had been there before. "When his heart stopped, the bleeding stopped. So there was very little blood on his shirt for anyone to notice."

"The shirt also happened to be dark, some sort of brown and blue pattern, so the blood that did leak out wasn't obvious anyway. Perpetrator had everything going for him. Murder wasn't discovered until two witnesses—older husband and wife from the neighborhood going out for their usual matinee and early bird special—trying to squeeze past him took a good look at the sleeping man blocking their way. Husband ran up the aisle to the ticket taker, who called the manager on his headset. Manager rushed over, and he and the husband ran back down to the body."

Brennan continued, "Manager takes one look at the body and calls 911. That's when he cleared the theater, including kicking out people coming in for the next screening, and shut down the coming attractions before they started. By the time the first units got here, there were only four civilians here: manager, the ticket taker, and the man and woman who found the body."

"And one corpse. Forensics?" Barbieri asked. "Anything?"

"Not a whole lot to work with. They have a dead body. Chest wound of some kind looks like the cause of death. No murder weapon. I doubt they'll find prints or shoe impressions the officers missed."

"And no witnesses," Barbieri added, without really needing to. "This guy's good."

"Maybe. Their good usually runs out, in my experience. It loses out to their stupidity. They talk too much, or trust the wrong person. Let's put it this way, Barbieri. If he gets away with murder, it won't be due to anyone in my squad missing something. I'll see to that."

"I have no doubt, Captain."

He walked away to answer his phone, then had a word with his investigators.

"Another homicide. Brownsville. My men are going to stay here and do some more poking around. Maybe we'll get lucky. "

"It's okay to let the detectives take over?"

"They know how to reach me. There's nothing I can do except write my report."

Interrogation over, Barbieri left the theater and headed back home to Fort Greene. By then it was late afternoon, rush hour, so she did not have long to wait for the train. While she knew the killer did not leave a single clue, not a smudge, for the police to work with, she was not so sure there were no clues pointing in her direction. Or that she had heard the last about this from either Captain Timothy Brennan or Gil Bauer's executioner.

Chapter Sixty-one

Mission accomplished. I'm home safe and sound. The house is exactly as it was last time I'd seen it, earlier in the afternoon. I hadn't entered a parallel universe. *Well, that went pretty well*, I'm thinking. I should've been surprised, I guess—this is new territory for me, murder one—yet I'm not. All the planning and prep weren't for naught, after all. They were simply applied to a new kind of enterprise, and successfully, too. I did what I'd set out to do. Better late than never, maybe, but business as usual.

This is the rational side of me, cool, calm and collected. The emotional side of me, meanwhile, was bordering on elated. I read somewhere if you take a life, part of you dies, too. Maybe it's true, except in my case, the part that didn't die is feeling pretty good. Of course, I can't tell my wife why I'm so damn happy all of a sudden. Takes away some of the fun, but I have no choice, do I? Besides, I'm home, in my safe place. If I can't keep it together here, where can I?

First thing I do when I close the door behind me is see if she's home. She's not. I check the garage and the basement, and I'm indeed alone. It's Monday, though, so I'm pretty sure she'll be back before long. Monday evenings we usually spend at home, reading or watching cable news after dinner.

I go straight up to the bathroom, strip off my clothes, and take a quick shower. Maybe to wash the guilt off me, I suppose, if not any evidence of the crime I hadn't noticed. Earlier, on the way home, I'd checked several times and knew I hadn't gotten any blood or anything on my clothing.

Just to be on the safe side, I put everything I'd worn into a shopping bag and put it way back in my closet. Out of sight, but not out of mind. I plan to drop them off at the Goodwill later, maybe to atone for my sins. Until then, I don't want Helen anywhere near them. The shirt and pants are nothing special, certainly nothing that would draw attention from anyone who may have noticed me at the crime scene, and I'm hoping over the next few weeks Helen wouldn't notice clothes I no longer wore.

I also hide the murder weapon in the closet, which I once again put in the pocket of an old jacket I'll never wear again. I remind myself I have to toss the knife miles from here, way out of the city, next time I go out for a drive by myself. I figure Helen won't go rummaging around in my closet until then, so this is as safe a place as any to hide the knife.

My sins showered off, I get dressed again, in my signature white-middle-class-male shirt and slacks, go back to the living room, and sit in my usual easy chair. Only then do I take a breather and look back at what I'd done. The elation I felt a few minutes before changes just like that to a feeling of overpowering sadness and regret. Fast as I'm talking to you right now, the horror of what I've done sinks in. I've transformed myself from an ordinary law-abiding citizen into a stone-cold killer. Me. The guy sitting with my feet up, wondering if there's anything good on TV.

What the hell have I done? What the fuck have I become?

Chapter Sixty-two

Of course, I don't want Helen to know how bad I feel. She'd only pepper me with questions for which I'd have no answer. I'm not sure why, but I get up off my easy chair and stand by the front window to watch for her car, maybe to make sure she's not bringing an armada of NYPD police cars with her. Already I'm breaking my routine. Not a good omen.

After about a half hour, her car pulls into the driveway and I rush outside to meet her. That's break-in-routine number two. My wife can read me like a book, and I've given her a not-so-subtle hint something ain't right. I give her a big hug even while she's reaching into the car to grab her purse.

"I'm tired of keeping our relationship a secret, Helen." I'm trying to keep it light to keep her off guard.

"David? What's gotten into you?" I can't tell if she's pleased or startled, but she hugs me back anyway. When I pull away, she's giving me a puzzled look as if she were asking "who *are* you?" I've clearly screwed up with my happy act. Instead of acting depressed, which is how I feel, I'm acting like a puppy. Either way, I'm giving her plenty of ammunition to use against me.

"Nothing. Working on my house husband skills."

"Well, whatever it is you're drinking, pour me one. I have to go inside."

I think I just dodged another bullet, the first one being my temper tantrum in Soho. Why am I acting so out of character? I don't know, and Helen decides not to let it go. We go into the house and we go our separate ways, me to the living room and her to the kitchen. She opens the refrigerator door, then closes it without looking inside and walks back to me. I know what's coming, and all I can do is brace myself.

"David, what's going on? You lost it with the delivery man on his bike, and now you're acting like a kid with a crush. One extreme to the other. You've never done that before."

I'm sitting on the sofa, fiddling with the remote, and she's standing over me. Last thing I need is for her to start questioning me. I've seen her subject people, perfectly innocent folks like supermarket checkout ladies, to withering interrogations, and believe me, it isn't pretty. I'm afraid I'd confess even before she began.

"I take your point, hon." The easiest thing to do is defuse the situation. Simply agree with her and nobody gets hurt. "I'll stop with the public displays of affection."

"It's not that, David. It's like you're having mood swings." Now she's sitting beside me on the sofa, her body language going from confronting me to consoling me.

"No, I'm not. Soho was when? Last week? This is Monday. Pretty far apart for mood swings."

"Okay, maybe they're not. I'm not a psychiatrist, but it's something you should keep an eye on. Both of us should." Once again my wife's giving me a way to escape her wrath, letting me know whose side she's on. "I'm getting whiplash trying to follow them."

Tough-love session over, she pecks me on the cheek and goes back to the kitchen. I go back to not watching the TV.

In the first hour after the murder, I'm acting differently than I usually do. That's not a good thing. My goal is to not draw attention to myself, and I just drew Helen's attention again. Mucho stupido. I think I can write off the motorbike thing as simply protecting a damsel in distress. I took my chivalry act a bit too far and lost my temper, yet people go ballistic all the time. I also think I had good reason to act giddy around her. She'll never know why, but I do. If she's right, and I am having mood swings out of nowhere, then by definition I'm wrong and I need help.

~ * ~

222

What I can say for sure is, so far in the immediate aftermath of the murder, I have good reason to jump for joy.

No investigators come knocking at my door that night, asking me to account for my whereabouts on that particularly eventful afternoon, or looking to tie up a few loose ends for their reports. More important, they aren't asking Helen to account for my whereabouts. Later, much to my surprise, I don't toss and turn and stare at the ceiling all night. Instead, I go right to sleep, not a care in the world.

Following morning, a Tuesday, I read the papers and watch the local news to see if my handiwork was newsworthy. It was indeed. Seems a body was found in the Albion Theater the day before. Murdered. No witnesses. No suspects. No clues. No nothing. The NYPD spokeswoman declined to reveal the victim's identity, or how the man was killed, or even whether there were any promising leads.

Naturally, it becomes a topic of conversation for Helen and me, as it does for all the good citizens of Pleasantville. Everyone's trying to ferret out who the victim was, ready to check how many degrees of separation stand between themselves and him. Everyone we know is asking each other the last time they'd been to the Albion, who they went with, where they sat, did they ever notice anyone acting suspicious, et cetera, et cetera. They don't have to ask each other if they'd ever go there again, certainly not by themselves.

I'm guilty of the same thing, of course, although it feels a bit strange discussing the victim as if I'd never met him, and referring to the killer in the third person. It's all an act I have an almost too easy time performing. Or maybe it's what psychologists call compartmentalizing, allowing my good egg half to live side by side, happily ever after with my inner demon half. It's kind of a defense mechanism people who find themselves in a whole lot of trouble use to keep from going off the deep end.

I find myself talking with Helen about the murder over breakfast the following day. It's the lead story on every local news channel, and she's as alarmed as everyone else. She knows I'd gone to the movies alone the day before the murder, yet she doesn't seem to connect the dots.

"They haven't said how he was killed, have they?" She's referring to the talking heads on the news.

"No. How the hell do you kill someone when you can't even see him?" I'm playing devil's advocate, as I already know the answer.

"How can you kill someone in front of so many witnesses? Was the killer sitting behind him or next to him? Did he even know the victim?"

"No idea. Whoever the victim is, he didn't make a sound. So maybe he was smothered."

"Or strangled." *Some imagination you have.* "How many times have we been to the Albion? Fifty?"

"At least. We're not going back anytime soon, that I can tell you. Where were the police?" I'm playing the role of anguished citizen.

"You want them at the movies, Dave? Seriously?"

"The NRA says to put guns in schools and churches. Why not?" I think I just took my role-playing too far and dial back. "Forget what I said. I don't want kindergarten teachers packing heat."

"So now no one can go to the movies?"

"We have to be careful, I guess. Go when nobody's there and sit squarely in the middle of fifty empty seats." I try my best to steer the conversation in another direction, not sure how much longer I can play innocent. "What's on your agenda today?"

"Not the movies." My clever ploy failed. "This afternoon I have to help a girl prepare for a biology final. Then I'm free if you want to do something."

If I'm at all tempted to go to the cops and confess, this would be the time. Save the police a lot of trouble. Also it would make me stop lying to Helen, which I'm having a hard time accepting. At this point I don't know the name of the man I killed, anyway. I find out later the police usually withhold the murder victim's identity until his family can be notified, so the cops can break the sad news to them in a private, dignified way, not hear about it on the local news like everyone else. I think I'll know soon enough, though. It isn't every day someone dies of other than natural causes in the middle of an afternoon movie.

I'm right. I turn on the news a few hours later and…bingo! The authorities put a name to the recently departed. Computer wiz name of Gilberto Bauer. Goes by Gil. Nobody I know, or Helen knows, thank heaven. Funeral will be held at eleven the next day at the Gardner Funeral Home on Beverly Road. Convenient, I think. Thanks to Facebook and LinkedIn, of course, I know it would be only a few hours at most until every nook and cranny of this Bauer fellow's life is put on public display.

"Helen," I ask, picking up the conversation where we left off earlier, "feel like going out for Chinese later? Thai, maybe?"

"We sure can. What's the occasion?" she asks.

"No occasion. I don't feel like staying home tonight. Call the Martins. Maybe they haven't made dinner plans yet."

Truth is, I want to celebrate the blessed event, at least a little. Maybe do a happy dance. Celebration may be a bit premature, or totally inappropriate, I know. I crossed the line from upstanding citizen to outlaw, but I feel putting a name to my victim makes the murder I've committed more of a done deal, like a critical piece of me was no longer missing. Validation, maybe. My success is real, and a specific individual, a man with a name and a career and a family, is no longer with us.

Chapter Sixty-three

What's it like to actually kill a person? Until the moment I actually did it, I had absolutely no idea. When I was choosing the weapon, I imagined how I'd use it, but not the actual death it would cause. I guess ninety-nine point ninety-nine percent of us are pretty ignorant in that regard.

Until I got into this whole escapade, I'd never really thought about what committing murder *feels* like. Is it thrilling? Depressing? Terrifying? Do you even know what you're doing? I'd have to say Gil's murder wasn't any of that, at least not to me. Seems kind of strange for me to say, and people might find it strange to hear, but I found the stabbing action to be pretty, well, ordinary. Yes, that's the right word, ordinary. Mundane. It's mere mechanics: the hand, arm, and knife motion were all simply the means to a grisly end.

Before you jump down my throat, there's a good explanation for feeling this way. If you separate out the exclusively physical act of plunging a knife into a human body from the final result of the action, which is ending the life of a living, breathing human being, it's an ordinary action, a motion you do without a second thought every day. You push a door open to enter a room, reach for a book high up on a bookcase. You don't think about it. You do it. Not an emotional act, but a physical act. A simple act. Some people who just had carnal knowledge of each other say it was only sex, a physical act with not an iota of love or even like. Same thing.

In the days before the murder, I practiced the stabbing motion over and over till it became robotic. Nothing more than muscle memory. Once I gave my arm and my hand holding the knife permission to launch, I just got out of the way and let them take over. I was merely an innocent bystander at that point, not feeling much of anything in terms of emotions.

In the few seconds before I did it, I did feel a little anxious, to be honest. The fears and doubts I'd been wrestling with were definitely still there, yet they were well under control. Breathing and heartbeat both normal, like I said. There's this restaurant scene in *The Godfather*, where Michael is going to lose his virginity by shooting the cop and that other mob boss, and he's tormented so much his body's almost shaking. That's what I was afraid I'd feel like, honestly, while the truth is my fear was kept pretty much in check. Calm as can be. I was one stone-cold motherfucker, for maybe the first time in my life.

Right after I plunged the knife in, I have to be honest, I was a little concerned for a second or two that my victim wasn't going to die as instructed. Again, not enough to cause panic or anything like that. I knew if I waited long enough to make sure he was dead, it would be okay—and it was. The murder was simply a physical action I'd rehearsed a thousand times, and I executed it successfully. I'd succeeded, and I was satisfied with my success.

Now, I'm not going to apologize for not feeling bad about what I've done. That's how I feel. There's nothing I can do about it. It isn't a conscious decision I made to feel nothing. It just isn't there. I do have a little remorse that a nice gentlemen had to make an early exit thanks to me, so maybe I'm not a total bastard. Right after I killed Bauer, at our brief moment sitting together at the movies, the only feeling I had was the satisfaction that all the homework I'd done had paid off. Just like the old days.

Chapter Sixty-four

Barbieri was not assigned to cover the Bauer murder. She had not expected to be, and not only because she was on Cavanaugh's shit list. *He had no choice, did he? I was there during the crime, making it at least possible I'll become part of the story. He had to reassign it out of concern about my objectivity.* It was a good call on his part, one she would have made herself if she were in his shoes. Of course, she also understood if the killing ever merited some kind of investigative reporting later on, maybe with a human interest angle, she would be ready. If, that is, Cavanaugh ever decided to stop getting in the way of her career plans.

It seemed to her he had not made the connection between the letters and the murder at the Albion. At least not yet. Or if he had, he chose to keep quiet and keep the *Daily News* out of it. There was nothing in it for him if his employer landed in hot water. Still, the murder had grabbed her in a way all the others she had covered had not.

I can't let it go. It won't let me go. Not being assigned won't stop me. I still have my press credentials. They're a license to ask around, authorized or not, for anything that might lead me to the man who made me tag along to the murder he committed.

One witness who could always be counted on to provide crucial clues about a murder was the victim—or rather the lifeless body the bad guy left behind. That is why the morgue was always off-limits to reporters like Barbieri, drawn like moths to a flame by homicides. As a forensic pathologist, the medical examiner knew how to persuade a reluctant corpse to give up its secrets. If the information an autopsy provided was at all useful to the police, it was usually to secure a killer's conviction after his arrest. Once in a blue moon, though, it could also help the cops find him. *Maybe something in their report will help me ID the killer before the police do. Then what? Do I tell Brennan or some kind of NYPD tip line?*

Her first stop was the office of Dr. Linda Fletcher, the ME who had performed Bauer's autopsy, whom she interviewed under the guise of researching a story she was writing for the paper.

She took the subway over to the ME's office on First Avenue in Manhattan the next afternoon and found about what she had expected. It was a pretty depressing place, mostly sterile autopsy tables in sterile examination rooms, and sterile refrigerators filled with bodies in sterile body bags, patiently waiting their turn to be sawn open and sewn back together again. The smell of decay was not nearly as sickening as she had anticipated, perhaps because the bodies were already refrigerated—unlike all the ones at homicide scenes.

Dr. Fletcher herself was anything but sterile. The ME was not the gray, drab figure Barbieri expected, numbed by interacting with corpses all day. Instead, she radiated vibrancy from head to toe, a full-time resident in the land of the living. Dr. Fletcher counter-programmed her white lab coat with bright red lipstick and colorful pendant earrings, with bright red stockings and Manolo Blahniks below. She had a terrific smile that promised excellent bedside manner, ideal for patients who needed a little cheering up. Barbieri was tempted to ask her how an MD wound up working on people who did not much care about bedside manner, but instead she skipped the pleasantries and went right to Bauer's autopsy. As often as she had covered murders, she had never actually been to one, so this interview was a teachable moment for her.

As Dr. Fletcher reviewed the report for Barbieri, she took an occasional glance at her computer screen to refresh her memory. Barbieri sat across the desk from her, taking notes as she spoke. Womansplaining here was okay.

"I performed the autopsy of Mr. Bauer on Monday, approximately eighteen hours after his death, Miss Barbieri." The formal address seemed appropriate, given the seriousness with which she viewed her job.

"I understand you didn't find anything the investigators didn't already know."

"No, we did not. First thing, we confirmed the identity of the deceased. His race, sex, age, hair color, eye color, and identifying scars told us he was indeed Gilberto Bauer," she explained.

"No chance of mistaken identity?"

"Doesn't happen. That part's sort of a formality. Next, we took pictures of his body with and without clothes on, then X-rayed it for foreign objects, which we always do in murder cases."

"By foreign objects you mean bullets?"

"Ninety percent of the time, yes. The other ten percent, you don't want to know. We examined his hands, also SOP in homicides, and took residue and fingernail samples. Could tell us if he fought back. He didn't. In addition, we looked for trace evidence like paint chips and hairs. There were none."

To Barbieri, this teachable moment was veering into a case of TMI, yet she remained quiet and continued taking notes. Nothing she had been told so far would lead her to the killer. While Dr. Fletcher had performed the same steps on countless murder victims, this was the first time Barbieri had heard all the gruesome details.

"We measured and weighed the body and then performed what's known as a forensic autopsy, which we employ where homicide is suspected, as opposed to natural death. We examine the body for bullets, trauma, internal injuries, poisons—"

"Knife wounds."

"In Bauer's case, yes. We found the stab wound we knew had to be there and measured its thickness and depth. We determined the blade entered the body at a downward angle in the intercostal space between vertebrosternal ribs one and two, and severed the victim's thoracic aorta."

As she spoke, the ME pointed to her own rib cage to help Barbieri understand the anatomical jargon she was using. The reporter welcomed the little show-and-tell moment, keeping her eyes focused on the doctor's hands as she explained her findings.

"His aim was good, for sure."

"If his intention was to sever the aorta, I'd say his aim was perfect."

"When you say 'downward angle,' do you mean the victim was struck from above? The killer was standing over him?"

"Not necessarily. It may have also been the raised position of the weapon in the killer's hand. We also checked the body's lividity, rigidity, chemical changes, and stomach contents to determine time of death."

"Why stomach contents? What does that tell you?"

"If we know when he ate last, how much food was digested can help us confirm time of death. We estimated it to be about eighteen hours earlier, which matched the time provided by the police. When we were done, we put all his organs back where we found them and sewed him back up. Bottom line, Gilberto Bauer's death was the result of a major hemorrhage following the severing of the aorta with an unidentified sharp instrument."

"Knife of some kind?"

"The really sharp kind. Like a scalpel." Dr. Fletcher glanced at her watch. "That's about it, Miss Barbieri. Now I have to kick you out. My services are needed again."

Barbieri thanked Dr. Fletcher for her time, closed her notepad, and made her way back into the land of the living. The interview confirmed Bauer's autopsy did not help the investigators one iota, and would not move them, or her, any closer to identifying the murderer.

This guy's pulled a world-class disappearing act. I'm stuck. Totally. NYPD with all their computers and investigators and snitches is hitting a brick wall. Has he disappeared for good? Or is he just lying low for a while?

Chapter Sixty-five

Sitting on a park bench near the Cloisters in Upper Manhattan at three o'clock on a warm, muggy afternoon, Kim Barbieri was hard at work crafting a story she had exactly twenty minutes to complete. She had not been banished from the paper for good, as she had feared; Cavanaugh had simply stopped using her until he could sort the matter out with the higher-ups. He was still furious about the danger she put the paper in, he had texted her, yet he had decided her reporting abilities outweighed her one lapse in judgment. He knew full well he had a better chance of nailing stories the first time with her than without her.

Her second story of the day—the first was about an Orthodox rabbi in Borough Park exhibiting a somewhat unorthodox sexual preference—was about a fire that had been deliberately set in an apartment house nearby. She was determined to get it right and send it over, yet her mind was not cooperating. She could not stop thinking about the killer, and the chokehold he seemed to have on her.

Barbieri: Inwood fire: 3:00 p.m.

A 39-year-old man suffered third-degree burns when he was trapped by a fast-moving blaze in an apartment building on Dyckman Street, near Fort Washington Avenue, in Inwood.

I should've thrown out his letters. Every last one of them. I'd have saved myself a lot of trouble.

Arson is suspected, as an unidentified man was seen running out of the building shortly before the fire was detected.

How am I going to find this guy? Autopsy told me nothing.

The victim, Enrique Cortez, was treated by paramedics at the scene and transported by ambulance to the Harlem Hospital emergency room. He remains in the hospital burn unit, in critical condition.

Why do I want to find him, anyway? He carried out his threat. He's Brennan's problem now.

Firefighters were unable to reach Mr. Cortez in time to rescue him before flames engulfed his fourth-floor apartment. "The collapsed stairwell restricted our firefighters from reaching the fourth floor," FDNY spokesperson Catherine Milton explained. Eighteen other residents of the building were rescued, unharmed, by FDNY personnel.

He's got to pay for what he did to me, that's why.

Fire marshals suspect the blaze was the result of arson. "There is evidence of an accelerant, specifically a container with gasoline residue, which was left on the ground floor of the building," reported Milton. The suspected arsonist remains at large.

Beast has claimed one victim. I'm not going to be the second.

Barbieri finished the copy and emailed it over with time to spare, but only after double-checking that none of her internal turmoil, her determination to find the killer, had somehow found its way into the story. It had not. The story was solid. She had kept her personal side, her desire to seek revenge, completely out of it. Impartial observer.

At least my professionalism's not shot to hell. That's something.

Chapter Sixty-six

If there was one person to whom Barbieri could open up about the whole mess without fear of being judged, or misjudged, it was Aunt Estelle. The woman was as ready to say "there, there" as she was when her niece did something naughty back in elementary school. On her next home visit Barbieri walked right to her assigned seat at the kitchen table. No hug, no hello. She remained still, not saying a word, her only gesture taking small sips of espresso. Her aunt knew when to keep quiet, and she did. She took the chair across the table from Barbieri and waited.

After a few more moments of stony silence, Barbieri gave herself the green light and opened up. She confessed all—the letters, how she and Delaney figured out where and when the attack would occur, and the murder itself

"I screwed up royally, Aunt Estelle. A good man is dead, murdered, and I was practically invited to intervene by the bastard who killed him."

"This is what you're beating yourself up for? Somebody killed somebody?"

"I was probably a few rows away at most, Aunt Estelle, maybe ten or twenty feet behind them. Or across the aisle. I still don't know. I didn't see a thing. Neither did the cops." She neglected to tell her aunt why the officers were there, and Estelle did not ask.

"Albion. I used to go there."

"I still do. It was about as professional a hit as I've ever seen."

"Which explains why he hasn't been caught, Kim."

"He won't be. Chances are pretty close to zero, I'd say."

"What about the letters? Have you given them to the police? The

234

killer did what he said he'd do."

"There's nothing in them to help the detectives identify him or track him down." Barbieri hoped her aunt didn't notice that she didn't answer the question directly.

"Fair enough. You're probably right. Let's move on. You want to catch this man so bad because…?"

"I don't know why, exactly. I wish I knew. To see him go to prison, I guess. There's nothing in it for me."

"Except maybe a scoop for the paper. It'll be a big story for you."

"Maybe, but I don't think a story in the paper's worth it."

"Not at all. You know what I think? I think it's about what he did to *you*, not Bauer. Am I right?"

"Bastard put me through hell." *Cut right to the chase, Aunt Estelle. Damn you're good.* "He outsmarted me. He's been playing games with my head. If I ever meet him, am I supposed to ask him about his childhood, or stick an icepick in his eyeball?"

"Careful what you wish for, Kim…although I think I agree with you. You should confront him. It's good for the soul. Let me ask you. Where would you go after taking a life? Return to the scene of the crime?"

"That's a lot of malarkey. Total cliché. Criminals tend to go back to their usual haunts, which makes them almost too easy to find and arrest. Or they take off to another city or some cheap motel in the middle of nowhere, which makes them a little harder to find. Not much harder since they're usually caught, even if it takes a few days more for the cops to track them down."

"Not the brightest bulbs, are they? What about the funeral? Don't killers sometimes go there? Or is that just a cliché too?"

"No, it's been known to happen. Morbid curiosity." Barbieri was well aware cops, and even crime reporters like her, sometimes staked out funerals. Cold-blooded murderers tended to overdose on their own bravado and take one little risk too many. "Maybe just a sick need to see how much suffering they caused for all the victim's friends and relatives. Bonus points."

"When's Bauer's funeral?'

"Tomorrow, I think. I'll check online." *Good a place to start as any. My pen pal may be inclined to press his luck.*

Barbieri got exactly what she had expected from her aunt, a combination of comfort and wisdom. Before the conversation switched to more mundane concerns, like who the reporter was seeing, Aunt Estelle offered her niece one final thought. "Please, Kim. Leave the icepick at home. One funeral's enough."

Barbieri gave her aunt a small smile and poured herself another cup of espresso. She was in no hurry to leave the old neighborhood.

Chapter Sixty-seven

Barbieri made sure to get to the Gardner Funeral Home, in Midwood, a little early, giving her time to eyeball the mourners as they arrived and started to mingle with family members, friends, and colleagues of the dear departed Gil Bauer. It was fairly new, as funeral homes went, a refurbished single-family home a stone's throw from Brooklyn College. That was where she got her BA, the free public college created to turn the children of dirt-poor immigrants into teachers, accountants, and scientists—and at least one reporter.

The campus, a compact sanctuary hemmed in on all sides by homes, businesses, and railroad tracks, was a big reason why Midwood had been largely left alone, unaffected by the upheavals some of the city's other neighborhoods had endured. Respectable one hundred years ago. Respectable today.

She took off her raincoat, which had made a valiant yet futile effort to protect her from the morning's downpour, and stood off to the side of the front door. She was trying her best to look like she belonged there. Barbieri had been to enough funerals to know she could not go wrong with a simple black dress and black shoes. She was right. All the women wore the same uniform, more or less. *Everyone here seems to assume I know the deceased. There's some connection, they're sure, and they're perfectly okay with being unable to figure out what it is.*

Unsurprisingly, there were three plainclothes officers attending the funeral as well. She spotted them a mile away, and even knew one by name, yet pretended not to recognize them. Reporters blowing their cover was simply not done. Even for off-duty reporters.

Inside the chapel, all the actors assumed their assigned roles: the immediate family huddling together, relatives quietly greeting one another, lots of hugs, and a little nervous laughter. Barbieri was watching for the man she imagined the killer to be, based on the glimpses she had had before. An unremarkable, middle-aged, middle-class individual whose only distinguishing characteristic would be he did not speak to anyone because he did not know anyone. She could not count on seeing any scars to identify him, nor any habits or tics that would give him away.

She did not see him, or anyone else who looked like a depraved monster, yet after a few minutes she began to sense he was there, in the funeral home. It was not quite the sudden panic she had felt back at the gun show, but rather a slowly growing uneasiness inside her that something was wrong. She searched among the cookie-cutter mourners who were quietly mingling and grieving together. Only one gentleman merited a second glance—older, maybe sixty to sixty-five, with short gray hair and wearing black horn-rimmed glasses. *Him? Was it the man walking by me at the Albion? He looked way younger. What about the gun show and the post office? I didn't get a good look, so I'd have to say no.* Every time he approached another mourner, it looked to her like he was introducing himself, as if he were a stranger to them. No one came up to him first and greeted him like an old friend.

Barbieri's curiosity about the older gentleman was dispelled a moment or so later. He was sitting himself in the back of the sanctuary when a woman approached him and began talking with him. She could not hear what they were saying, as they were well out of earshot, although based on their gestures they seemed to have known each other a while and were getting reacquainted. *I'm right. Not him. Harmless.*

With zero likely suspects, Barbieri concluded that the aura she was feeling may not have been triggered by the killer himself. This time, it could have been because his handiwork was on full display. She chalked it up to that and let it go.

Once it was clear everyone who was going to attend had already arrived, and everyone took their seats and the service began, Barbieri decided to stay if only out of respect for the deceased. Given how she took some responsibility for the death of Gil Bauer, if only due to some kind of negligence on her part, staying for the service was one way of atoning for her sins.

The officer she had recognized gave no sign he knew her, not even a nod, and all three officers left empty-handed about halfway through the service. It was pretty much routine, and when it ended, the goodbyes and hugs went according to script as well. She declined to go to the actual burial at the cemetery out in Queens. *If the killer decided to skip the funeral service, he wouldn't push his luck by going to the cemetery.*

Other than the one older man she had briefly eyeballed earlier, there were no persons of interest to Barbieri. *No one looked like a killer, particularly the image of the killer I've created in my own mind.*

~ * ~

I sort of look forward to going to my victim's funeral. Probably a strange combination of cojones I'd show my face to his family, and respect for the deceased. Or maybe evidence I am indeed just a weird fuck. I don't know.

Before I went over there, I changed my appearance a little, to make myself look maybe ten years older. A few more gray hairs, pair of black glasses. If I ran into the reporter there, I didn't want to set off any alarms on her part: Who is this guy, and why do I keep running into him?

The interior of the funeral home on Beverly was standard-issue funeral décor: deep gray carpeting on every floor to muffle noise, walls painted all somber gray and brown. The steady rain coming down the whole morning only made the place even more somber.

By the time I get there, a little before eleven, it looks like about ten people had already settled in and begun the quiet greetings and small talk funeral services bring out in mourners. Gil Bauer's immediate family, my best guess.

One mourner is a man who appears to be about Gil's age. Looks nothing like him, but I assume he's his brother anyway. He's talking quietly with an older couple, much older. The parents, no doubt. They're speaking very softly, almost in a whisper, and in the little I pick up I detect a slight Spanish accent. Bauer was apparently Hispanic, not that it makes a difference. I have nothing against them. He was the one who happened to show up at the movies.

They're soon joined by a couple of women who look maybe five years younger than Gil, along with their husbands. My guy's kid sisters, in my estimation. The deceased is on display in his coffin in the front of the chapel, surrounded by flowers and photographs. Slowly throughout the morning, the immediate family is joined by Gil's extended family—cousins and uncles and nieces and nephews—as well as by colleagues from work, old friends from college, and new ones from the neighborhood. As new mourners arrive, I try to figure out how they're related to the guest of honor, based on who they came with and stay close to, and how they interact with other mourners.

Gil's passing drew a pretty big crowd, which I take full responsibility for. Silently. Like hearing his name on the news for the first time, their coming together to mourn his loss and celebrate his life only serves to validate what I've done. I can't claim credit out loud, of course, yet it's something I feel anyway. Perverse, I know. This whole project of mine is definitely taking a turn for the weird.

All the mourners hug, and whisper, and cry, and shake hands, and air-kiss, as is the protocol for such events. They all catch up with one another, share little anecdotes about Gil, and reinforce to each other he'll be missed, his life was cut way too short, it's only a matter of time before his killer is caught and will get the chair if the state ever brings back the death penalty, the motherfucker.

It seems besides the funeral director and his minions, everyone at the funeral home had some emotional connection, and a strong one, to Gil Bauer. Except for the plainclothes detectives, who don't go out of their way to blend in. There are three, they clearly know nobody here besides each other, and they're discreetly keeping an eye on the mourners. I've never heard of a killer going to his victim's funeral before, but apparently they do. Although I don't know if they expect the killer to show up, they're clearly ready if he does.

And except for the reporter. She doesn't seem to notice me, maybe due to my clever disguise. Yet once again, I gotta give her credit for due diligence. I chose wisely.

I'm not sure why, perhaps because I seem so ordinary, but the detectives don't pay me any more attention than they do the other mourners. I do notice one of them eyeballing me as he scans the room. He stops, gives me the once-over, then moves on to the next mourner-slash-fugitive-from-justice. I look perfectly normal. My behavior is appropriate for the occasion. I'm a nobody, just another mourner at just another funeral, which is fine by me. Nothing happening here, move along.

Of course, I don't go out of my way to direct their attention in my direction, either. I try to blend in as well as I can, introducing myself to mourners I've never met before and making small talk about the deceased. A little awkward, I have to say, but it's what you do at funerals. I'm a little afraid the police might take notice, yet they continue to ignore me no matter how hard I try to blend in.

My disappearing act hasn't gone entirely unnoticed, though. I'm sitting by myself in the back row of the chapel when a woman, looks to be about thirty, walks over and takes a seat alongside mine, and makes a clumsy attempt at what passes for small talk.

"I guess you're not family. Like me." she says to me, offering her hand to shake. "Sarah. How did you know Gil?"

"Martin. Marty. Nice to meet you." Not my real name, of course. "I never knew Mr. Bauer, sorry to say. Never met him before. Seemed like a nice guy, from what people are saying. When I read about what happened, I felt I had to be here. Could've been me, you know? I go to the movies by myself all the time, since I retired. Sometimes at the Albion, now that they've fixed it up."

"Your loss, not knowing Gil. I worked with him almost two years, app development mostly. Nicest guy in the world. You know how an office is, a bunch of little cliques competing for attention. Gil was the one guy we all wanted to hang with, and the guy we all wanted to be our mentor. Maybe it was because he was the only guy who was twice our age. Wicked sense of humor, though. Some people didn't get him, but I did."

"Sounds like I would've liked him. His passing like this, it reminds me I've got to be a little more cautious with strangers," I respond.

She points to a woman about Gil's age standing with two others a few feet from the coffin. "His wife. Karen. Everyone calls her Kay. She's over there with her sisters." I'd mistakenly taken the two women to be Gil's sisters, not his wife's.

"I was wondering. I'm not sure if I should introduce myself to Karen, offer my condolences." I have no intention of doing either, except it seems like the right thing to say.

"I'm about to myself. I think she'd want to know how much we liked working with her husband. Nice meeting you, Marty."

"Nice meeting you, too. Take care."

Sarah leaves my side and approaches Gil's wife. I can't make out what they're saying, but it's pretty clear Sarah was right about Kay. His wife is smiling, even laughing a little, as Sarah talks about a side of her husband she never really saw, the mentor side.

The funeral service goes on as planned, on autopilot, with the wife and friends letting go of their grief with personal stories about Gil and the priest providing the solemnity he's offered a thousand times before. I didn't notice it at the time but the three detectives left in the middle of the service, apparently concluding no person of interest would be making an appearance.

After, when the service was over, all the mourners slowly say their goodbyes to each other and the victim's immediate family leave the funeral home, try to stay dry as they walk to their respective cars, and join the long, slow procession to the cemetery. I don't join them, though. It seems to me like a victory lap, like I'd be rubbing it in by seeing Gil Bauer in the ground. I take their departure as my cue to gather my coat and umbrella, nod politely with a tight, forced smile to the stragglers, the way you do at funerals, and leave quietly.

No one seems to notice I didn't sign the condolence book.

Chapter Sixty-eight

"Captain."

"Barbieri."

"I expected to see you here today. I hear City Hall isn't pleased."

"Washington isn't pleased, I'll tell you that. The mayor wants me to make it go away."

"The *News* is beyond pleased. This story is good for business. A nice juicy homicide could keep a reporter busy for months. Bauer. Progress?"

"You'll be the first to know."

She and Brennan were standing outside an arraignment courtroom in Brooklyn Criminal Court, waiting for the bailiff to call the case of a citizen of Burkina Faso under arrest for killing a transvestite. Brennan was not in the habit of handling anything as common as the murder of a lowlife, except when foreign nationals were involved. Foreigners meant diplomats and negotiations and international incidents. Foreigners meant the brass wanted him there to make sure the United Nations and the Police Department of the City of New York did everything by the book. The incident must not give the Ministry of Defense of Burkina Faso a pretext to commence hostilities against the United States of America.

The indignant consular officials in the Burkina Faso embassy declared the accused killer had diplomatic immunity and were ready to fly him out of the country on the next plane. The State Department claimed they never heard of him and wanted him to stay put. It was a Mexican standoff, and the judge decided to break for lunch.

"I'm going out for Chinese, Barbieri. Nothing going on until two. Place on Joralemon?"

"Can't, Captain. Sorry. I've got some witnesses I need to

interview." The reporter actually did. She had no reason to tell a white lie this time.

"I'll come over later. I believe you have some more documents relevant to the Bauer murder."

~ * ~

Later the same evening, he let himself in at eight, as she expected. The key to her apartment was an early benefit of their friendship. He found Barbieri in her usual spot on the sofa, engrossed in a book while listening to an opera she doubted he would recognize, and she barely looked up as he bent down to kiss her on her forehead. He then went to the kitchen, took out two wineglasses from the cabinet, and poured a little merlot in each. He gently took away her book and replaced it with the glass of wine, then sat alongside her on the sofa.

"Let's have them," Brennan said, holding out his hands. Barbieri took it as more of an order than a request.

"You'll give them right back to me?"

"I'll decide after I see them."

She took the binder, now with all six letters, out of her messenger bag and handed it over. He leafed through them in order, each one spelling out the next step in the killer's plan and inviting her to tag along as he proceeded to stab an innocent man in the heart. Brennan was clearly impressed now that he was seeing them all, laid out in chronological order.

"Man's thorough. I'll give him that."

"And smart, and pure evil."

"He's outsmarted my men, so far at least. He's given us nothing to go on. Absolutely nothing"

"Anything you can use?"

"Nope. Nada."

After reading them, and rereading them, he returned the binder to her. Brennan did not show any anger at her, or disappointment, or condemnation. Instead, he offered her a different way to atone for her sins. A form of redemption.

"Anyone could've written those letters to me."

"Right. Doesn't narrow down the list of suspects, certainly."

"Your men don't have a personal stake in this, Timothy. You don't, either. I do."

"I can see that. Is there is a little masochism going on here, maybe? His pleasure, your pain?"

"I'm not buying I'm a masochist, Brennan. It's total bullshit. I'm not enjoying any of this, believe me. I want him gone."

"Point taken. He is a sadist, though."

"No kidding. He's one sadistic motherfucker, only to Bauer, not to me. Not anymore."

"Okay, but there is something interesting going on here, at least from where I sit."

"Which is…?

"You'd make one great criminal, Kim. Think about it. All he did was tell you he was going to kill someone. It's the only admission he actually made. Not a crime. Then you went to work. You figured out the victim, an adult male, and you were correct. What weapon he was going to use. Correct again. You were right about the crime scene."

"All true." She did not tell Brennan it was all figured out by the dynamic duo, herself and Delaney. It was not because she wanted to hog the credit. There was no point in both of them being in jeopardy.

"Your stakeout came up a little short, maybe, though overall, pretty good detective work, Barbieri. I should know. You should be giving yourself a medal, not beating yourself up."

"Man's dead. His killer got away. I let him. I went along with his lunacy."

"That's where you're wrong. He didn't need you to kill Bauer. He didn't need you to get away."

"I could've brought you in from day one, Timothy."

"I doubt it would've made any difference. We couldn't have stopped him. Maybe scared him off. Then he'd find some other victim in some other location. We don't have enough cops to be everywhere. He was going to get away."

Barbieri did not say anything. Intellectually, she knew what he was saying was true, yet it did not make a dent in her frustration. *This guy outed me. I'm not a reporter. I thought like this murderer, which means I'm an evil bitch who knows how to take a life. Or I'm a great detective who figured out how to stop him but didn't. Either way, I was a patsy. His patsy.*

"I'm a control freak, am I not?"

She looked at Brennan, not understanding where he was going with the admission. "Yes. Your way or the highway, I believe the saying goes."

"Except with you. Why?"

"I won't let you."

"And I know you won't let me. Works for both of us. So let's seize control from him, Barbieri. You want to get this guy, right?"

"You bet your ass I do, but there's nothing we can do."

"No. There is something. Remember what I said about stupidity, Barbieri. It never fails."

He said his piece, and she said hers. Barbieri trusted Brennan more than anyone, and she found his confidence reassuring. Misplaced, perhaps, yet definitely reassuring,

She refilled their wineglasses, and as the wine took hold, they spent the rest of the evening doing nothing except listening to the second and third acts of *Tosca* by Giacomo Puccini.

Chapter Sixty-nine

Friday, May 5
10:15 AM

So close.

The deed was done. She had failed the challenge, and a person unknown had gotten away with the murder of an innocent victim. Barbieri had not expected a seventh note from the killer, and a part of her wished she had never received it. Yet seven days after the last one, it arrived. Unlike the others, though, this one was delivered not to her mailbox, but to the inbox on her ancient Dell laptop.

It was the morning she had decided, finally, to stop putting off the task of filling up the computer's trash can icon with old files and apps, and emptying it out. *This isn't a trip down memory lane for me. I'm just hoping it'll run a little faster if I take out the trash.* Her editor had not yet contacted her, and she looked forward to a whole day of doing not much at all. The only item on her agenda was waiting for the snail mail to come—hopefully without another letter from the killer.

Fortified with some strong coffee, she began the morning sprawled out on the sofa, still in her pajamas, reading the *Times* while watching cable news. *I'll get to it. I will.* Just reading an actual newspaper set her apart from her millenial neighbors, who no longer read anything that was not online. If it made her a relic from an earlier age, she at least thought of herself as a well-informed one.

When the first part of her morning ritual was done, she went on to the next: the crossword. Friday's was the toughest for her, and she kept at it until the last box was filled in. She thought of the puzzle as a contest between herself and the writer who created it, a war of words playing to two of her strengths, logic and language. It was a contest she would never allow herself to lose, and as usual, she prevailed.

The crossword solved, she was now out of excuses. *Suck it up, Barbieri. Let's get this over with.* She turned off the TV, forced herself up off the sofa and shuffled down the hall to the study. After moving over a pile of yellow writing pads to make room for her coffee, she sat down at her desk, booted up the Dell, and began the search-and-destroy operation.

In the middle of identifying the files most deserving of a proper burial, a new email alert popped up on the display. She had long ago deleted her personal email account from the computer, yet had never bothered to delete her @nydailynews.com account.

The alert was as good an excuse as any to take a break. She logged on, went to her new mail folder and clicked on the incoming message. She did not recognize the sender's Gmail address, though that failed to set off any alarms. She was used to getting emails from total strangers. The subject line was a simple "Important Information." *A little blind yet harmless.* The second Barbieri saw the content—*So close*—she knew exactly who had sent it. *How did he get my email address? Wait. How can this bozo be stupid enough to use his personal email? Now he wants me to find him?*

Her sense of relief that she had finally caught a break was only fleeting, of course. It abruptly ended as soon as she came to her senses. *He got my address from the* Daily News *website. He saw how the paper's employee email addresses were formatted, and entered my name the same way. I've done it myself on other sites. He no doubt closed his account the second he emailed me. Gone forever. Probably destroyed the device he sent it from, too. It's as if the account, and the killer himself, never existed.*

She noted he had not texted her, which probably meant he did not have her phone number…at least not yet. Still, she sensed him reaching her by email was somehow more sinister, or at least more intrusive, than by snail mail. Either way, there was nothing she could do about it. The email had no attachment, yet that did not ease her anxiety any. The old PC had only primitive antiviral protection, not enough to thwart the latest generation of viruses. *Why didn't I open his email on my Mac? PCs are a lot more vulnerable to viruses, aren't they? What if he just stole all my files? What if I just let him breach the paper's network?* Barbieri was no geek, although she did not have to be to see her old computer was now officially more trouble than it was worth. *It's made me and my online existence both more vulnerable. Screw sentimentality. Toss it. Our long-term relationship has to end sometime.*

Opting for complete security from a risk she did not fully understand, she unplugged the Dell's internet cable, inserted a sanitizer disk to remove every single bit of her personal information from the hardware, and dumped it in the garbage. *Done. Good riddance.*

The damage contained, at least in her mind, she went back to the message itself —*So close*—quickly noting this seventh communication was as anonymous as the first six and wouldn't bring her any closer to finding the killer. *Will this sadistic fuck keep writing to me in order to keep me involved? Does he want to make sure I'm implicated if he's ever caught? The cretin should realize by now that's not going to happen.*

While she had hoped, with the murder done, her involvement with the killer would be officially over, she did not want to end their relationship just yet. She definitely had issues needing closure. *Unbelievable! Jerk's not used to women like me. He's still trying to control me. He clearly hasn't caught on I'm done with him. Once I tear him a new one, then he can take a hike.*

She wanted to speak with him. She had to speak with him. She knew she would be lying to herself if she claimed her motivation was not personal at all, but entirely professional. She had interviewed plenty of criminals, and she would not have minded the opportunity to do so with him. Beyond the Journalism 101 questions all crime reporters must ask, there was one other she would demand be answered by the killer. Question number one would be *"Who are you, really?"* Question number two was *"How did you pull off the perfect murder?"* Question number three would be more open-ended. *"Why?"*

It was question number four she was most afraid of asking him, because she might not be ready to hear the answer. *"Am I next?"* While she was certain she would not be, Brennan was not so sure. Criminals had no use for star witnesses. She convinced herself the killer wanted his story told, and chose her to be the storyteller. She had been wrong before.

~ * ~

I was just having a little fun, sending the reporter an email instead of the usual letter. Break in the routine. It had nothing to do with the chance postal inspectors would get their hands on the mail I sent her. The only evidence they'd find would've been left by all the mailmen who handled my mail, not by me.

I was pretty sure she was still spooked by the whole thing, and I wanted to let her know I wasn't done with her even though I'd done what I set out to do. Didn't take much. Just went to the library, where they have computers anyone can use, opened a phony account, sent her an email to her address at the paper, and closed the account. No way to trace it back to me.

I really am a sick puppy.

Chapter Seventy

Senior Mobile Application Developer. New York City. $125K. Get Bizzy. Click here.

Standing next to dead bodies day in and day out, interviewing relatives and colleagues, Barbieri was only too aware of the ripple effects murders could have. Kid suddenly had one parent, not two. Woman lost a cousin close enough to be her sister. In Gil Bauer's case, a mobile app company might unexpectedly have an empty desk to fill. It was only a hunch, yet in a matter of seconds, she found the ad confirming it on indeed.com. *Didn't take them very long, did it?*

Acting on her own as her paper had assigned the Bauer story to another reporter, Barbieri decided to interview the head of Bauer's department at Get Bizzy. The interview might, just might, give her something to go on, an insight able to point her toward Bauer's killer. If not directly, then by giving her an idea that could get her wheels turning. The alternative was doing nothing.

His ex-boss was a woman named Miriam McConnell. Barbieri had told her over the phone she was a reporter for the *Daily News*, which led the exec to believe she was being interviewed for a story that would appear in the paper.

Barbieri intended to say nothing to straighten her out. At two in the afternoon, six days after the murder, she went up to Get Bizzy's offices on East Twenty-First off Fifth, in the Flatiron District. There was no receptionist to point her in Miriam's direction, so she asked the first person she made eye contact with, a young woman sitting alone on a sofa, legs tucked beneath her, staring intently at her laptop. She pointed to herself. "You're right on time."

After the introductions and the obligatory exchange about how sorry they both were to have to meet under such circumstances, Miriam walked Barbieri to a small conference room, the only one with a door in the whole place. Sitting across a small table from Miriam, Barbieri glanced at the woman's left forearm and noticed a tattoo going all the way up to her shoulder, some kind of oriental flower design with Japanese characters. *At least it's not something morbid like a skull or a devil. I've had enough of death.*

On the way to the conference room, they passed through a workspace a world apart from the ADA's. It was not so much an office as an industrial-strength playpen, a free-for-all replacing an organization chart with a clear pecking order. One big open space rather than walls and doors and cubicles. Many women and a few men young enough to remind her of how obsolete she was. *Probably neighbors of mine. Did I see her at the health food store? Wait, wasn't she at the funeral?* Pool tables and coffee bars if they did not feel like working. Humongous computer screens on every surface for when playtime was over.

"The app work Gil had been doing still needs to get done," his old boss explained, "and we began looking for someone to replace him right after the funeral."

Barbieri felt it was a little harsh, Miriam not mentioning upfront how blessed the company was to have Gil work there. Trying not to steer the conversation one way or another, Barbieri just listened and took notes. *With the door closed, maybe nobody except Miriam will notice I'm the only person here using pen and paper rather than a keyboard. I'm a dinosaur.*

"Projects have deadlines," Miriam continued. "Clients want it today, not tomorrow. They don't want to hear about our personnel or workload issues. We learned this lesson the hard way on more than one occasion. They want what they paid for and don't really give a crap about all the other deadlines we're facing at the same time. Or how everyone on our A team is too burnt out from too much overtime to think straight."

"Deliver, or we'll find someone who will," Barbieri said, getting to the gist of the executive's point. Paraphrasing was a proven way to keep people talking.

"Right. So, business being business, we bribe another hotshot app developer away from a hotshot competitor to take his place. Our gain is the other shop's loss. Now the other shop has to find a replacement for the gal we lured away, so they go out and bring in someone new from a third company."

"Hopefully not yours," Barbieri said, if only to confirm she was listening. So on and so on down the line. Empty desks needed to be filled, managers with titles got their hands dirty, and HR execs worked past five for a change. Nobody can't be replaced. Round and round she goes.

"I couldn't help but notice the staff is mostly female, and a lot younger than Gil Bauer," Barbieri said. "How did he manage to fit in?"

"There's no reverse sexism here. Big no-no. If you're good, you fit in, and Gil was damn good. Besides, we all needed a mentor, and he was the only one experienced enough. We all loved the guy." She paused for a moment, wondering if she had said too much. "Anything else I can help you with?"

"Not right now," Barbieri replied, putting away her notepad and rising from her chair.

"Great to meet you, Kim. If you know any mobile app superstars, tell them we're looking." Miriam got up to escort Barbieri out of the office.

"I'll do that." Barbieri thanked Gil's old boss for her time and told her she would discuss the article about this part of the deceased's life with her editor. She would not do any such thing, of course, since she was going rogue here, Cavanaugh-free. She had called the meeting to see if it could help her track down Bauer's murderer. It did not. The killer had gone off the grid. No identity. No description. No last known address. She still had no clue.

Well, this was a complete waste of an afternoon. I'm no closer now than I was this morning.

One thing came out of it, though. Barbieri did not know much about the software business, other than app developers were living large and she most definitely was not. She had no idea exactly how many of them were playing the latest version of corporate musical chairs, maybe a dozen or so, yet there were more than enough chairs in New York to go around. A number of Bauer's ex-colleagues would be finding themselves in new jobs in new companies with better titles and nice bumps in salary—and they had a mystery murderer to thank for it.

If I ever catch up to this guy, I'll tell him all the new Richie Riches he created should throw him a party.

Chapter Seventy-one

For several weeks now, there had been a killer on the loose in her fair city, and Kim Barbieri was the only one to have even a vague idea of who he was. More like a wisp of an idea. *Like the detectives who caught the case, all I know about him is that he's gotten away with murder. Could be anybody, even the harmless old fart sitting at the next table, trying to make a cup of coffee last for another hour.*

She was at Gregory's Coffee on Carlton Avenue, a few blocks from her home, trying to figure out her next steps. *Why on Earth did I think it was a good idea to violate rule number one in the reporters' code of conduct? Never become part of the story.*

Until the sixth letter, when she decided she had had enough and was determined to turn the tables on the killer, she paid a pretty steep emotional price for her sins.

It was irrational. Crazy even. He killed Bauer. Without me. He was going to kill Bauer even if he never wrote me.

The old doubts, the self-questioning, were beginning to creep back. She knew better, yet still found herself unable to prevent them. *Did I aid and abet the killing of Gil Bauer? No. Not at all. So why am I banging my damn head against the fuckin' wall again?*

Chapter Seventy-two

One thing I've learned after the little dustup at the Albion. If you want to feel you have things well under control, you might want to think about something else besides executing a guy you never met before.

It's supposed to be the absolute control, isn't it, being able to dictate whether a person lives or dies? I have yet to figure out why I feel I need it, this sense of control. Was it missing in my life? Wasn't I always master of my domain at work? I had all the autonomy I needed to do my job, and the bosses learned to just stay out of my way. I delivered, and they got rich.

At home, my wife and I never had a problem deciding who wore the pants. She did, if only by default. When I worked fourteen-hour days it was up to her to run our home, call the plumber, keep the cars running, all that. My sensitive male ego never felt threatened by her, not in the least.

After I did the deed, I did in fact feel more in control, in all senses of the word. Can't deny it. I had the power of life and death and acted on it. I took someone's life away. By myself. I controlled the whole enterprise. I did everything I had to do to plan the crime, make a clean getaway, and keep my role secret from everyone and it was all flawless. It's like the power of God, a supernatural force, and I had it.

Textbook case of narcissism.

Kind of heady, I have to admit. To be honest, though, my inner control freak wasn't able to savor the moment for long. This feeling of control came at an almost unbearable price. The fear of being found out somehow, the fear of my wife discovering I lied to her, and the fear I was a deranged monster all became a part of me I couldn't ever shake off. It made me afraid I was losing control of my faculties and I didn't like it one bit. I couldn't think straight.

The force was with me, true, although it turned out to be a very dark force indeed.

~ * ~

Was the murder my mystery man committed an act of cowardice or of courage?

A lot of people Barbieri spoke with, inside and outside law enforcement, thought the guy was a complete coward for killing a defenseless, unarmed man who was totally unprepared for the attack. If this is not the act of a total coward, nothing is.

But then she took the trip back inside the killer's head and looked at the whole thing from his point of view. It was a bit of a stretch for her, because she was no shrink, nor a man, but at least it was an opportunity to move away from the usual focus on who, what, and where of her job and delve deeply into the why.

What the killer did was actually pretty brave on his part, considering. *I'm a solid citizen who committed one act a little out of character. I thrust myself way out of my comfort zone. Out of almost any decent citizen's comfort zone, for that matter.* This took guts, to put it mildly.

He also acted alone. There was no one there who had his back if things went south, or to share the blame with. *I alone risked the victim fighting back. I alone risked dying in prison.* There were also no mitigating circumstances his lawyer could offer as a defense. He had committed as unwarranted and cold-blooded a killing as anyone could imagine. Not even a hint of an excuse was possible. Plus, the crime could have been witnessed by hundreds of people, if he miscalculated how long the screen, and the theater, would keep him unnoticed.

Thinking like the killer, Barbieri gave herself plenty of reasons to make the transition from condemnation of a heinous act to admiration of a job well done. *On the other hand, maybe it's all nonsense. All the bravery rationale I can conjure up doesn't change the fact I took the life of a defenseless man who didn't deserve to die. It wasn't a fair fight at all. It was the act of a schoolyard bully.*

Meaning I'm also guilty of cowardice, not just murder.

Chapter Seventy-three

I sort of expected one victim of the murder I'd committed would be myself.

I know I'm damaged goods, haunted by the knowledge I'm now a stone-cold assassin with one confirmed hit under my belt. I try to tell myself I'm not a murderer, but rather a normal guy who committed one murder. To be honest, I underestimated how much I'd be changed by my one act of malice.

The me everyone knew, including myself, was smart, deliberate, considerate, talented. I could've easily described myself as accomplished, kind, reliable, and moral. Not a Boy Scout by any means, but all good for the most part. True, I had one or two character flaws, yet I think it's fair to say I came across as a pretty decent fellow. It's how I saw myself, and hopefully how I was seen by others.

The new me, post-homicide, is all that still, although with an added layer of darkness unseen by the outside world.

It's as if I'm keeping a secret I have no intention of sharing, and that feels good as well.

The other change for me is I've learned a new science, having taken a crash course in anatomy. I also mastered a new skill, homicide. I acquired it the old-fashioned way, with a lot of preparation and some hands-on experience. I can't boast here, either. So although outwardly I'm the same guy everyone knew, or thought they knew, inside I've acquired a whole new dimension, a whole new level of complexity. And evil. And power. It's as if I became a superhero in reverse. If you push my buttons I wouldn't change into my costume and come to your rescue, I'd pull out a knife and take your life.

It's one strange feeling, this power of life and death.

I'm keeping it all to myself, with everyone I know totally unaware of my dark side. Needless to say I have no one to talk to about this personality quirk, no one to lean on or share with, even if I wanted to. I don't mind a bit, which may be the scariest part of the whole thing.

Chapter Seventy-four

Brooklyn South Homicide was feeling the heat. Bauer's murder, exactly the kind of high-profile crime that tended to give voters *agita*, got noticed by City Hall. The city fathers, who did not like it when voters got angry, put a lot of pressure on the brass at One Police Plaza. Who in turn put pressure on Captain Timothy Brennan. Who relayed it to the six experienced detectives he had put on the case.

For weeks, those investigators did everything by the book. They knocked on hundreds of doors around the Albion Theater: on homes, businesses, churches, and synagogues. Nobody saw a thing. Nobody heard a thing. The investigators looked into Gil Bauer's life in the days and weeks before the murder, interviewing his friends and relatives, his colleagues at Get Bizzy, to see if anyone noticed anything out of the ordinary right before he was killed. They had not. The investigators set up a tip line, hoping a nice fat reward might induce someone to drop a dime on the killer. They tracked down several anonymous tips, but there was nothing there. Waste of time.

No evidence of any kind had been left at the crime scene. No clues were going to come from any lab. No leads came of all the investigators' intense, thorough efforts. Unless the killer walked into a police station and gave himself up, it appeared the crime was headed to the cold case file.

Captain Brennan was not pleased. He always took it personally when it looked like an idiot was about to escape the justice he richly deserved.

~ * ~

This brutal killing, the murder Barbieri came close to preventing, had given New Yorkers a nasty reminder of the way things were years before, a climate nobody had any nostalgia for. Who did the good citizens blame? Cops, of course. It was their fault for not assigning an officer to sit between Gil Bauer and his murderer.

Morale inside the NYPD, especially among the homicide detectives in Brooklyn, had taken a real beating in the weeks since Gil Bauer had met his maker. Not catching the perp only made it worse: the political pressure to clear capital cases and get killers off the streets matched by the determination the detectives put on themselves. Barbieri could not help but feel their pain. *Cops take these cases very personally, and they hate to leave a crime unsolved. Can't let them go. Open cases eat away at them, sometimes for years.*

That was one reason Brennan and his detectives were totally out of joint. They had no suspect and made no arrest. The case was open, taunting them to no end. The other reason was detectives operated under the assumption all criminals were morons, thugs, dumb as a bucket of hair. They hated to think they had been outsmarted by an idiot. *Anyone who knows a cop, especially a commander, knows it's true.*

The murderer himself thought he was the exception to the rule. He was no idiot by a long shot. Yet the detectives trying to find him did not know that. They took it as a given he was too stupid not to get caught sooner or later. He would make a stupid mistake or blab to the wrong person. They always did, the shmucks. This had not happened—yet. The killer no doubt realized he was not any smarter than they were, just not any dumber, either. No mistakes.

Chapter Seventy-five

The killer's still at large. He hasn't been arrested or even interrogated. He hasn't confessed. He's still living somewhere in the city, most likely not far from where I am right now, 336 Vanderbilt, between DeKalb and Lafayette, apartment 1B.

The morning paper was filled with the latest installment of political outrages and sex scandals and wasteful spending. Bauer was yesterday's news. As Barbieri had every morning since the murder of Gil Bauer, she went straight to the metro page crime blotter.

She hoped to read about the killer being stopped by a police officer while shopping or jogging. Either that or a convoy of huge, angry armored personnel carriers would converge on his house one night, and a huge, angry SWAT team would tase him into submission and drag him away. Her letters, and her involvement, would not be of any consequence. *He wouldn't talk.*

Those expectations were misplaced. The investigators continued hitting one dead end after another. Every day the killer remained a free man, he probably felt a little more comfortable with the idea he had actually succeeded.

She knew when police hit a brick wall they sometimes sent a message out to the community asking all the good citizens to be their eyes and ears. "Have you seen this man?" "He may be armed and dangerous." That sort of thing. She had been at 1PP a number of times to hear detectives reach out to the media, so she was not at all surprised to find the story she had long expected would be there.

BAUER MURDER: POLICE ADVISE CAUTION.

Captain Timothy Brennan, Commander of the Brooklyn South Homicide Squad, reported today that the investigators of the Gilberto Bauer murder had hit a wall and were no closer to finding the killer than they were on the day of the homicide.

Bauer, fifty-four years old at the time of his passing, was found stabbed to death in the Albion Theater, on Flatbush Avenue and Albemarle Road, on April 28th of this year. The detectives have not found the murder weapon, presumed to be a knife. Witnesses at the theater did not report any altercation or disturbance and were not even aware the crime had occurred.

Until the killer is caught, Captain Brennan advised anyone living and working in the city to be extra cautious. "If you're going to a public event like the movies or a baseball game," he warned, "you should be alert and aware of people sitting nearby. If they're acting suspiciously in any way, notify an usher or security guard. Likewise, at public spaces such as Times Square and Orchard Beach. Until we apprehend the suspect, we're allocating more police resources to these areas, flooding the zone if you will, ready to respond rapidly to your 911 call."

Noting that Bauer was Hispanic, Captain Brennan cautioned, "Members of the Latino community should be extra careful about whom they socialize with. I want to remind everyone there is no evidence at this time the killer is targeting the Hispanic community in particular, but we can't be certain he isn't, either."

The captain urged anyone with any information about the murder to call the NYPD anonymous tipline, 800 577 TIPS, or visit https://crimestoppers.nypdonline.org. He noted the reward for information helping the police department identify and capture the perpetrator has been increased to $50,000.

Chapter Seventy-six

Can you mourn the death of someone you killed? I think I do.

Far as I can remember, I hadn't even once crossed paths with Gil Bauer before that afternoon at the Albion. My company never did business with his. He and I didn't travel in the same circles. He was Spanish, true, but Helen and I weren't prejudiced.

On some level, I guess, I regret I killed a good citizen like him, rather than some worthless bum or junkie a little more deserving of the death penalty. Would it have eased my guilt if I'd done a good deed and taken out some lowlife society won't miss?

I want to know more about Gil Bauer. I know it's kind of macabre, taking an interest in someone you recently dispatched. I mean, the last thing you want to do when you take someone's life is to somehow make the act more regrettable than it already is. Yet I can't help myself. Gil wasn't a public figure of any kind, so there's very little for me to get from the news reports—only the name of his employer, apps he developed, that kind of thing. There's his Facebook page, which nobody's bothered to take down yet, telling the world which college buddies he kept it touch with, which movies he liked and which causes he supported. It was what he wanted people to know about him. His more private side he chose to keep to himself. I can speak with people he'd been close to, real flesh-and-blood human beings. Chatting up his wife seems to be a little too risky, as far as not arousing suspicion is concerned, but I figure his mom and dad might be more than willing to talk about their son. Safer for me too, I think.

Six weeks after the murder, I call his parents at their home number. They probably don't even have a cell, neither of them. I figure by now they've had enough time to deal with their loss and move on, if that's even possible when you outlive your child.

Anyway, when his father picks up, I introduce myself and tell him Gil and I had been college buddies who had lost touch, and I'd only recently found out about his passing. I tell him how sorry I am for them, and would they be willing to meet me over coffee and talk about their son? Maybe reminisce about our friendship back then and find out from them what I'd missed not seeing him all these years. I guess it sounded plausible enough, and he agrees, certain he was authorized to speak for his wife, too.

I also tell him I'd missed Gilbert's funeral, unfortunately, as I was out of town. I don't really expect him or his wife to remember me being there, given their emotional state at the time—and my clever little disguise. If they do, I know I'll be able to talk my way out of it.

Few days later, ten in the morning, the three of us are sitting at a booth at a diner his parents suggested near their home. It's almost a clone of the one in my neighborhood, where I hang out. Same mirrors everywhere, same counter, same vinyl seats, same aromas all the Glade in the world wouldn't remove. These generic diner designers sure knew what they were doing. It feels like I've been there a million times. I can't say for sure, but my guess is Mr. and Mrs. Bauer chose this particular place for us to meet precisely because of the comfort level. It's someplace they know well. I bet they practically raised Gil there, comparing child development notes with all the other moms and dads and grandparents congregating there.

On the morning we agree to meet, I commandeer a booth by the window, facing the front door, and recognize the Bauers as soon as they walk in. I wave them over. Luckily, neither of them shows any sign they recognize me from the funeral. One bullet dodged. Mr. Bauer is, I guess, seventy-five, seventy-six, Mrs. Bauer a little younger, maybe seventy-two. They may actually be not quite as old as they look. They must've aged plenty in the last few weeks. They're both pretty somber, no surprise there, as they're clearly still in mourning. Probably always will be.

They introduce themselves and sit down next to each other, across from me. I'd been right about the funeral. Their English was close to perfect, though I could detect a slight Spanish accent. Just a trace. Sitting so close, I can't help but notice each one's resemblance to Gil. How much pain their eyes reveal, too. Weary, beaten, empty.

After our waitress comes over and takes our order, I thank them again for agreeing to meet with me and remind them Gil and I had last seen each other way back in college, maybe twenty-five years ago. I ask Gil's mom and dad—it's how I thought of them, as if he were still with us—to talk about whatever they wanted about their boy. Right as they begin to respond, our waitress comes back with our orders—bacon and eggs for me, a bran muffin for each of them—and fills our coffee mugs. As we all begin eating, I simply listen to them, not even thinking of interrupting their reminiscences of the son they'll never see again.

They tell me Gilberto—it was his given name, and they stuck with it—was a wonderful boy who never caused them a bit of trouble. Not much different from the eulogy I'd heard a few weeks before. They also tell a few anecdotes the eulogy didn't mention, like how great he was in Little League, the volunteer work he did in the hospital. His mom and dad also bring out some pictures of their son as a child, as a teenager, at his wedding, the usual highlight reel of a normal, happy life. I can't tell if they erased any bad memories they'd had of their son, or even if they ever had any. Gilberto was just a great kid, who grew up to be a good man, good student, good husband, good computer guy. He would've been a great father too, if fate hadn't had other plans for him. Nothing much more to say.

I tell them all I know about his case was what I'd read in the paper, and they both assure me the police are holding nothing back. They're as much in the dark about the investigation as everyone else. I then venture into very dangerous territory, for me anyway, considering the weird role I'm playing in their life.

"What would you two do if the killer is caught? Demand the death penalty?"

It takes them a minute or two to think about my questions, which they clearly haven't heard before, and formulate their answer. His dad replies. "If he's caught? We've wondered about it, although we never agree on anything."

I let that hang a bit, waiting for his mom to elaborate.

"Part of us wants the man dead, naturally. We also want him to suffer in prison for the rest of his life. One punishment's worse than the other."

"Either would do."

I offer to break the tie and give them my choice of punishment, life or the chair, and they decline my offer. I was tempted to tell them New York State doesn't have the death penalty anymore, yet I didn't. Let them have their fantasies. If there was a death penalty, though, I'm not sure I'd choose it even then. I don't want to be killed by the state about as much as I don't want to spend the rest of my life in maximum security.

After about an hour of this reminiscing I call the waitress over and ask for the check, making it clear to Gilbert's mom and dad breakfast is on me. As the busboys take away our now-empty dishes and clean up our table, I thank his parents for seeing me, they thank me for the opportunity to talk about their son, and we say our goodbyes. I come away from our meeting a little shaken, believe me. While I'm fully satisfied with the successful conclusion of my project, it turns out I'm a little troubled by this particular aspect of the hit.

I've decimated his mom and dad, broken their hearts, and they deserve better. They truly do. I took their little boy away from them, and I'm not ever giving him back. I should've anticipated it, did anticipate it in fact. I mean, I told myself early on the family my victim leaves behind is of no consequence to me. People lose loved ones all the time and get over it. So the impact of a son's death on his parents wasn't a deal-breaker as far as my project went. Now, though, the conversation with Mr. and Mrs. Bauer really rattles me.

Looking back, the chance I'd be taking the life of a living parent's child didn't stop me from committing murder. Maybe, just maybe, it should have.

Chapter Seventy-seven

One morning, during my ritual passage from bedroom to coffeemaker to kitchen table, I find myself looking in the bathroom mirror, trying to understand the person staring back at me.

I take a really good hard look at myself, as if I'm eyeballing a complete stranger for the first time, a more intense examination than I've ever given myself before. I look into his eyes, expecting pure evil to be looking back at me. I look at his face, his hands. I can't see beyond the surface, but I thought somehow I'd see something, *anything*, that wasn't there before the person staring back at me evolved from Mr. Nice Guy into a homicidal maniac. A monster who committed first-degree murder.

I'm half expecting to see a new person, an individual who's undergone a transformation of some kind. Is he bipolar like Helen said back on the day of the murder? If he is, would he look any different? Would he carry himself differently? Would his inner demon turn into an outer demon, ready to scare the shit out of anyone he saw?

I was afraid I'd see in my reflection the monster I'd created, yet the person who's looking back is definitely only me. Nothing unusual. Nothing different. Not pure evil, like I'd feared. No danger to the community. My hands don't look like they could be used to kill anybody.

No monster. Me. About the only difference are the teeny-tiny changes in skin and hair and eyes you get from being a day older than you were the day before.

Notice I say I'm studying *him* in the mirror. Third person. I'm not sure there's any deeper meaning, though I'm well aware of the way I'm viewing the killer. It isn't me, it's him. Like I'm not taking responsibility for my actions. I know it's all bullshit, in that I'm one hundred percent sure the killer is me. I'm no schizo. I merely want to see the person others see.

Another coping mechanism, I guess.

I have indeed reinvented myself, yet the transformation is completely internal, invisible to the outside world. I also know deep inside the change isn't permanent. I feel completely normal, leading a completely mundane, unremarkable life. I blend into the background. The good citizens I share my city with have nothing to worry about from me, I swear.

~ * ~

Took a while, but soon after I gave Gil Bauer his termination papers, it was as if nothing happened. The murder stopped being topic number one, and the murderer, yours truly, is back to being the friend and neighbor and customer everyone knows.

Seems everyone decides to get on with their lives, including me.

One day I take the car in for a tune-up, long overdue. Garage is over on Flatbush and U. The mechanic and I talk while he checks under the hood, me trying my best to sound like I know what he's tinkering with. I don't. He knows I don't, but it's the game we're both in on, always been in on, making me feel like I know as much about transmissions and suspensions as he does. Probably the same game he plays with every customer who brings their pile of junk in for service.

On my way home, I stop at the same lawn and garden place on Nostrand I've gone to every Saturday morning forever. Again, nothing. No fingers pointing in my direction. No wife suddenly pulling her husband close and whispering urgently in his ear. It's like I'm invisible. My dark side sure is.

One night, Helen and I go out for Italian with Zoe, George, Cherie and Mike. We go back a long way, the six of us. I don't give anything away. There's no tell from me, just a normal evening out with friends. Life goes on. Either it's a massive conspiracy everyone I know is in on, or they really are clueless. Murderer's on the loose. They're all talking with him, joking with him, complaining about their bursitis and crooked repairmen with him, dissing mutual friends with him. Marriage is the perfect camouflage. If they only knew.

I've become completely comfortable with living normally after taking another man's life. Is this something a sane person would do?

~ * ~

As she did every Thursday morning, Barbieri picked up a bottle of water at the deli on the corner of Dekalb and Carlton, then took the subway out to her aunt's home in darkest Brooklyn, making sure to stop off at the diner on Coney Island Avenue first.

Sitting on her usual stool at the end of the counter, nursing her tea, she noticed the table right behind her was occupied by the same group of regulars. Four middle-aged friends. Like this particular table was theirs, not the diner's. One of them ordered the same breakfast he always did, iced coffee and key lime pie. *They're always here when I'm here. Creatures of habit.* She did not pick up any stalker vibes from any of them, she was sure of that.

She overheard them discussing the same guy stuff they did last Thursday morning, and the Thursday morning before that. The economy, the playoffs, the primaries—everyone weighed in with his two cents every so often, like always. Everyone listened and either nodded like he was a sage or dismissed him with an insult to his ancestors, like they did a thousand times before.

In terms of everyone's day-to-day routine, post-murder became no different from pre-murder. *Remarkable.*

Chapter Seventy-eight

One insight her job gave Barbieri, which the killer might not have factored into his calculations, was the number of times police officers and average citizens were in the same place at the same time.

If the killer is indeed a little on the paranoid side, he'd have to go about his affairs under the assumption that eventually the police will be canvassing his own neighborhood and stop him for questioning. Have to, if they're getting nowhere. In which case he better be prepared.

Officers in radio cars were cruising the streets all day, every day, either making their presence felt or looking for anyone who might be trouble. Even rush hour, when they were more interested in drivers behaving badly than pedestrians behaving badly. While their minds might be on keeping cars from T-boning each other, they were still keeping an eye out for specific bad guys wanted by the detectives. *At least the gung-ho rookies are. Couple of ride-alongs I've taken, they actually spotted one and brought him in. Higher-ups noticed, too.*

Having an unsolved homicide like Bauer's on their hands made cops even more vigilant, the reporter knew, and more determined to put the killer behind bars. Police officers and their families didn't want a bad guy ruining their day, either.

The killer's probably already created a list in his head of the questions the detectives would likely be asking him and rehearsed the answers he expects to give them. He no doubt knows as well as I do cops ask trick questions just to trip suspects up. In which case he'd have to improvise and make stuff up without a tell.

The problem for the killer was he knew every last detail about the murder the investigators were trying to solve, more than they did certainly. *He knows what the murder weapon was and where it was dumped. He knows why Bauer was killed, which was no reason at all, and he of course knows the murderer very well.* Given all that, though, he probably thinks he is smart enough to convince any detectives he is not their guy and to take their questions elsewhere. He would not play games here, or give them answers just a little off-kilter.

When the cops sent him on his way, he wanted himself off their radar permanently.

~ * ~

Fuckin' police are everywhere.

I mean, you can't walk down the street or go to the supermarket without being followed by a lot of eyeballs. Before I entered the dark side, I was glad they were there. They protected me and my family from evildoers. Not now. Now cops are the last people I want to run into. What if I'm questioned by cops assigned to investigate the murder of Gil Bauer? I know they have absolutely no reason to suspect me, yet there's no reason I couldn't be stopped at random, on the whim of some detective who'd run out of solid leads and was just clutching at straws.

I may have been a little paranoid here, although not without reason. Which is why I've rehearsed, over and over again, the dialogue I imagine I'll be having if I do get stopped. I want the questioning over quickly, and I want the police to walk away convinced I'm the wrong guy.

"Sir, got a moment? Ask you a few questions?" I've never actually been questioned by police, although I've seen enough cop shows to anticipate how they'd begin.

"Me? Sure," I'd answer without a moment's hesitation. Open and cooperative, nothing whatsoever to hide.

"April 28th? Remember where you were that afternoon? 'Round three, three thirty?"

"April 28th? No idea. It was a while ago." I'd act like I was trying to think back and come up empty. "What happened on April 28th?"

"Incident we're investigating." The detectives wouldn't be giving the game away, hoping I'd mention the murder first.

Then it would come to me. "Oh geez, you're looking into the murder at the movie theater," I'd reply in sort of a surprised way. The investigators wouldn't respond right away. They'd just stare at me, hoping I'd give them a straight answer for once so they could end the interview and move on to the next non-suspect on their route. "I think I was at Kings Plaza, shopping for a raincoat. I remember it was a waste of an afternoon after finding nothing I'd ever wear." Straight answer, and a perfectly plausible one, I hope. I wouldn't have to produce a receipt, and there's nothing for them to corroborate with Helen. Given that they have no description of the killer to go by and I'm just a random average Joe, I doubt the police would check out security camera recordings at any of the men's stores to see if I was there.

"Okay. Anyone you know was at the Albion Theater? Nobody say anything to you about going there?"

"No, sir. Sorry. I'd remember something like that," I'd answer. Again, quick and unambiguous.

"Okay. Thanks. Hear anything, let us know," they'd say, handing me a business card I'd make a point of putting in my shirt pocket for safekeeping.

This would be the extent of my interrogation, at least in my mind. Police would probably do a lot of asking around in the Bauer case, due to the fact that it's a high-profile murder of an upstanding member of the middle class, and get much the same answers to the same questions time and time again. Seen nothing. Heard nothing. Know nothing. What if the detectives see something in me that looks a bit sketchy? A nervous gesture, maybe, sudden sweating, or something in my voice. A tell noticeable to them but not to me. If the polite, strictly-a-formality questions become more like an interrogation, would I be able to keep my cool? I don't know, and it's a little troubling to me. Not being able to think things through doesn't sit well with me at all. I've always been able to maintain a pretty good poker face when I'm sitting across the negotiating table, but that's when only my company's profit margin is at stake. Would I able to do so when it's my freedom on the line? Or my life? I don't want to find out.

One scenario I've imagined over and over actually gives me nightmares. What if I get caught? What if I'm too clever for my own good and leave a teensy clue behind, pointing the cops right to my front door? I haven't yet, since I'm still a free man, yet there's always the possibility my perfect crime could've had just a slight imperfection that turns into the break the detectives need to find the guilty party. Then what?

Well, I'd answer the doorbell one day, and there'd be two detectives at my front door ready to bring me in for questioning. If their evidence holds up, if they've got me dead to rights, the DA who catches the case would do whatever it takes to make sure I spend every single day under lock and key for the rest of my damn life.

Chapter Seventy-nine

Once the investigation into Gil Bauer's murder comes to a complete standstill, it'll stay there for good. I know that as much as anybody. There are cold cases that all of a sudden get hot again after a DNA search, but this won't be one of them. The killer was careful not to leave any of his behind.

To Barbieri as much as to the NYPD, it was as if the perpetrator had disappeared into thin air. She knew from all her years on the job the chances of an arrest got worse by the day. Cops were assigned to new crimes that needed solving. Enough time passes by and the chances of clearing the case drop to zero. The Bauer case would be as cold as they come. Eternally open. Filed and forgotten, gathering dust in some basement somewhere.

It doesn't matter if the statute of limitations doesn't apply in murder cases. He'll remain a free man forever.

The killer still had not shown up on police radar. *Why would he, after all the work he's done to make the police clueless?* All the leads the detectives pursued led nowhere. They knew of no one who had a grudge against the victim, or would profit from his death, or would reap any financial windfall from his insurance.

I don't care what Brennan says. The perp isn't stupid enough to be caught, and I'll never get to interview him. Or stick an icepick in his eyeball.

From the messages the killer sent her, Barbieri came to believe the murderer was both very methodical and very sick, with the latter trait canceling out the former, given enough time.

She was determined not to share her letters with the investigators, now or ever. Brennan would not, either; he gave her his word. She also knew the detectives who caught the case would retire or die or be promoted to uselessness at some point. Brennan thought the guy was so stupid he would get himself caught, eventually. If they were making progress, they were keeping it from her.

She checked in regularly with the *Daily News* reporter covering the case, the one staff writer left on the metro desk. She followed the story in the *Post* as well as all the crime news websites, and shot the breeze from time to time with the detectives who caught the case.

They were well aware they did not have to talk to her. It was not her story. They had heard rumors she was no longer in the employ of the *Daily News*, followed by rumors she was back. They also knew she was at the Albion when the murder went down and wanted some kind of closure. So they kept her in the loop, even feeding her information they usually held back from the public. Loyalty ran in both directions.

The detectives, she surmised, did not have much to go on. All she was able to glean from her sources were the basic facts about the case.

The deceased was a Hispanic male named Gilberto Bauer. He was a mobile app developer, employed at Get Bizzy. He was fifty-four years old at the time of his death, and married. There were no children, natural or adopted. The victim was first-generation American, a child of Panamanian immigrants.

The crime occurred at the Albion Theater on Flatbush Avenue, on April 28th, at approximately 3:20 p.m. The cause of death was trauma to the heart: in particular, the severing of the thoracic aorta, which led to rapid, massive internal bleeding. The hemorrhaging, in turn, reduced the flow of blood to his brain cells, starving them of oxygen.

The death was the result of homicide perpetrated by person or persons unknown, rather than of suicide. The medical examiner determined the wound was caused by a knife or other sharp instrument, and was very neat, very precise. Almost surgical, in fact. No murder weapon was found near the body. It had yet to be recovered.

No potential sources of DNA evidence, such as friction ridges, hair, blood, or saliva, were found at the scene. The seats, the armrests, and the carpet underneath offered investigators nothing.

The body was discovered by a married couple named Marie and Philip Hemphill, 1745 Beverly Road in Kensington. They had no relationship to the deceased. They were simply going to a movie and happened to notice the victim's body as they were exiting the theater.

There were no witnesses to the murder. By the time the police got there, virtually everyone at the movie had gone their separate ways without realizing a crime had been committed.

The few who stayed and talked to the cops had not heard or seen anything, had not noticed any kind of dispute or fight, and certainly could not give a description of the killer. It all happened in the dark, too dark for anyone to see anything.

That was about it. From what Barbieri could gather, it was almost a given Bauer's killer would be charged with murder in the first degree. If he was ever found.

All the elements seemed to be there. The perpetrator unlawfully killed the victim. The perpetrator acted with malice aforethought, deliberately and intentionally. The killing appeared to be premeditated rather than impulsive. The perpetrator seemed to have fully considered the act and its consequences beforehand. The crime took place at a known location.

Because there had been no commotion or argument anyone noticed, it seemed logical to everyone else who touched the case that it was a planned hit by a stranger, rather than a crime of passion by someone the victim had known.

The deceased's wife, Karen, was quickly ruled out. In the murder cases involving husbands and wives Barbieri had covered, the spouse was almost automatically a suspect in the early stages of the investigation. In this case, Mrs. Bauer was able to fully account for her whereabouts on the afternoon in question.

The deceased's coworkers and clients were ruled out as well. Interviews with the police gave the impression Mr. Bauer was well-liked by everyone he worked with and had never screwed over a colleague or a client. A good guy, everyone agreed.

The deceased's friends were ruled out. The members of the Latino community who knew the victim all spoke well of him. None of the informers the police had embedded in Hispanic neighborhoods reported hearing any rumors about the crime.

No one spoke ill of the dead Gil Bauer.

This is where the case stands. This is how it'll stay.

The reporter held out hope that even if the cops never tracked him down, she would. *It's not to make sure he gets caught, tried and convicted. It's simply to make him answer all the questions keeping me awake at night. I want to make him pay for all the bad he did to me.*

Yet she knew in her gut this was not going to happen. He was gone for good—unless he decided to taunt her with another letter, post-murder.

Chapter Eighty

By six months or so after I expelled Gil Bauer from the land of the living, I'm one hundred percent sure I'll never be caught. The investigators have no doubt given up on finding Bauer's killer, and moved on to murders they can actually solve. Clearing cases makes them feel like they're actually accomplishing something, and looks good in the reports they send to headquarters.

I'm also no longer possessed by the idea I'm nuts. I continue to talk and act like a normal individual, and nobody reacts to me as if I'm going insane. Remember the mood swings Helen was worried about? If I had them back then, I haven't had any since. Which leads me to believe I've had nothing to worry about all along.

Although I've been a model citizen since the Monday matinee, I'm not quite done with the idea I'd been ill in the months before the crime. Not now. Then. A cured case of temporary insanity. The fear I hadn't been in full control at the time has become a loose thread the logical side of me simply can't stop pulling. I'm clutching at straws here. I still need proof, one way or the other. I can't go to a doctor to diagnose me, since any symptoms would be buried real deep, and I'd be given a clean bill of health. I think.

I'd have to diagnose myself, which means being honest with myself. I could put one over on the shrink, but what would be the point of deceiving myself? No, I'd have to be brutally honest with myself, including the whole thing about why I left the company. Did I take out my feelings about that prick Kelleher, and the whole damn company on some innocent stranger? Is there really anything to this? I'm not going there, believe me.

I do the next best thing. I take an online self-diagnosis test. It may be pointless in terms of diagnosing my mental health back when I killed Bauer, but at least it could put to rest any lingering questions I have. Amateur hour, I know.

Turns out figuring out if I have all the makings of a psycho is pretty easy to do. Just answer a few yes or no questions about how you view yourself and add a little personal history. Give it maybe five minutes and you could be on your way to straightjacket city. Your score tells you you're either nuts, normal, or a psychiatric hypochondriac.

The one disorder the test said I might actually have turns out to be a pretty minor one. Narcissism. Figures. All I did was confirm what I already suspected.

Strictly by the numbers, I'm no psychopath. I don't have enough yes answers to qualify. The more times you answer yes or maybe, though, the more likely you're a psychopath. So based on my few yes answers, the most I can conclude is, if I am a psycho, I'm only a minor one.

That's a relief, I guess, not being a psycho killer. Though I know I'm only scratching the surface in terms of mental illness. Concluding I'm a narcissist doesn't rule out a thousand other types of bonkers I barely understand. Avoidant personality disorder, dissociative identity disorder, obsessive compulsive disorder, dissociative amnesia, bipolar disorder. More crazy diagnoses than you can shake a stick at.

It's clear to me, at least, I'm not much for introspection. That's all a big fat waste of time, far as I can see. I'm not interested in exploring my feelings or delving into past traumas. The shrink's all-time favorite question—*How does that make you feel?*—makes me cringe. That's how it's always made me feel. If I have any neuroses, I don't obsess about them or let them run my life. You can be damn sure if I do ever see a shrink, I'm not about to tell him anything useful. Screw patient-doctor confidentiality. If he tries to find something interesting about me, I won't give him much to go on.

Frankly, my dear, I don't give a shit. Make the best of the situation you're in and soldier on.

~ * ~

So am I the narcissist I think I am? I killed Gilberto Bauer because I think I'm so special?

This is what the online test told me. It's also what I told me. Couldn't blame anyone at all for thinking that, as it's the one diagnosis I just might agree with. There's always the chance I could've accepted it not because it's the most accurate, but because the symptoms of narcissism are so easy to grasp for an amateur like me.

In the textbooks, it has a fancier name. Narcissistic personality disorder. No idea why, but apparently it's a lot more complicated than merely admiring yourself a little too much, which isn't me at all. It's a little too late to ask people who know me, though I bet the last thing they'd ever call me is vain.

To qualify for acceptance in the narcissistic personality disorder society, there's a whole slew of personal tics you have to be guilty of. More you have, the more likely you're a certified narcissist. Shrinks have set a pretty low bar for membership. If you meet the behavioral threshold, you're in the club. Not even a probationary period.

Other diseases, they had a lot of symptoms too, though I think I'm guilty of just a couple of them, if any. Not with narcissism.

The textbook definition says you use other people to reach your own goals. I did, no question if you call taking Bauer's life the same as using him. It also says you have fantasies about power and success. Think you're the bomb. Again, guilty, since I certainly wanted power over someone's life, and I wanted to kill him without getting caught. In my new area of expertise, that's exactly what success is. The symptoms include not giving a crap about the feelings of others. Which I didn't, as far as Bauer was concerned, although I admit I do feel pretty bad for his mom and dad.

Also having a strong sense of entitlement, which I think means you feel you have a rightful claim on something you don't deserve. Which I sort of do, since I feel I was entitled to stab some guy in the heart and take him out of circulation. You also value yourself more than other people. In Bauer's case, I did indeed. His life had no value, far as I was concerned, save as a means to an end.

A few other symptoms of narcissism I don't have, but those I definitely do. Definition says you're impulsive, which I'm not, at least in this case. It was no rash decision on my part. You're also aggressive, you can't stand criticism, you expect special treatment, you need constant attention, and you're self-promoting. Again, not me in terms of my life before and after one lovely afternoon at the Albion.

Do the math, and I'd say I am around fifty percent narcissistic. I understand perfectly well this diagnosis may be way off, since my feelings of superiority applied to just one person. Otherwise, I have no such feelings, none I could see anyway, toward my family, my friends, anyone. So it just may be the case I need to put a label on something I simply don't understand.

Again, this is me diagnosing myself. That in itself isn't in any list of symptoms of narcissistic personality disorder I've found, yet even thinking I know enough to diagnose myself could be yet another sign I'm a narcissist. Jury's still out, and it's just as well it stays out. If I am in fact a narcissist, it could even be a form of temporary insanity I came down with it a few weeks before the murder and had a full recovery right after. Fuck knows.

Chapter Eighty-one

"Hello."

"Kim Barbieri?"

The call came in November, more than six months after his last message, while Barbieri was on her way to visit a friend a few blocks away. It was almost Thanksgiving, the temperature a lot colder than just a few days before, and she was wearing her down coat and lined gloves for the first time since March. She did not recognize the number on her phone's caller ID, yet it did not stop her from taking off her right glove and pressing the green "accept call" icon. Curiosity trumped her usual caution.

She had never heard the voice before, yet she had no need to ask the caller for his name. She knew exactly who it was. *How did he get my number? Is he watching me? No point trying to trace the call. It's a burner he picked up ten minutes ago.*

Before responding, she stopped walking, forcing other pedestrians to walk around her, and anxiously looked up and down the block to see if he was behind her, or across the street, or sitting down the block in a parked car. He was not. She was safe for the moment.

"This is she."

"It's about time we meet, I believe. Do you agree?"

It was definitely a man's voice. Husky. A little scratchy. Other than that, it told her nothing about him. She imagined the voice speaking the words in the letters he sent. He sounded intelligent enough, and she was unable to detect any particular accent, except maybe generic white adult New Yorker. Probably not from the South, or Boston, or Nebraska.

Oh Lord, please don't let him be Italian. I'm begging you. That was about as precise as she could make it. Still, she noticed a slight disconnect between his speaking voice and his writing voice.

"I do, yes. I'm not going to bother asking you for your name."

"Better for both of us. If I'm going to confess my guilt, it won't be in a way that will hold up in court. I hope you understand." *If it's him, he writes more formally than he speaks. Like me. Like a lot of people. Keep him talking to be certain.*

"Bauer's dead. You killed him. You're guilty of murder."

"Not legally. I got away with it. Remember?"

"So far."

"I'm more optimistic than you are. I have reason to be."

"Okay. Where and when? It has to be outside, in a public place."

"It is. Playground on Prospect Park West and Ninth Street. Just inside the entrance. You know it? Park Slope?"

"I do." She had a lot of good friends in Park Slope and knew the area well.

She tried to pinpoint his age from his voice, but failed. She tried to imagine what a person with that voice would look like but could not. The way he spoke did not seem to match the man who had been stalking her—or the man she only imagined had been stalking her.

"Benches right outside. Near the fountain. Eleven tomorrow morning."

"Got it."

"Alone."

"Just me. Can I ask you something before we meet?" *Keep him talking. Keep him talking.*

"Shoot."

"Why did you send me the letters? Not anybody else?"

"I wanted someone to chase me, just not catch me. They worked."

"They did. You were always a step ahead of me, though."

"That was my plan."

"Why me in particular?"

"I'm a good judge of character. See you tomorrow."

"I'll—" The caller cut her off and ended the call. She stared at the phone for a second, put it back in her purse, and continued walking. *Knowing him, he's already taken the burner apart and dumped the pieces in the trash.*

Barbieri's involvement in the murder of Gil Bauer had been over for a long time. Other than her editor, Cavanaugh, who did not make the connection, and her lawyer, Simon, only Delaney and Brennan knew about the letters and their link to Bauer's murder. They were not going to say anything. The killer knew. Nobody else.

He already had her home address, obviously, although she had no idea how he got it. He had her email address. Now he knew her cell number as well. *Is this what it's like to be tracked down by an investigative reporter? If he wasn't batshit crazy, he'd make a great one. What else does he know about me? Does he know about me and Brennan? Does he know when I leave the house and when I get back? Does he know where Aunt Estelle lives?*

Am I still being stalked? Does the killer plan on murdering me as well? Am I going as a reporter, or as his next victim?

If I were interviewing him for a story I'd make sure I knew the facts, and ask questions that showed it. Yet there are no facts here.

She hated the guy. Had for months. She felt okay now, finally, though for way too long he had driven her crazy. He had manipulated her, and she let him. He had outsmarted her, despite her frantic efforts. She never liked feeling vulnerable, and that was exactly how he made her feel. If the killer wanted her dead, she would be dead already. He had plenty of chances. There was no use looking over her shoulder, or walking only with others, or sticking to crowded streets.

What did I just agree to? This man's a ninja. He's already proven he knows how to kill in seconds and disappear. If he attacks me like he attacked Bauer, I'll be dead before anyone has a chance to stop him. I must have a death wish.

Barbieri was putting herself out there. Alone. Unarmed. Against a man who already killed once. All she had was her faith she would not be murdered in broad daylight, in a park, where kids and their parents could see.

Was her faith enough?

Chapter Eighty-two

I'll tell you why I started writing that reporter, Kim Barbieri.

It wasn't a hidden urge to be caught. Way I figure it, there was no chance I wasn't going to pull this off. Nothing was going to go wrong. I left nothing to chance. I had no wish to have someone stop me before I killed someone. The murder itself, becoming a murderer, was just the end result of a process I wanted to see to its conclusion. Nothing more than a job well done.

While I didn't want to get caught, or even become a suspect, I did want it known the victim was killed, and his killer was still at large. He was never going to get caught. I also wanted recognition from someone who worked with the police but wasn't a cop himself, herself. Someone who'd understand how difficult it is to take a stranger's life if you've never done it before.

I wanted her to realize the murder would be committed by a professional who thinks everything through. That's why I made sure to write the letters as carefully as I used to write at work, like a corporate honcho would. Not exactly the way I talk, as you might've noticed. I couldn't speak as elegantly as I write if you put a gun to my head.

The real reason I wrote her was I wanted my story told without revealing my identity. She was the perfect vehicle—a crime reporter. I read the *News* just about every day, mostly for the local goings-on the *Times* doesn't bother with, and I'd seen Barbieri's byline on just about every crime story. Her writing was always fair. She got the facts right and tried not to let the sensational details slant her stories one way or the other. By leading her on, by baiting her into planning the murder along with me, she could give her readers a first-person account of a crime in progress. I was right about her, too. I gave her a personal tutorial on how to commit murder. Barbieri did everything I did, made every decision I made. Everything except stick the knife in Bauer's chest herself.

I guess that's why I wrote her those letters, and called her to ask if we should meet. After all this time, she's had plenty of opportunities to hand the letters over to the police. Still, I felt in my gut she hadn't. A decent reporter, like she was, would never allow herself to become part of the story. Besides, she was in it way too deep. They'd want to know why she waited so long to tell them. I didn't know for sure, but it's what I believed.

I could trust her not to call the cops.

Chapter Eighty-three

The next morning at eleven on the dot, Barbieri was in Prospect Park, sitting on a park bench outside the playground off Ninth Street, kept warm by her down coat and a cup of hot cocoa she had picked up from a street vendor just outside the park entrance. She had walked there from her home, a mile or so north of the park, to give her time to experience a completely normal morning in the neighborhood before the ordeal awaiting her. *I must be nuts, agreeing to meet him. Why on Earth would I trust this man? Am I committing suicide here? What was I thinking?*

The bench was on a winding path going roughly east to west, through several grassy areas and under an overpass, from the main park roadway to the park entrance a few blocks down on Fifteenth Street. She was sitting across from a playground where about twenty little boys and girls were equally divided on the swings, slides, and merry-go-round. *They're not going to come to my rescue.* They were all laughing and yelling and calling out to each other despite being all bundled up against the chill, hidden inside thick winter coats that no doubt made play exhausting. Almost all were white and were watched over by an equal number of adults, almost all women. They were not quite as white as the children. The ones who were not, she assumed, were nannies from Jamaica or some other Caribbean island. *They might, only after I'm dead. This guy's already killed Bauer in front of witnesses who saw and heard nothing. What's it like to be killed in plain sight?*

Sitting a few feet off to the right of Barbieri were a couple of young women, maybe eighteen or nineteen, glued to their cell phones, totally oblivious of her. College kids. *They texting each other?* About twenty feet to her left, a middle-aged man wearing filthy rags, apparently homeless, was intently organizing and reorganizing a shopping cart of his worldly possessions. One bench over, a fortyish woman was reading the *Daily News*. Barbieri had always been intrigued whenever she caught someone holding a copy of her own paper, perhaps reading an article she herself had written just a few hours earlier. *Did she read the whole thing? Does she like my writing? Did I leave anything unanswered?*

Barbieri clearly had come to the rendezvous before the killer did, and she realized she had put herself at a real disadvantage by doing so. *I have no idea what the killer looks like, while he knows exactly what I look like. Terrific.* All he had to do was Google her. She was no doubt weaker than him. She could always hold her own in any battle of the sexes, just not when it came to sheer physical strength. *I've left myself completely vulnerable here. He could overpower me in a second if I let myself get caught off guard.*

The path was pretty busy, more alive than usual. It was a beautiful, brisk, late autumn day, giving just about anyone looking for an excuse to drop what they were doing indoors and head outside. Every minute or so, pedestrians walked down the path in her direction, mostly couples holding hands or moms and dads pushing strollers. A few were women by themselves. Dog walkers. *Is that him? What about him? What if he's not alone? What if he's got a partner?* She suspected the killer might already be nearby, just out of view. If he was not, he would be approaching her bench from either the east or the west.

Barbieri waited, and watched. She stared blankly at a couple of men about twenty yards away, landscapers wearing hard hats, oversized workmen's gloves and safety goggles: one up in a cherry picker pruning dead branches and one below, keeping an eye out for passersbys. *They're not going to stop this guy. They're too far away.*

She stared intently to her right for a few seconds, toward the underpass, as if focusing her eyes would conjure up some sort of bogeyman lurking behind the bushes. She then slowly turned her head and looked left, toward the park entrance. From either direction, men who were walking alone just kept walking. No one appeared to recognize her, or walked directly toward her, or sat near her.

After twenty minutes of nothing, Barbieri gave up. *He's not coming. I'm being stood up on maybe the biggest date of my life!* She gave one last look in both directions, got up from the bench, and walked toward the Ninth Street entrance. About fifteen feet from the entrance, she felt a tap on her shoulder and heard a familiar male voice.

"Kim Barbieri?"

It was the voice she had heard just yesterday on the phone. Barbieri had, of course, been expecting to meet him today and had convinced herself she was fully prepared for the encounter. She was nonetheless shocked. She had met killers before and interviewed them one-on-one, but only when they were already in custody, behind bars or in cuffs. *This one is free, and standing right behind me. Close enough to kill.*

Chapter Eighty-four

Barbieri turned around slowly and came face-to-face with a killer. *The killer.*

Before saying a word she looked the man over. He appeared middle-aged, maybe fifty-five or so, an inch or two taller than she was. She had to tilt her head up, if only slightly, to look him in the face. He was white. He did not look particularly Italian to her—*grazie a dio!*—or Jewish, or Irish, or German, the usual white ethnic suspects. His hair was salt-and-pepper, short, and neatly combed. Clean-shaven. He looked to be in good health, at least physically, because he had no obvious disabilities she could see. He was wearing a heavy brown field jacket, khaki Dockers, and clean Nike running shoes. Peeking out from under his jacket was the collar of a blue oxford shirt. On his left hand, he wore a wedding ring, the only piece of jewelry she could see. If he wore a watch, it was hidden under the sleeve.

Her powers of observation took in a lot in just a second or two. She did not know what the mystery man would look like, and had expected to see pure evil. Here, in person, there was absolutely nothing evil about him, and she was taken aback by how unremarkable he looked. He was just an average, totally ordinary man, without a single distinguishing mark or characteristic an eyewitness could give to the police. Truly, she could not pick him out of a line-up. Until a lightbulb lit up. No, exploded.

Holy shit! He's the man I saw before! The realization she and this man, this killer, had crossed paths caused panic inside—the same visceral reaction she had felt whenever she sensed he was nearby—yet she managed to keep her composure on the outside.

"I had to make sure you were alone."

"I am."

"Mind walking, Kim? May I call you Kim?"

Was he following me this whole time? Was I following him?

Walking side by side was a bit easier for Barbieri, as it allowed her to talk with the killer without having to face him the whole time. The less eye contact, the better, she felt. Their meeting was already unnerving enough.

Barbieri leading the way, they turned back into the park.

"What choice do I have? First, let's get this out of the way. Where have I seen you before? I know I have."

"At the Albion. You were there. I saw you on my way out. It was too dark for you to get a good look at me."

"Before that."

"Other places. Funeral home. Gun show."

"In Pennsylvania? You were there? You were following me?"

"I wasn't. Believe me. We were just going in the same direction and made the same stops along the way. You were checking out weapons, just like I was. I was right about you. You planned the murder the same time I did. "

"Not quite. My goal was stopping it. Stopping you."

"Well, you failed. Bauer's dead. I got what I wanted."

"Playing me for a fool? Driving me nearly insane? Tricking me into committing a felony? Is that what you wanted?"

"Not at all. I didn't want that, and I am sorry, Kim. Really. It was the thrill of the chase I was after. I'm not a stalker. I don't know anything about your family or your bank accounts. Nothing personal. I'm not interested. All I know about you is you work for the *News* and you're a good reporter."

"Okay." Barbieri usually appreciated praise, but not coming from him. "When did you come up with this brilliant idea to stick a knife in someone's chest?"

"Let the interrogation begin. Beginning of the year. I'd just retired and was looking for a challenge."

As they walked deeper into the park, she noticed the number of people nearby kept changing. Fewer people up one path, more people down another. She was okay with fewer people, but not with none.

"You consider committing murder a challenge? Seriously?"

"Anything is, if you haven't done it before."

"Why Gil Bauer?"

"He was there. I was determined to kill an adult male, remember? We agreed on that. He was the one who happened to make himself available." She paid close attention to his choice of words and his speech pattern. *He wrote the letters. I'm sure of it.*

"I didn't agree to anything. Clear?"

"If you say so."

"You wanted to. Doesn't mean you *had* to. Nobody was putting a gun to your head. I mean, there are people I've wanted to kill sometimes, yet I never actually did it."

"No, I had to. I had the urge to kill, and I refused to contain it. I think I may be mentally ill. Narcissism. I don't think it's an illness myself. Still, there's an official medical diagnosis for it. A disorder."

"Narcissism. That's it?"

"Simple self-indulgence. I killed him because I willed myself to learn all there was to know about taking a life and getting away with murder. Ultimate ego trip. Sound crazy to you, Kim? Does to me."

They were alone, almost. Just the two of them and a handful of others too busy to take notice of an ordinary-looking, middle-aged couple out for a stroll. Barbieri subtly steered them back toward where they started, by the playground. At least there were a lot of people there. The killer went along, apparently unaware they were slowly and gradually reversing direction, a small measure of control she was exerting over him.

"Sounds like you're a sadistic monster. You were crazy just to think you could get away with this, in my opinion. Don't you think maybe you should've seen a psychiatrist? Gotten help? Bauer would still be alive if you had. Maybe."

"That's just it, Kim. I didn't want help. I didn't want anyone to talk me down. I didn't want anyone to get in the way."

"You're sane enough to have pulled this off, obviously. Certainly sane enough to plan it all, right?"

"A tremendous amount of planning did go into it, as you well know. I'd like to think I avoided the trip upstate due to all the prep I did before I actually did the deed. This was one crime where everything, I mean every little detail, every possible screw-up, was fully thought through by me. And by you as well, I might add. The police could find nothing to point them in my direction, because I left them nothing. No DNA or prints, certainly. Everything worked out exactly as I'd planned, and I'm a free man. A soulless psychopath, maybe, but definitely a free man. It's all fine and dandy with me, not getting caught. Heck, I don't think I've even come under any suspicion. Far as I can tell, the police don't know I exist. Not then, not now. I'm rather proud I'm a person of absolutely zero interest to them. I'm not about to give myself up, that's for damn sure."

"You killed someone. In cold blood. In some states you'd be executed for what you did."

"I did murder someone, Kim, but I'm not a murderer anymore. I'm no serial killer. No one's in any danger from me."

"For now."

"For forever. I swear. The fear I had, the dread I wouldn't be satisfied with one victim, has turned out to be groundless. It's been six months, and I can say in all honesty I have no intention of taking another life. One is enough. I'm done. I'm the same person I was before all this happened. Almost the same. My life is completely normal. I'm the same guy I've always been. I'm the same husband. Same upstanding member of the community. Nobody knows a damn thing otherwise, besides you. The only person besides you who knows I'm a little different than I used to be, is me. I've stopped giving myself a hard time about it."

"How nice for you."

"Play nice, Kim. Please. The homicidal fantasies I used to have, they've vacated the premises for good. Maybe the only ones getting me angry were the occasional idiots I had to work with. Now that they're out of my life and unable to ruin a perfectly beautiful day, the fantasies are gone as well."

"The cops may be somewhat skeptical."

"If they ever find me. The what, where, and when of this little caper I pulled, they were no secret. Never were. A rookie cop could've gotten that right a few seconds after getting to the scene of the crime. Yet the questions the police haven't come close to answering—who did this, and why—those'll never be answered."

"Until now."

"Until now."

"Detectives are pretty frustrated. I'm sure of it. I know them. I've interviewed them. The police tried real hard, put a lot of men on the case, worked a lot of overtime knocking on a lot of doors trying to find someone, anyone, who might know something. Nothing."

"Give them my regards next time you run into them. No, maybe you better not. I read the paper every day for months after the crime. Detectives hit one brick wall after another. No clues to run down. No third degree, no arrest, no trial, no jail time certainly, no executioner ready to pull the switch. Nothing. I still can't believe it myself, frankly. Still."

"Where's your computer? And printer?"

"Long gone. I donated them to Goodwill right after I printed the last letter. They're probably in some classroom in the Congo somewhere."

"I knew you'd make sure of that. As long as we're on the topic, why did you send me the last email? It didn't help me any."

"No, but it could have. I actually debated leaving the account open and giving you something to track down. I didn't. Too risky."

~ * ~

"Perfect crime."

"Perfection indeed. I got away with first-degree murder. It was perfect, in my humble opinion, save for one minor detail. The law of unintended consequences bit me in the butt, hard, coming way too close to costing me my marriage, and my sanity. I could be batshit crazy to this day, for all I know."

"The case is still open. You could still wind up in prison. There's no statute of limitations for murder."

"I know that. I mean, the fear never goes away. I guess a part of me is always expecting to get a call one day. Tap on my shoulder from out of nowhere, like I just gave you."

"I have to tell you, I was pretty damn angry at myself for not stopping you. Hopping mad. Still, I thought about what you'd done and sort of admired how you did it. Not the murder, which is just plain wrong, but getting away with it."

Once Barbieri and the killer were back at the playground, they stopped walking. They now stood facing each other. Barbieri struggled to maintain eye contact with him, if only to prove to herself she was not intimidated—another small measure of control over him.

"Tell me you didn't get a vicarious thrill from this, Kim."

"The exact opposite. It depressed the crap out of me. Every damn minute of it."

"Maybe it was just me, then. I'm still trying to figure out what led me to even try such a thing. I was a real success story, worked hard all my life. Earned more money than God. Paid my taxes. All that's true. I've done enough soul-searching and found nothing to change my mind. No point. I'm okay with what I did."

"Never mind you committed a felony. What about basic human decency? Thou shalt not kill. It's in the Bible."

"I don't need any lectures from anybody 'bout right and wrong, Kim. Sanctity of life. I know I did something terrible. I've decided I can live with it. Look, there's no sugarcoating what I did. No possible excuse. I crossed a line that just shouldn't be crossed, ever, by anyone, at any time, under any conditions. Believe me, I get it. I can't go back and change history. It's done. The actuarial tables tell me I could live another fifteen years maybe, and in all likelihood, I'll be taking my secret to my grave."

"You sure messed up Bauer's mom and dad, and his wife."

"I did. It's my biggest regret in this whole escapade, hurting them.

Not because I violated the most basic rule of society. On that level, at least, I can tell myself my conscience is intact. I'm not proud of what I did at the theater, believe me. There's no honor in it. It went against everything I'd ever believed in, yet I did finish the job, and here we are."

"Maybe, until you make a dumb mistake. Trust me, a lot of killers have. Prisons are filled with them. I've met one or two myself."

"I made no mistakes. None."

"There's always a first time."

"I wouldn't bet on it."

"Are you going after me next? Am I one last loose end you need to tie up?"

"No, Kim, you're not. I'm done."

"How about an apology, then? I didn't ask you to drag me into this. I felt trapped by you. I almost lost my job. You had me questioning my sanity. I was fuckin' miserable thanks to you. I told myself plenty of times if I ever ran into you, I'd kill you."

"I'm not worried. I'm not sorry, either. I should be, maybe, yet I'm not. You go on with your life, I go on with mine. That's how this story ends."

"I do have one question I've been meaning to ask. Do you treat your wife this way, too? Bully her, I mean. Make her do things she'd never do because you ordered her to."

"That's really none of your business, is it? Sorry, but there's a side of me I'd like to keep private. What I can tell you is I don't make a habit of it. I happen to have a question for you as well, if I may."

"You may."

"I kept looking for your stories in the paper, hoping to see one on the Bauer murder. An inside investigation into a perfect crime type of piece. There were articles by other reporters, but none by you. Was it your choice not to write any, or your editor's?

"Mine. My decision entirely."

"Why? I assumed you'd want to write a crime story only you could write."

"You assumed correctly. And I did, for about a minute—until I decided a piece of shit like you wasn't worth it. I wasn't ever going to give you the satisfaction. Call it payback."

"Ouch. Let's move on. You still have my letters?"

"I do. Why'd you send one every week?"

"To keep you wanting more. Admit it, you looked forward to Fridays, didn't you?" He didn't give her any time to respond. "Let me ask you something, Kim. Why didn't you ever bring them to the police? I know you didn't, not even after Bauer was dead. Don't bother answering. The reason is you couldn't without implicating yourself. All they'd have to do is ask, 'Why did you wait till now to come forward?'"

"I still have them." She did not mind lying to him in this case. She had given them to Brennan, but why disabuse him of the notion? *If he believes I didn't, let him keep on believing it.*

"Burn them. They're not going to do either of us any good."

"Maybe, but I'm going to hold onto them. They're a souvenir of our time together. You'll forgive me for saying I hope I never see you again."

"Oh, I'm sure our paths will cross, Kim. City's a pretty small town. Although not at the Starlight. Now that you've seen my face, I can't go back there."

"And leave the guys?"

"I'll find a new place and take them with me. I'm the alpha male."

With that, the killer turned around and headed back toward the entrance. Barbieri stayed right where she was a second or two, paralyzed, then started walking in the opposite direction.

After walking five or six seconds, maybe twenty yards, she turned her head around to see if the killer was following her. She could not see him. He was blocked from her view by the five undercover cops surrounding him and putting him in cuffs: the two landscapers, the homeless man, one of the female college students and one of the nannies. She turned back around and kept walking, looking up only to make quick eye contact with the commanding officer of Brooklyn Homicide, Captain Timothy Brennan.

Chapter Eighty-five

"Aunt Estelle, they got him! He's in jail!"

"Oh, wonderful! How'd they catch him? Did he kill anybody else? Why did he write to you? They found his DNA, right? Why did he do it?" Estelle couldn't wait for one question to be answered before blurting out another.

The call to her aunt was the first thing Barbieri did when she got back to her apartment after her walk in the park with the murderer of Gilberto Bauer. It was not just because she wanted her aunt to stop losing sleep over her. It was also a matter of self-preservation: She knew she would never hear the end of it if her aunt learned about the arrest from the local news first. Barbieri told her what she could about the arrest, and her role in it. She described her cooperation with Captain Brennan, careful to leave out any mention of their relationship. That was a topic for another day, maybe.

Her aunt listened intently to every word, of course. She was a vacuum cleaner when it came to gory details about heinous crimes perpetrated by despicable animals, especially when she learned about them before anybody else did. This particular heinous crime, though, was different. It struck a little too close to home, so Barbieri wanted to assure her aunt she was safe. Finally.

"I'm proud of you, Kim. You did good. You didn't stick an icepick in his eye, I hope."

"No, Aunt Estelle, I didn't. He went to jail in one piece."

"This murderer, Kim…what's his name?"

"You'll know when I know." For Barbieri, the killer's arrest was a happy ending to one ugly, hideous, and sickening chapter in her life. The healing had begun.

Chapter Eighy-six

Was I surprised? Yeah, you could say that. I never thought a bunch of cops would outsmart me.

All along, I must've been fooling myself about how perfect this perfect crime was. Maybe that's an actual symptom of narcissism. Sure fogged up my thinking, whatever it is. What I was afraid of actually happened. I wasn't totally in control of my faculties, and here I am.

Doctor here has a prisonful of conditions a lot worse than whatever bullshit personality disorder I have. A lot of men here are out-and-out nuts. Psychotic. If they're not criminally insane, officially, they just missed the cut.

One thing I learned about narcissism, though. There is a cure. Guards who can barely walk upright treating you like shit for a decade or two.

Does *doing* something abnormal make me an abnormal person? A nutcase? I just don't know. Still don't. I mean, I feel normal. I act normal. I'm not psychotic, at least not like half the inmates here. I have a fairly firm grip on reality, in my humble opinion. I'm not talking to myself or wandering around in my skivvies. I don't rant about the CIA sending me signals through my dental fillings. Still, here I am, locked in a box by myself twenty-three hours a day.

There's no head doctor here, which is fine by me. I'd rather be kept in the dark about my mental health than go through any kind of psychoanalysis.

As far as rage goes, I'm just angry at myself for getting caught. No point getting pissed off at the other guests here. They're a whole lot meaner than me, and they all carry homemade shivs. I'm not about to commit suicide-by-inmate. As you know, I'm all too aware of the damage a sharp object can do to the human body.

I still don't know where I made the mistake. Or who dropped a dime on me. I'm always circling back to Barbieri, then circling away. Not much to do up here besides think, and I rack my brain every waking minute. I'm not penitent, that's for certain. I did it. Can't undo it. The state can punish me, is punishing me, but they're not going to rehabilitate me. There's nothing to rehabilitate. I'm done with killing, yet I'll never convince the parole board. Bastards are going to make sure I die here, and there's not a damn thing I can do about it.

Anyway, thanks again for coming all the way up here to my country home. You've given me a chance to vent. Lord knows I don't have much to say to anyone here. Helen's gone. Divorce. I think she'll be hating my guts forever. I can't blame her.

If you find out where I screwed up, let me know, okay? You know where to find me.

Chapter Eighty-seven

Cocaine dealers, illegal aliens, and assorted gunslingers all call Miami home. Kim Barbieri was just days away from becoming their neighbor.

Miamians always found a reason to end up in court for something, and she would no doubt keep busy courtesy of her new employer, the *Herald*. The paper had lured her by offering her a position as an investigative reporter, and she looked forward to finally writing the stories she was always meant to write. *Move over, Seymour Hersh.*

She had told Cavanaugh she was leaving two weeks earlier, and they both knew she could be replaced. She already had, based on the crime blotter articles she had seen the past few days. He had begun teaming Delaney up with other reporters, his role in the Bauer murder still hidden from everyone at the paper. At the moment, her ex-partner was getting ready for a camera safari in the Okavongo Delta. He was going as a tourist, not a tour guide.

The reporter was in her living room, surrounded by moving boxes waiting their turn to be filled, taped up, and labeled. The place was otherwise just about empty, ready for its new owner. She had already seen to it all the furniture she had adopted over the years was placed in good homes. Only the most important family heirlooms, including her dad's record collection, would be relocating with her. They would be among the last things she packed.

To make her last days at home a little more tolerable, she was playing Bellini's *Norma* on the turntable. Loud. *My parting gift to the neighbors.* True, the strong female character did come to a tragic end, but not before a number of intense "hell hath no fury" moments. Barbieri could relate.

Starting over in Miami meant starting over without Brennan. *This is as good a time as any to end what I should never have started.* When she felt she was losing control to the killer, she had used Brennan to get it back. Now that the killer was no longer a threat to her, she could finally move on. It was the same old record she could never stop playing: Get close, then pull away.

Leaving on her terms was another sign the Bauer murder was well behind her. *Last message I got from the sick fuck was the last one I'll ever get from him.* The killer was locked away upstate in Clinton, the maximum-security prison closer to Montreal than to New York City, with a less-than-zero possibility of parole. He had been convinced by the cops it was not Barbieri who set him up. The police got an anonymous tip, he was told, and the detectives tapped her phone. Idiot bought it. He was considerate enough to call while the cops were listening in, and dumb enough to confess to her. *Brennan was right. Criminal stupidity. Maybe that's an offense in itself.*

Brennan had fed the media the baloney about reaching out to the community and raising the reward for information, only to give the killer a false sense of security. Maybe he would be stupid enough to let his guard down and make a mistake. He was. He did. Now he had all the time in the world to find the flaw in his otherwise flawless crime.

The CO did thank her for doing her civic duty. He got her to let his surveillance team tap her phone and she got the killer to admit his guilt. She also let herself be the bait in the trap he was setting. She had resisted at first, but he was a hard guy to say no to.

He kept his promise to keep her out of it. He called in a favor or two to see to it her name did not appear on any legal document. Quiet authority again. The letters remained their secret: The killer's confession was all the DA needed to seal his fate. Even if he got out decades from now, on some kind of made-up technicality, he would have no reason to come after her.

The story the murderer wanted told would not be told by her. She was not going to write a brilliant piece about him, and nobody would marvel at his brilliant plan. *No point in telling the world what a total jerk the killer turned me into.*

Still, she had not come to terms with her role in his arrest. Putting murderers behind bars was a good thing, she knew. And here, the punishment definitely fit the crime. Murder one equals life. Yet there were questions still swirling inside her head that would not let her be.

Did I cooperate because Brennan asked-slash-ordered me to? Or was it for another, entirely selfish reason? Revenge. Did the punishment fit the crime he'd committed against me?

Barbieri felt like she had been gaslighted on an industrial scale. She never took crap from anyone, yet Bauer's killer had practically buried her in it. Time would help the healing process, she knew. Still, maybe adding a bit of revenge might speed it up.

For months, I felt manipulated by him. I knew better, and I let him. I hated myself for being his patsy. Yet I couldn't stop blaming myself for going along with the sadistic bastard. Until the day I decided I'd had enough of playing the female victim.

I outwitted Bauer's killer. I beat him. Badly. I made sure he's going to be some other inmate's bitch for the rest of his life, then die behind bars.

Figlio di puttana chose the wrong woman to mess with!

About the Author

A lifelong New Yorker now living in Manhattan, Sid Meltzer took a couple of worthwhile detours on his way to becoming a crime fiction writer. He first served as a Brooklyn Supreme Court Probation Officer, a job that helped him see things from a criminal's point of view. He then switched careers and went into advertising, where he learned to craft a compelling story.

VISIT OUR WEBSITE
FOR THE FULL INVENTORY
OF QUALITY BOOKS:
http://www.roguephoenixpress.com

Rogue Phoenix Press

Representing Excellence in Publishing

Quality trade paperbacks and downloads
in multiple formats,
in genres ranging from historical to contemporary romance,
mystery and science fiction.
Visit the website then bookmark it.
We add new titles each month!

www.ingramcontent.com/pod-product-compliance
Lightning Source LLC
Chambersburg PA
CBHW061938170626
46813CB00006B/2447